SUNKEN DREAMS

LIBRARY OF CONGRESS CATALOGING-IN-PUBLICATION DATA

Names: Kuehn, Steven R., author.
Title: Sunken dreams / Steven Kuehn.
Description: First edition. | Waterville, Maine : Five Star Publishing, 2016. | Series: A Jake Caine archaeology mystery
Identifiers: LCCN 2015050627 (print) | LCCN 2016009781 (ebook) | ISBN 9781432831677 (hardback) | ISBN 1432831674 (hardcover) | ISBN 9781432831646 (ebook) | ISBN 143283164X (ebook)
Subjects: LCSH: Archaeology—Fiction. | BISAC: FICTION / Mystery & Detective / General. | FICTION / Suspense. | GSAFD: Mystery fiction.
Classification: LCC PS3611.U346 S86 2016 (print) | LCC PS3611.U346 (ebook) | DDC 813/.6—dc23
LC record available at http://lccn.loc.gov/2015050627

First Edition. First Printing: May 2016
Find us on Facebook– https://www.facebook.com/FiveStarCengage
Visit our website– http://www.gale.cengage.com/fivestar/
Contact Five Star™ Publishing at FiveStar@cengage.com

Printed in the United States of America
1 2 3 4 5 6 7 20 19 18 17 16

SUNKEN DREAMS

STEVEN KUEHN

FIVE STAR

A part of Gale, Cengage Learning

GALE
CENGAGE Learning·

Farmington Hills, Mich • San Francisco • New York • Waterville, Maine
Meriden, Conn • Mason, Ohio • Chicago

SUNKEN DREAMS

CHAPTER ONE

"Archaeology, more than anything else, is like putting together a puzzle with missing pieces and only a vague idea of what the picture is supposed to look like."

Professor Jacob Caine paused to let his words sink in. He surveyed the classroom for evidence of interest, confusion, or boredom in the faces of his undergraduate seminar students. Every seat was occupied, a typical occurrence during the last few classes before finals week. Some of the students showed signs of life, which he found encouraging.

"I know I've said this more than once since class began, but with all the specifics we've covered on different sites, pottery and point types, stages and phases, and every other aspect of North American prehistory, I think it's a good idea to take a step back and envision how the pieces mesh together. If you want to see it in a more dramatic light, picture yourselves as history detectives, solving mysteries with relatively few clues, lots of misleading information, and no way of knowing if you've solved the case when you're done. After all, none of the people we study are around any longer to confess. Pretty impressive work for a bunch of oddball archaeologists who study dead people's garbage for a living."

That brought a round of laughter, so Jake decided to end on a high note. "Okay, let's wrap it up here, folks. The final exam is next Thursday at one o'clock. Heather and Scott will be in the grad student office tomorrow and all next week if you have any

7

questions. For anyone who wants to talk to me, I'll be around tomorrow afternoon and off and on after that. Leave a note on my door if you want to make an appointment, or send me an email. Assuming the system doesn't crash again, I will respond as soon as I can. Thanks."

With a clatter of folding lap desks, the students cleared the room save for a few stalwarts with questions or meeting requests. Jake knew from past experience that most would wait until the last minute to speak to him about the exam.

"Well, I've got three meetings lined up already for tomorrow," Scott said as he joined Jake and Heather at the front of the room. "Guess it's a good thing I finished my research paper on the Overton ceramics."

"Oh, the girls know you're a big softie and will probably give them a copy of the test to look at over the weekend," Heather said. Scott turned red and began a garbled protest, but she cut him off. "Relax, I'm just kidding. You've got to lighten up or grad school will give you a nervous breakdown."

"She's right Scott, so pay attention," Jake said. He suppressed a slight grin as he gathered up his lecture notes. "Maybe Heather can tell you about one of her legendary meltdowns during her first couple of semesters."

It was Heather's turn to blush. "All right, that's enough, I give up," she said, raising her hands in mock surrender. "Just trying to give Scott the benefit of my vast grad school experience, that's all."

"Since that's settled, let's plan on grading the exams right after the test," Jake said. "We'll put in a couple of hours, then grab some dinner and go over the plans for the field school at Waconah."

"You're buying, right?" Heather said. Scott looked surprised at her cheeky reply, but he had only been one of Professor Caine's grad assistants for one semester while Heather was a senior graduate assistant at Wisconsin State University.

"Fair enough, I guess," Jake said, smiling. "After all, I can make the money back by working you two harder at the dig."

Jake passed the balky elevators and climbed the well-worn stairs to his third-floor office in Eddings Hall. One of the older buildings on campus, it had been renovated some twenty years before with less than stellar results. The elevators jammed at least once a week and the poor wiring led to numerous power outages and computer system crashes. He walked down the hallway, greeting his colleagues and students as he went.

As one of the younger faculty members in the joint Anthropology and Archaeology Department, Jake served as an advisor for a large number of students and was required to teach more than his share of classes each semester. A popular instructor, his efforts were responsible for the recent upsurge in interest in the North American Archaeology program, a fact not lost on the senior faculty. Rounding the corner, Jake was not surprised to see someone sitting in the chair outside his office. The frail, gray-haired woman perched uncomfortably on the plastic university-issued chair, however, was decidedly not a student.

"Can I help you, ma'am?"

"Are you Professor Caine? I'm Linda Wardell. I think I've found what you're looking for," she said, tapping the box next to her.

Unlocking the office door was a bit tricky as he balanced the heavy box in one hand, but Jake managed and ushered Mrs. Wardell inside. "You'll have to excuse the mess in here, Mrs. Wardell. I had assumed I'd need to arrange a time to drive out and examine your daughter's notes."

"My niece was coming into the city and she offered to drive me. I found the papers you asked about and saw no reason to have them sitting around on my dining room table." She glanced about the cluttered office with a raised eyebrow, and then settled onto the now-emptied chair as Jake shifted boxes and piles of books out of the way.

"I was a bit surprised when I got your call, Professor Caine. Not many people inquire about Jacklyn's old affairs anymore, although I certainly think of her every day."

"Well, I hope it wasn't an inconvenience for you, Mrs. Wardell. As I said on the phone, I'm going to be conducting a field school at the Waconah site and unfortunately a lot of files seem to be missing. I was just hoping that some of them might have gotten mixed into her personal effects, after the accident."

Mrs. Wardell stared at him as if startled by his ignorance. "My daughter didn't die in a boating accident. She was murdered."

CHAPTER TWO

"That lake took my baby, Professor Caine. But someone else was to blame, of that I have no doubt." Mrs. Wardell gazed out the window, eyes focused on the manicured lawn and stately trees of the campus, but seeing only the rolling waves and whitecaps of far-distant Taylor Lake.

"Mrs. Wardell, forgive my confusion but it was my understanding that Jacklyn drowned in a boating accident, while running a field school at the Waconah site."

"Well, that may be what the sheriff thought at the time," she countered, refocusing on him, "but that doesn't make it so. My daughter was a strong, smart woman. My husband Jack—god rest his soul—and I raised her right."

"I meant no disrespect, Mrs. Wardell," Jake said. "Truth be told, it seems a bit odd to me that she would have been out on the lake on a night like that."

"That's just it, Professor, she wouldn't have. Besides, Jack practically lived on the water, fishing and boating. Jacklyn knew how to handle a boat and she had more than enough sense not to take a boat out with a storm coming. No reason at all that she would have gone out during a storm. None at all."

The certainty in her voice left no avenue for rebuttal and Jake saw no reason to argue with her. He had little firsthand knowledge of Dr. Wardell's death roughly a dozen years earlier. Old department gossip and the scraps of info he picked up since he began researching the Waconah site excavations made it all seem straightforward. Young Professor Wardell drowned as a result of a boating accident while conducting a field school at the site. She was interested in surveying some of the small islands in Taylor Lake and had taken a boat out to do some preliminary testing. A storm blew up and she was caught out in the middle of the lake. The body and fragments of the boat turned up a few days later. A significant loss for the department and the end of work at the Waconah village.

"My husband Jack and I spent years trying to convince people of the truth, but some folks just won't accept the obvious when it stares them in the face. He passed on three years ago. He had heart trouble, you know. And now all I have left are my memories. That damn lake and whoever put her out there took all our dreams away."

"I'm sorry if my call caused you any grief, Mrs. Wardell. I didn't—"

"No, no, I'm fine." She turned her attention to the unopened box poised on the edge of the desk. "Anyhow, I went through her old papers and this should be everything that relates to her work at the university. If what you need isn't in here, you're out of luck, I guess."

Jake removed the lid. The box was full of jumbled papers, folders, and envelopes. He grimaced as he paged through the top layers. "It may take some time to go though all this, I'm afraid. If it is all right with you, I'll have copies made and then see about returning it to you, maybe in a couple of weeks."

"As far as I'm concerned you can keep it all. Nothing in there is personal and it probably should have stayed with the university in the first place. Jacklyn would have preferred it that way, I'm sure."

"You're probably right, and thank you. I read a few of Dr. Wardell's articles back in grad school and she was a very thorough, detailed archaeologist. I'm sure these notes will prove invaluable."

She brightened at that remark. "Well, thank you for saying that, Professor Caine. I think Jacklyn would be glad to see that someone who appreciates her work was taking over at her site."

Jake saw Mrs. Wardell to the elevator, made sure she reached the ground-floor lobby, and returned to his office where he began sifting through Jacklyn Wardell's files. Before long, several new piles had sprouted on his desk and the adjacent table. Trays of artifacts, research papers, and class assignments were restacked to provide additional space. A woman's photo, two tiny robot figurines, and a few other special treasures managed to retain their designated spots on the desk, but they were the exception.

As the contents of the box were redistributed in the office, Jake realized that much of the missing information had in fact ended up with Mr. and Mrs. Wardell after their daughter's death. The absent feature forms, several maps, and copies of the artifact inventory log were all there. Jake also found a small stack of artifact illustrations with Jacklyn Wardell's initials in one corner. He recognized several decorated rim sherds from his examination of the Waconah artifact collection stored downstairs. A few images were unique, including one of a large, broken piece of clamshell carved into the shape of a fish. Similar fish lures or decoys made of shell had been found at other prehistoric Native American sites in the region, but none so large. Even with only half the artifact present, it was considerably larger than any others Jake had seen. *Use for report cover - check Unit 28 for other half* was scrawled next to the initials.

A timid rap at the door caught his attention. "Excuse me, Professor Caine, are you busy?"

"No, not at all Michelle, come on in. What can I do for you?"

"I had a couple of questions about the Archaic-to-Woodland

transition, and . . . geez, you're busy with something, aren't you?" she said, noticing the papers and folders strewn about. "I can come back if you are."

"No, please, I'm never too busy to help out. Besides," he said with a grin, "I only scatter stuff around like this so I look busy, in case the dean saunters by."

Michelle smiled and took a seat. The next half hour was spent discussing the key factors used by archaeologists to distinguish between the more mobile Archaic foragers and the more sedentary Woodland mound builders.

Michelle took copious notes, and Jake tried to focus her efforts on topics he planned to cover on the final. Jake searched for her student file as they talked and eventually found it sandwiched between two overdue library books.

"I see you're signed up for the Waconah field school. If you haven't decided on a topic for your senior thesis paper, we might be able to find something from this summer's dig that would do the trick."

She stopped writing and chewed on her pencil. "Yeah, I'm sorry but I just haven't come up with any ideas so far. I've had a ton of classes this semester and lots of readings and homework. Half the time I feel like I'm just treading water, trying to stay caught up."

"Don't feel bad about it, Michelle. Most of the students are in the same boat. I don't think more than a few have even talked to me yet about their senior projects."

Michelle managed a weak smile, but doubt still clouded her big brown eyes.

"Anything in particular you're interested in, maybe pottery, or lithics? You did really well in the zooarchaeology section of the Archaeology Lab class last semester."

"The bone tools we looked at were really cool. Maybe I could do something with that?"

"Generally we don't see a lot of bone or shell tools at sites in Wisconsin. Bone doesn't preserve well, but they did have a fair amount of faunal material from Professor Wardell's field school. Hmm. Tell you what. For now, let's tentatively plan on you examining any worked bone we find this summer, and if there's time you can compare it with material from the original dig."

Jake glanced at his watch as Michelle left the room. Most of the afternoon had passed, but he decided to put in some time revising an article for the state archaeology journal. The deadline was weeks away, but Jake knew planning and packing for the upcoming field school would soon take all his available time. He entered some notes in Michelle's student file and a reminder to pull some articles for her to read when the fall term began.

An hour later, Jake was infuriated trying to address concerns raised by the two different reviewers, as they contradicted one another at nearly every point. For his own amusement, he wrote a few sarcastic comments about the parentage and personal habits of each anonymous reviewer and then made a few more minor changes before tossing the manuscript onto the top of the nearest pile.

Jake grabbed a soda from his small dorm fridge and settled back into his chair to decide what to tackle next. He spotted the box brought to him by Linda Wardell, put aside when Michelle arrived. Intrigued, Jake retrieved the box and continued sorting through its contents. Beneath the layer of artifact drawings, Jake found several bulky manila envelopes. The first contained nothing but receipts for campsites, food and gasoline purchases, and other expenditures relating to the field school. It was a bit unnerving to see one from a local resort, requesting payment from the university for the ten-foot aluminum boat and motor lost in the storm. It was dated only four days after Jacklyn Wardell's death. Kind of heartless, he thought, but at least the bill wasn't sent to her folks.

The second envelope was much more interesting. Nearly three-dozen large black-and-white photos of the dig tumbled forth. There were a nice variety of excavation photos, as well as some landscape shots with Taylor Lake in the background. The name "Droessler" was stamped on the back of each, along with dates corresponding to the original Waconah field school. He recognized a much younger Terry Schroeder in one photo and picked out a harried-looking Jacklyn Wardell in two others. Except for a broad-brimmed gray fedora and sunglasses, she didn't look all that much different than she did in the "Remembered Faculty" staff photo in the first-floor lobby.

The final envelope held Jacklyn's personal field notebook, a thick leather-bound journal. Jake skimmed through the book and found page after page of Jacklyn's thoughts on the field school, how the excavations were progressing, and comments about the students, grad assistants, and visitors to the site. Little sketches decorated many of the pages, along with smears of red and brown soil. She had obviously spent at least part of each day writing in what was essentially a diary. The last entry was made the morning of her accident.

Jake noticed that the journal contained no actual names. Everyone was referred to by a nickname or description, forming a simple code. "Kos" and "CatWoman" were most likely Alice Koster and Cathy Lorenzo, while "Curls" had to be Terry Schroeder, who until the recent onset of male-pattern baldness had a thick set of jet-black curls. While it might not baffle any code breakers at the FBI, it was obvious that Jacklyn didn't want her comments to become public knowledge should anyone snoop through her diary.

The phone rang, jarring Jake from his perusal of the notebook.

"Hello, is this Professor Caine? Ooh, you're so sexy! Any

chance I can do a little extra credit and boost my grade, handsome?"

"Hi, Amanda. How are things in La Crosse?"

"Geez, Jake, is that how you usually respond when hot young coeds call you like this? Talk about exciting."

"Sorry, honey, but it hasn't ever come up. You're the only one who does this, and you do it every semester."

"Still, it wouldn't hurt for you to play along once in a while, Mr. Romance. It's hard enough having a long-distance relationship without you at least trying to put forth a little effort here."

It was meant as a joke, but it still stung a bit. "Sorry. I've been stressed as hell lately, what with the semester coming to a close and trying to get everything finalized for the field school."

"I'm not surprised. You're teaching what, four classes this semester? Plus you've probably editing two or three articles and spending more time working with the students than taking care of yourself. Or writing dirty emails to your sexy girlfriend, for example."

Jake let her vent. Past experience had shown him that this was the easiest way.

"Oh, Jake, I'm sorry. I just miss you so much and with our schedules lately we haven't seen each other in over a month."

"I know, you're right, and I'm sorry too. We knew when we took these jobs we'd have some rough spots and I guess this is one of them. I'm just worried about making some progress on the tenure track. Did I tell you that they postponed consideration of my assistant professorship application until next fall?"

"Yeah, I remember. But like you said, it's probably because you're running the field school this summer. Didn't Dr. Chang tell you that it actually works in your favor, since this way the department has to officially take it under consideration?"

"You're right. Guess I keep forgetting I've got a few folks

around here on my side. Playing office politics just isn't my thing."

Amanda released a loud sigh over the phone. This discussion had stolen much of their limited time over the past year. "I know. That's why you're focusing on your teaching, working with the students, writing all those articles. Remember, the plan is to go with your strengths and not sweat the rest."

"You're really good for me, you know that?"

"Of course I am, honey. You're damn lucky to have me around, even if I am halfway across the state. Let's keep that in mind next time I call."

"So how is the sexiest curator of archaeology at the Northern Mississippi Valley History Center, anyway?"

"Pretty good, but the last few weeks have been pretty hectic. We always get lots of school groups in spring and with summer break around the corner they aren't always that interested."

"How are things going with the rock art exhibit?"

"Not so good. The director liked my idea, but the cost of creating a miniature rock shelter would really put a crimp in this year's budget, so it will probably get pushed back a year or two."

"Sorry. I know you put in a lot of research on that."

"It's all good, it's not like he said no. So now Sean and I are setting up a display on local industries from the 1800s."

"Sean?"

"Yeah, he's one of the historians, remember? He's great and so funny. You'd really like him."

"I'm sure." Jake suspected that wouldn't be the case.

"Anyway, we have artifacts from a family brewery and bottling company, a cranberry bog operation, and a sawmill. I wanted to include some items from shell button manufacture, but they already have some of those in the domestic living exhibit, so that idea got shot down."

"Still running into trouble with Ann, then?"

"Yeah. For some reason that woman just does not like me. Even if my exhibits have nothing to do with hers, she finds some reason to make a snide comment. I got back at her at the last staff meeting, though. I suggested that even the permanent exhibits should be given a yearly review so that signage can be updated or replaced, items can be rotated out of storage for display, and new information added in response to patron feedback. She stared at me like I had suggested painting over the Sistine Chapel with characters from the Simpsons."

Jake laughed at the image. "Keeping the exhibits up to date sounds like a good idea to me."

"Sean thought so too," Amanda said. "Dr. Holley thought it was a great idea and ordered the senior curators to set up a schedule for the reviews by the end of the week. He went on and on about the goals of the Center, how we have to think in terms of entertainment as well as education, and stay 'dynamic and timely' with our interpretive displays. He may come across like P.T. Barnum at times but he's the kind of director the Center needs to stay innovative."

"I take it Ann and her cohorts are less than enthusiastic about the idea."

"You got it. So now they have to produce these reviews rather than sit around patting each other on the back about how damn wonderful they are. And obviously Holley isn't going to accept any half-baked reports that say everything is perfect the way it is."

"Have to hand it to you, it sounds like you are really thriving at the History Center." Jake cleared his throat and took a sip of soda. "Everything still on track for you helping out with the field school for a few days?"

"Geez, I almost forgot. That's the main reason I called. Dr. Holley gave me permission to spend a few weeks at Waconah instead of the few days we originally discussed. I sort of convinced him that with more time there, I can generate more background info on the site, take more photos, and maybe even get some video footage of the field school in action. It should really make for a great exhibit when it's all done."

"That is great. Let me grab my calendar and I'll jot down the days you'll be there."

After finalizing the dates, Jake told Amanda about his meeting that day with Linda Wardell and summarized the contents of her daughter's box. He also recounted his surprise over her insistence that Jacklyn was murdered.

"Wow. Do you think there's any truth to it?"

"I don't know. I suppose it's possible, but you'd think they would have figured that out years ago, right after she died," he said, considering the situation. "But you have to wonder why any sane individual would take a small boat out onto a big lake like that, especially so late in the day, with a storm approaching. From what Mrs. Wardell says, her daughter would never have done something like that."

"Does seem pretty foolish, but it's a big leap to go from a dumb mistake to murder. Could be that she just can't let go of the fact that her daughter died at such a young age, at the beginning of her career."

"I suppose so. Maybe I'll ask Musket about it if I run into him. In any event, I can't see where it will cause us any problems during the field school."

CHAPTER THREE

"Here's one of the errant bastards, finally!"

The assistant curator's voice echoed through the dimly lit recesses of the curation area. Prior to its acquisition by the Anthropology and Archaeology Department, the room had been a maintenance area. Based on the rusty pipes and ductwork still visible in the shadows, Jake suspected it had originally housed the boiler system for the building.

A cloud of dust rose in protest as Erin Weiss unceremoniously set the cardboard curation box on a plastic pushcart. Brushing aside years of dust and cobwebs, she peered at the faded label and nodded in triumph. "I thought we might find some of your missing boxes back here. Nancy never comes this far back into the tombs. Let me see that inventory sheet again." She made a quick side-by-side comparison of the two lists. "Hmm, it looks like most of the stuff listed here is packed into one of these three boxes. Probably whoever had them kept them out for a while and that's why they aren't stashed with the rest."

"Might have been Mark Winters. See the *M.W.* scrawl down here? He was the primary author on the memorial volume written after Wardell died. Probably kept these artifacts for more detailed analysis. I wonder why he never followed through writing up the site?"

"Probably got busy with some other projects, I suppose," Erin said as she began pulling smaller boxes and artifact bags from the larger storage boxes. "Back then, from what I hear,

21

checking out artifacts for analysis was pretty casual. Nowadays, we lowly assistant curators do our best to keep you professors in line."

"Hey, give me a break," Jake said. "I always fill out all the paperwork, and do you ever have to break down my door to get any artifacts returned?"

"All right, fine. You're the one exception to the rule, I'll grant you that. Why else would I have agreed to root around back here to find your artifacts?"

A few minutes of additional toil, punctuated by dust-induced coughing, and the last two missing artifact boxes were pulled from the shelves. Soon all three were placed on a nearby table and Jake and Erin began pulling artifacts for the upcoming field school. Before long, a nice selection of decorated and plain rim sherds, stone tools, and worked bone and shell artifacts were set aside.

"Seriously, Jake, I wanted to thank you again for arranging it so I can work at the Waconah field school. The Crypt Keeper just told me again that they would likely cut my hours even more over the summer months."

"Not a problem. Having you run the field lab will be a big time saver down the road, and it'll help reinforce to the students that archaeology is more than just walking corn fields and digging up sites. Speaking of Nancy, how is everyone's favorite curator dealing with my request to pull some of the Waconah artifacts for use at the field school?"

"About as well as you might suspect. She may not say it to your face, but she was beside herself when your request came in. Went on and on about how it was 'highly irregular,' no security to speak of, the collection being in danger, stuff like that."

Jake looked around the dank, dusty hall with the crowded secondhand shelves, poor lighting, and uneven floor with a critical eye. "Yeah, I can see why someone would be leery of taking anything out of this pristine vault."

Erin nodded. "No argument here. Calling this place a curation facility is an insult to museums everywhere. I think she was trying to figure out some way to deny your request, but when the department head sent that note asking that your request be put on the fast track, she changed her mind awful quick."

"Well, Professor Chang is one of the few senior faculty members I haven't seemed to aggravate, and she owed me a favor for taking over her introductory archaeology lab mid-semester. Most of the rest are annoyed I haven't joined one side or the other in their stupid department politics. I was hoping a note from her would move things along down here. Obviously it worked, to a point."

"Nancy can never do anything quickly, you know that. I swear she must fill out a form before she relaxes enough to go to the bathroom. About the only thing she isn't anal about is taking her extended coffee breaks twice a day, so she can gossip with the rest of the hens upstairs."

"Well, I know I always have you to rely on, which helps a lot." Jake picked up a potsherd with a curved design, studied it for a moment, and then returned it to the pile. "I talked to Heather and Scott, and we decided that if you're willing, we'd plan on having you lead two or three of the evening lectures. This way we can get a nice balance between field and lab activities."

"Are you planning to have lectures every night?"

"No, just two or three times a week, depending on how things go. Any more than that and we'd have a mutiny for sure."

"Sure, that would be great."

"Don't plan on anything formal. We just want to keep the students thinking about what they are doing in the field and how it relates to analysis in the lab. Oh, and leave time for questions and general discussion."

"Are you still planning to rotate a few students in each week to help out with the artifact cataloging?"

"Yeah, but probably not until the second week. That should give you time to set up the field lab, and I want all the students out at the site when we first get started. After that, we'll shift people over so they can get at least a few days of lab time. Of course, everyone will be in when we get rained out."

"Is the building big enough to hold all those people?" Erin said. She packed up one box and returned it to the shelf.

"Yeah, it's actually a big recreation hall, put up by the forest service years ago. Sits on a nice high spot overlooking Taylor Lake. Besides the main classroom area, there's a full kitchen, some storerooms, and even a small bedroom for yours truly."

"Sounds pretty cozy, just you and some lucky young coed, while the rest of us suffer in Civil War surplus tents."

"It's not going to be that horrific, and you know it. The university is supplying a dozen five-person, cabin-style tents, practically brand new. Some rich alumnus donated them for one of those goofy corporate retreats, with all the deans, department chairs, chancellors, you know. Once the dust settled after that fiasco, they just patched up the bullet holes and cleaned up the blood spatter, and the tents haven't been used since. Guy over at Surplus Services told me about them."

"Well, that does sound pretty good, I guess," Erin said. "And I don't mind sharing with Heather, as long as she doesn't snore."

"You two will just have to work that out, I suppose. And the only time I'll have company in my room is when Amanda comes up on behalf of the History Center."

Erin's eyes lit up at mention of the Northern Mississippi Valley History Center. She had been trying to get hired there for the last few years, and hearing Amanda describe the place during her visits had only whetted her appetite. "Say, Jake, has . . ."

"I'm sorry Erin, but they're still not hiring at the Center. Amanda's keeping her ears open and will let you know as soon as she hears anything. Right now, the budget's pretty tight and none of the departments have any openings."

Erin nodded, but couldn't hide the disappointment on her face. "It worked out nice that the History Center is partially sponsoring the field school," Erin said as she continued to repack the artifact boxes.

"It works out well for everybody. The university gets support for the field school, and then a discount on curation costs at the History Center. They get to be involved in the field school and then have the artifacts and photos to use in their new archaeology exhibit."

Erin nodded as Jake handed her the final repacked box. "What about the artifacts from the first field school, the one Jacklyn Wardell did? Will that stuff end up at the Center, too?"

Jake had to think about that. "Hmm, now that you bring it up, I'm not sure it was ever specified. I think the agreement we have now is that they get all the Waconah artifacts from this year's field school only, once the analysis is completed. The rest of the assemblage stays here."

"Oh, okay. Thought I might hide myself in one of the big boxes and travel to La Crosse with the artifacts. You know, turn into the History Center phantom or something."

It was meant as a joke, but Jake caught the underlying bitterness in her tone. After years of slaving and abuse in the Social Sciences Archives Division, Erin was ready to leap at any possible chance to move on. Her career was stalled, and few among the senior archivists were interested in the fresh ideas and suggestions of the pert young woman. Their private joke for the establishment amounted to "the status quo is the way to go," usually enhanced with some choice curse words. While sympathetic as a kindred spirit, there was nothing Jake could do other than keep his ears open for job openings elsewhere and provide what opportunities he could at the university. He had felt much the same way not too many years earlier, bouncing from one short-term teaching appointment to another at a series of two and four-year colleges. When he finally landed the associate professor position at Wisconsin State University, his dreams had come true. Now, with tenure issues and his advancement to full professor apparently up in the air, he rued how easily dreams can turn into nightmares.

"Say, did I mention that Jacklyn Wardell's mother came to see me?" Jake said. As they straightened up the work area, Jake described the contents of the box she had brought and how adamant Mrs. Wardell was that her daughter had been murdered.

"Wow, that would be a great basis for a ghost story, don't you think? I can tell all the students how her ghost still haunts the site, and you can see a spectral light across the lake from the campground." As she spoke, Erin flicked off the backroom lights, plunging them into darkness before opening the heavy steel door.

"Be my guest, but don't say anything like that if Mrs. Wardell ever stops by. She still seems pretty broken up about it, although I guess my calling about the notes probably brought up a lot of bad memories."

"That's so sad, don't you think? Still hurting for her daughter after all these years."

"I suppose it's harder when someone young dies, rather than an elderly relative. When they're old or sick, you can always be comforted by the idea that they're out of their misery. For someone just starting out in life, it leaves all those dreams unfulfilled. And, if you believe they were taken from you intentionally, like a murder, it must be even harder to deal with."

CHAPTER FOUR

"Hey, Jake, mind giving me a hand here?"

The rasping voice came from behind a small tower of artifact boxes. To the casual observer, it might have appeared that the floating boxes had sprouted legs and were taking a break on the second-floor landing.

Jake hurried over, shifted half the boxes into his own arms, and tossed the Waconah files on top of the stack. Together the two men struggled up to the third floor. Both were puffing by the time they reached Doc Mahler's office.

"You know, Doc," Jake said as he shifted the load from one arm to the other, "if you'd just use the elevator you could have brought all this up on a cart."

"Do you know how many times I've gotten trapped in that damn thing?" Doc Mahler said as he fished his office key from his pocket. "And that was before they fixed up this old dump."

An archaeologist's office, almost without exception, is full of clutter. Books, professional journals, articles, and artifacts are the norm, but in addition there are always the odd bits of paraphernalia found during surveys, knickknacks and toys received as gifts, and varied items collected during years of semi-professional scrounging. In the same manner that the age of a site can be roughly determined based on the layers of soil positioned above it, the length of an archaeologist's career can be estimated by the amount of clutter present. Based on the plethora of items contained in his tiny third-floor office, one would gauge that Professor Carl Mahler had been an archaeologist for at least a century and probably longer.

"So, what do you have going here, Doc?"

"Oh, just pulled some of the better artifacts from that fur trader's cabin I excavated back in '75 and '76. Finally got up to Montreal and went through the original company books, and found some old journals and magistrate's records that confirmed Ignace Hebert was the one running the post. Just what I need to finish up my book, but I wanted to have some new artifact photos taken."

Jake set his load on one end of the long worktable and critically eyed the trays already overflowing with gunflints, jaw harps, broken crockery, and clay pipe stems. "Sure you've got enough artifacts?"

Doc Mahler's head snapped up, his wispy gray hair wafting high as he gave Jake a sideways glance. His eyes twinkled beneath his furrowed brow, though, and he returned Jake's grin with one of his own. "Hey, I think after working on this damn project for more than two decades, I can afford to take a little extra time to make sure all the best artifacts are photographed properly in the report. Look at these clay pipes, and these trade beads."

Mahler spoke at length about the colored glass beads and pipe bowls on the tray, several similar examples from other sites in the Great Lakes region, and on changes observed in these artifacts over time. Jake listened with interest, and marveled at the encyclopedic level of knowledge stored in the older man's head. If you ever needed information on any subject, "Musket" Mahler was the one to ask.

Jake's eyes flickered to the gold-plated flintlock musket mounted above the desk. Rumor had it this was an exact replica of the Brown Bess musket from which Doc Mahler had received his nickname. When he semi-retired a few years before and became director of the department's contract archaeology program, his colleagues and some former students pitched in and presented it to him as a tribute. According to campus legend, Mahler was in the midst of a show-and-tell portion of his Historical Archaeology seminar when the musket fired. No one was injured, but two glass display cases and a replica *Homo habilis* skull hadn't been as fortunate. His career survived the mishap and years later he was still considered one of the preeminent archaeologists in the state. Jake hoped he'd be this sharp and productive when he became an emeritus professor. Assuming he made it to that point, of course.

Mahler wrapped up his discourse on the beads and settled into his chair. "Any luck finding those missing Waconah site notes, Jake?"

"Actually, yes. I got in touch with Linda Wardell on the off-chance that she might have had them, and she showed up the other day with a box full of old files, notebooks, and some photos that should prove useful. I'll let you know what I find out."

"Sounds good. I'm still hoping to come up for a visit at some point, but I need to stay local in case Chang needs me for that highway survey project we've got in Bayfield County. With her serving her stint as department chair and you running the field school, it falls on me to keep an eye on our contract archaeology projects."

"The grad students should be able to keep the project on track, I would think."

"Yeah, but since the contract is through the university, they need at least one or two staffers to be around to deal with any problems that pop up. Unfortunately, Clark and most of the other professors tend to look at cultural resource management archaeology as something you scrape off your boots. Damn shame, really."

G. Clark Kelley was the senior North American archaeologist in the department and Jake's chief nemesis. "I'll say. Lots of good archaeology comes out of CRM and contract projects. I thought the days of academia versus CRM archaeology were pretty much over."

"Well, there's always going to be disagreements over how to view archaeology, as a scholarly pursuit or as a resource to be managed, with a business slant. Both sides have their champions and there are pros and cons to each. Likewise, you find good and bad work done by archaeologists in both camps."

Doc Mahler coughed, a harsh bark from deep in his throat. His doctor had told him to quit smoking, but he couldn't seem to break the habit.

"As long as the department is underfunded, though, and our contract work yields decent sites and material for the students to work on, I think the contract program is here to stay."

"Speaking of grad students, Doc, I wanted to ask if you know the whereabouts of some of Jacklyn Wardell's old students." Jake retrieved his Waconah file from the top of a nearby box. "Here's a copy of that memorial report on Waconah that came out after she died. I figure some of her grad students might be able to help me with some questions about the field school, if I can track them down. I know Terry Schroeder and I've met Alice Koster once or twice, but I've drawn a blank on the rest."

Doc Mahler scanned the list of contributors. "Well, other than Lorenzo and Griffiths, can't say for sure. Lorenzo is running a CRM firm in Kentucky or Ohio, I think. She had an article in the Ohio archaeology journal about a year ago. Jim Griffiths is teaching at the University of South Dakota. Not sure if the other three are even in archaeology anymore. Mark Winters pretty much dropped off the face of the earth, far as I know."

"That figures. He's the one I wanted to get in touch with the most. He was listed as the senior assistant for the project, and it looks like he wrote or at least edited most of this memorial report."

"Well, the department secretary might be able to help you track him down. Rochelle's been pretty good at keeping tabs on all our wayward students and alums over the years. And if she doesn't know where he is, you can bet she'll be able to get in touch with folks who probably do."

Jake stuffed the report back into the file. "Say, would Clark know much about the Waconah dig? He was just starting out here about that time, right?"

Doc Mahler searched his memory. "Well, Jacklyn and Clark didn't see eye-to-eye, really, and there was more than a bit of competition between them. The students sort of chose up sides, too, and didn't interact much. Clark was the senior investigator for the project, but I don't think he ever bothered to do any research on the site. They had to include a second staff member on the grant application, simply because it was going to be a long-term project and he had a few more years under his belt."

"I'm surprised he didn't follow up on the excavations after she died," Jake said.

"I don't think he was all that interested in the project, and Jacklyn did all the work anyway," Doc Mahler said. "Not to gossip, but I remember after the accident there was an incident in one of the grad seminars that was something of a minor scandal for the department. One of Jacklyn's students accused Clark of killing her. Clark blew his top and you could hear the yelling all the way down in my classroom. The department chair got it under control pretty quick, but it was pretty tense around here for the next few weeks. They brought in the counselors, again, and chalked it all up to traumatic stress following the death of a very well-liked teacher."

"Sounds like that student had a pretty specific grudge,

31

though, not just simple distress over the death of someone they admired."

"Maybe," Doc Mahler said with a shrug. "People react in weird ways when death is involved. Anyway, it all quieted down after a few weeks and that was the end of it."

Back in his office, Jake checked his phone and email messages and replied to those he deemed urgent. With that chore completed, he sent emails to Schroeder, Koster, Griffiths, and Lorenzo to inquire about the Waconah field school. On a hunch, he tried "Mark Winters" and "Mark Winters archaeology" on several Internet search engines, only to be rewarded with several thousand hits. A search for "Winters Wardell Waconah" brought in a more manageable fourteen positive hits, but all referred to the Wardell memorial volume or references to it in regional archaeological reports. With luck, one of Jacklyn's old students might still be in contact with him.

Jake made a brief attempt to straighten his office, spurred by a failure to locate his grading notebook for his Introduction to Old World Archaeology class. Once the notebook turned up, he spent an hour checking the notebook entries against those recorded on the official university database. As the day progressed, a dozen students from his various classes stopped by with questions and two of his grad students turned in research papers for him to review.

"Dr. Caine?"

"Yes? Oh, hi Janice. What can I do for you?"

"Rochelle asked me to bring you these purchasing orders for your field school, and some other documents that need your signature."

"Okay, thanks. I'll take care of them." He took the forms and set them on top of the nearest mound of folders.

The office assistant nodded, but made no effort to leave the office.

"Is there something else?"

Janice chewed on her lower lip. "Well, Rochelle gave me strict orders not to leave until everything was properly signed."

"Is this an implication that my office is disorganized?" Jake said with a smile as he made an exaggerated show of scanning the room. "I'll have you know, it may seem like a mess to the untrained eye, but there is order in this chaos and I can find anything I need. It might take a few hours, of course."

She giggled, and relaxed as Jake opened the folder and signed the documents. "Sorry. You know how Rochelle gets. I'm just following orders."

"Not a problem. I suppose there was a small possibility that I might have misplaced something," Jake said as he returned the forms. "Say, if you get a chance, ask Rochelle if she remembers a grad student named Mark Winters. He was here about ten or twelve years ago, and worked with Jacklyn Wardell. I'm trying to track him down."

Janice agreed and dashed out of the room. Jake glanced at his watch, pushed his work aside, and checked his email. Schroeder and Griffiths had both replied a few hours earlier but could offer little additional information on the original Waconah dig or the current whereabouts of Mark Winters. Terry Schroeder was of the impression that Mark had dropped out of the profession due to a drug problem. Cathy Lorenzo, likewise, had no idea where Winters might be but offered to send copies of her old field notebooks. An automated email reply came from Alice Koster's office stating that she was on sabbatical this semester and to contact the department secretary if it was urgent. Most of the remaining messages were from students requesting meetings during the upcoming week. Jake toyed with the idea of forwarding his spam email to Clark Kelley, especially the one promising to increase his member size by three inches (or more), but decided it probably wouldn't be a good idea.

Instead, he settled back in his chair with Jacklyn's field notebook and attempted to absorb all he could about the original Waconah excavations. Jake jotted down a few notes here and there, mostly snippets about feature locations and artifact concentrations. He skimmed through the personal comments, grinning to himself in sympathy as she groused about problematic students, arguments with one of the local landowners, and some caustic comments about other archaeologists who were giving her grief.

Nearly every page contained some doodles or a tiny sketch, some of which demonstrated the depth and natural skill of a talented artist. A few full-page drawings portrayed the site itself, both in its then-current state and as it might have looked when occupied by the Oneota inhabitants. Jake laughed at one image, a dead-ringer of Clark Kelley floundering in Taylor Lake as sharks and turtles circle menacingly. He stopped smiling a few pages later, when he found a sketch of the lake with the three islands visible in the distance, and *"Survey these A.S.A.P.!"* scribbled underneath. From that point, all Jake could think of was frail Mrs. Wardell in his office, insisting that Jacklyn had been murdered, and an image of Jacklyn Wardell struggling in her tiny boat as the storm raged around her.

CHAPTER FIVE

From Jacklyn Wardell's journal:

June 4. Work is finally underway at Waconah!!! Great bunch of students and my grad students can't be beat, even if they are some crazy oddballs sometimes. Finding a few features but taking some time to get through the old plow zone; maybe I should have scheduled a backhoe after all(?).

Thought I would be rid of The Dark One when we left campus, but even long-distance he is a major pest. Two calls yesterday, and one so far today. Yes, Dark One, I do know how to excavate a site, and recognize a pit feature, and how to screen dirt, etc. Maybe he will lighten up after his "inspection" next week. Doubt it.

And yet another thrilling visit from our northern neighbors today. Grand Professor Snootypants (boo) and his assistant Lady Margaret came down from "on high" again to complain about our dig. He should talk, rooting through mounds with his stupid "exploratory trench" and his ham-fisted approach to archaeology. Thousands of sites in Wisconsin and we have to be right on top of each other. JERK!!! Bet he was the one who complained to the State about our screening. Maybe I should let Snowman and Curls toss him in the lake like they suggested. Would serve him right. Well, we'll see who's on top when the season is over!

Weird seeing Lady Margaret again. We had all those classes together as undergrads, but I don't recall her ever being very friendly. She seems to remember it differently, though. Oh well, guess if I was working for Professor Snootypants I'd be looking for a friendly face, too.

A few weeks later found Professor Caine, graduate assistants Heather and Scott, and over two dozen students bustling about the Waconah site. The sun shone over the treetops to the east, the promise of a warm summer carried in the gentle breeze. Enthusiastic students were put to work removing brush and clearing spaces for digging while Jake, Heather, and Scott set up a grid for mapping. The meadow grasses and thorny bushes were soon removed, quickly replaced by a forest of wooden stakes, nails, string, and small pin flags. Baby ducks bobbed among the reeds in the weedy shallows, herded to safety by their mothers as the students' ground-clearing onslaught advanced. Small collections of turtle eggshell, bird feathers, the odd piece of fishing tackle, and unusual rocks accumulated on the folding picnic table set up on the edge of the gravel parking lot. Aside from the occasional beverage can or bottle, modern trash was scarce, reflecting the limited use of the boat launch since the more recent one had been constructed at the north end of the lake.

Around lunch, work came to dramatic halt as cries of "snake" erupted at the north end of the site, followed by a mad scramble of students rushing toward the vehicles. Jake identified the culprit as a piece of black rubber tubing, likely a discarded fuel line from an old outboard motor. As they settled in for lunch, Jake took the opportunity to remind them all that no venomous snakes were found in that part of the state and they should be more concerned about ticks, wasps, and other pests.

In the afternoon, Jake decided a tour of the area was in order. Relying on a copy of Wardell's field map, he described the presumed layout of the site and what he expected to find this summer. Moving north, the group crossed a log bridge over a small stream and then followed a rugged hiking trail up to the top of the nearby terrace. As they paused for breath after the steep climb, Jake gave them a summary of the location.

"The Christianson II site is located on this terrace," Jake said. "The mounds, some of which are visible over there, were first identified in the 1920s and some excavations were done right after World War II. Lots of Late Woodland pottery but no Oneota material, indicating Christianson II was occupied before Waconah, by a different group of people. Chapman College dug here around ten years ago, about the same time as Dr. Wardell was at Waconah."

"How do they know the two sites were used by different people, and not just the same group using different pots and stuff?" Andy said. He was a sophomore with an interest in Archaic spearpoints. "I mean, what if the two spots were used for different activities?"

A few students had similar comments, so Jake led the group in an impromptu comparison of Late Woodland and Oneota peoples, pointing out how differences in the archaeological record at sites could be used to distinguish one group from another. He reminded them of the concept of an archaeological signature, through which a prehistoric group was recognized by the distinct characteristics of the pottery, stone tools, house structures, and other artifacts and features they left behind. Using examples from the Christianson II and Waconah sites, Jake constructed distinct artifact classes for the inhabitants of each locale.

"So how come Wardell never came back here?" Dale said as he crumpled a soda can under his boot. He was a lanky junior with a deadpan sense of humor. "She find a better place or something?"

"Well, archaeologists often put in a lot of time at different sites, looking for evidence relevant to their research interests.

Those interests change over time, um, or they find new opportunities or sites they can't pass up. Other times they get involved with one site and never get around to returning."

His voice trailed off as Jake noticed the frown on Heather's face, her hands raised in an attempt to get his attention. "You might as well just tell them," Heather said. "They're going to find out sooner or later."

Most of the students looked confused, at least those who were attempting to follow him. "In this case, though, Professor Wardell died before she could come back to the site." Jake sighed. "She died right here at Waconah, in fact."

The uncomfortable silence lasted for a few scant seconds.

"Here at the site? How? What happened?" Jake held up his hand and the clamor of questions ceased.

"There was a boating accident. She went out to survey some of the islands," Jake gestured past the students to the tree-dotted forms in Taylor Lake. "And a storm blew up. Her boat must have overturned, and she drowned. Her body was recovered a day or two later."

Jake noticed a few whispered comments between some students, but most stared out toward the lake or at him, waiting to hear more.

"Part of the reason we're here now is to follow up on what Professor Wardell started. Other than the Anthropology Department report I gave you as part of your class packet, the results of the first field school were never written up. Most of the artifacts were never fully analyzed and right now there are more questions than answers when it comes to Waconah."

Several students still had questions. "How come no one else ever came back here? You know, to continue her research?"

"Some established professors will groom their students to follow up their research," Jake said, "while others prefer to send them out on their own to find their own sites and develop their own interests."

"You have to realize, too, that there are literally thousands of archaeological sites out there waiting to be investigated," Heather said. "There's not much money for research projects. Most sites are excavated as part of CRM projects, with government funding, but less time for analysis and research, usually."

"That's true," Jake said. "Strict academics have to be pretty choosy. The smart ones combine contract work and research whenever possible. Jacklyn Wardell was fairly young when she died and her students pretty much made their own paths after that. When no one took an immediate interest in the material she collected, all the notes and artifacts went into curation. Anyway, that's enough sightseeing for today. Let's head back to the site and get back to work."

Heather and Scott were a bit surprised at Jake's abrupt shift in plans, but assumed he was eager to get started on the field investigations. It would likely be a multi-year project and good results during the first season would entail better funding down the road.

Jake was anxious to make significant progress during the upcoming season, but at present he found himself more than a little upset by the callous comments he overheard from some of the students. He chalked most of it up to the insensitivity of youth, but since his meeting with Mrs. Wardell he felt a certain odd kinship for the dead professor he was replacing at Waconah. And if her death had not been an accident, as her mother so adamantly believed, he supposed it was understandable that he might feel uneasy when the subject arose. At least he hoped that's all it was.

CHAPTER SIX

"Say, isn't that one of the Forest Service vehicles up by the hall?" Heather said as the truck maneuvered through the tree-lined gravel road.

"Looks like it," Jake said. "Not many vehicles painted that awful green color. Yeah, I see Bob Jingst out there talking to Erin."

The caravan of vehicles pulled to a stop in front of the recreation hall. Jake and Heather hopped out of their vehicle and shook hands with the DNR property manager while the students dispersed across the campsite.

"Hi, Bob. Good to see you again."

"Hey, Jake. I see you've got your students all settled in," Bob said, gesturing at the various tents scattered across the group campsite in the yard opposite the building. The half-acre landscape was dotted with tents, roughly distributed around a large central fire pit. The female students were set up on the south side while the males occupied the north half. The two tents occupied by Heather and Erin and Scott, positioned a few yards from the fire pit, marked the boundary between the two groups. Field boots and dirty sneakers were set outside most of the tents, while towels and field clothes hung on nearby ropes strung between the trees.

"I aired out the hall for a couple days before you showed up," Bob said, "and dropped off the extra supplies I mentioned. Should be plenty of firewood in the bin by the storage shed, too. I'll stop by in a few weeks to restock, but if you need anything in the meantime just leave a message on my cell."

"Thanks. We should be fine," Jake said. "Heather, Scott, Erin, and I came early with tons of food and our field supplies, so we had a chance to get situated before the students arrived. I appreciate all your help."

"No problem at all. We don't get too many big groups wanting to use the group campsite, so it was nice to be able to rent it out for so many weeks this summer." Bob looked around the area, his attention drawn to a boisterous group of kids setting up a volleyball net between two trees. "Speaking of big groups, though, and I hate to bring this up, but occasionally we get folks over at the single campsites who complain about the noise from the group sites, especially if young folks are around."

"I understand. We spoke to the students and they know they have to stay in line if they want to pass the class. After a long hot day digging, I don't imagine we'll have any trouble enforcing the curfew. Besides, this group of kids is pretty mature."

At that moment, two shrieking girls in bikinis ran past, followed by three screaming boys, all headed for the beach. Jake rolled his eyes and Bob scuffed at the gravel with his boot as he smothered a laugh.

"Sorry about that," Jake said. "Today was our first full day and they're probably blowing off some steam. Clearing brush and laying out nails and string for excavation units can get pretty boring."

"Don't worry about it. I got a couple of teens of my own," Bob said, still smiling. "So, you expect to find much during your dig?"

"I hope so. The other field school showed that Waconah was a fairly substantial Oneota village. Lots of features, pottery, good bone preservation. We plan to open up some hand units first, and then bring in a backhoe to remove a portion of the old

41

plow zone, so we can see a larger part of the village. That'll give us a better picture of the overall plan of the village and guide us as we continue the excavations."

"So you'll be coming back again next year?"

"Most likely. If we find enough artifacts and features, we can argue that more research is needed. And if more research is warranted, we can get grant funding for more analysis and testing."

"I was just starting out here during the last dig. Shame about the lady professor who drowned. I figured the site had some bad voodoo tied to it, which is why no one ever came back."

"Wardell had planned a multi-year project, but it all fell apart after her death," Jake said. "Unfortunately, there are lots of projects and old sites that get forgotten, and collections sit around waiting for someone to analyze them. And money is always an issue, too."

"Don't have to tell me about money issues, that's for sure," Bob said. "Our budget gets trimmed every fiscal year but we still have to do the same amount of work, or even more work with less people, usually."

"Yeah, I noticed the old boat landing and pier by the site is in pretty bad shape."

"Now that we have the new landing a few miles to the north, by the intersection, there aren't any plans to maintain the old landing. A few of the locals still use it but none of the tourists. Eventually the pier will rot out and collapse and that'll be the end of it."

Bob's phone rang, a sharp clang similar to an electric cowbell. After a few moments, he hung up and turned back to Jake.

"Gotta go. Some fool missed his parking spot and hooked the axle of his trailer on a stump." He shook his head in disgust. "Another typical day in the park. See ya."

Jake waved as Bob drove off, and walked to the bathhouse to

clean up. He mentally reviewed his planned remarks for the post-dinner meeting, offhandedly wondering how Jacklyn Wardell ran her field school. All the effort put in, so many little details to fret over, and all for nothing because of a stupid boating accident.

CHAPTER SEVEN

The next few days went smoothly enough as the students picked up the nuances of archaeological fieldwork. Some caught on quicker than others, and on several occasions Jake, Heather, and Scott had to remind them all to slow down. The idea of archaeology as a destructive process, as sites are destroyed through excavation in order to collect the information they contained, was stressed in the field during the day and in the evening lectures and lab sessions. To drive the point home, Jake put a large sign on the kitchen wall that summarized his message:

> *Archaeology isn't about the artifacts; it's what the artifacts can tell us about the people.*

Despite a few minor problems, by the beginning of the second week things had progressed under the watchful eye of Jake and his graduate students. More often than not, a minor suggestion coupled with a compliment or two had the best results. The students found enough interesting artifacts to keep morale high and each new discovery drew a curious crowd. Observations and note taking improved as more and more artifacts were found, and the pace of excavation slowed as the students carefully troweled off each new layer of soil. This gave Jake more opportunity to examine the excavation units scattered across the site, work with the students individually, and plan out further work based on their initial finds. Taking a late-morning break, he drew Heather and Scott aside to evaluate their excavation strategy.

"Scott, are they still finding lots of pottery in the northern units?" Jake said as he studied the large field map taped to an oversized drawing board.

"Some." Scott leafed through some wrinkled, dirt-smeared field forms. "The sherd count in Unit 9 has doubled over the last two levels. About the same in Unit 8, too."

"What about Unit 10?"

"Can't tell. Sarah and Lisa started that one last week but they're both in the lab now. Remember? Lisa got a bad sunburn so you put her in the lab, and sent Sarah along to help Erin."

Jake nodded, and wrote "delayed" next to the unit on the big map.

"Do you want me to put another crew on that unit?" Scott said.

"No, it can sit a few days until they come back," Jake said. "When they hit the sterile soil in Units 8 and 9, have them open up some adjacent units on the west, after they draw the profile wall. Walk them through it, if you have to."

"How are things progressing on the big block?" Jake said to Heather, who supervised a group of students digging a series of extended test units in the center of the excavation area.

"Pretty good. Most everyone is getting the hang of digging and screening, but I'm still getting lots of 'Is this something?' questions," Heather said, rolling her eyes. "Oh, and get this. I was telling Andy and Dale to start opening up the unit to the north of where they are now, and Bryant hops over to throw in his two cents. Little jerk, trying to show me up."

"He's Clark's first-year grad student, right?" Scott said. "The one who had zero field experience when he arrived last semester?"

"Yeah, that's him. Suddenly he's a big expert on stratigraphy and features. He told half the students around him that they're missing features, or that rodent holes are posts marking houses. Just to warn you, I wasn't exactly polite when I told him to mind his own business."

Jake suppressed a laugh, recalling how he had done something similar on more than one occasion when he was a grad student. "Well, try to go easy on him. Could be he's just enthusiastic and wants to make a good impression. I'll talk to him if things don't improve."

Heather mumbled something under her breath, but Jake didn't pursue the matter further. "Anyway, Paula and Brooke have reached the sterile subsoil in their unit and I need to know where you want them to dig next."

"Let's see, they were just north and east of where we figure Wardell's old Unit 12 was located . . . hmm. What was their artifact count like?"

Heather made a quick scan of their paperwork. "Not much, really. About a dozen flakes, a few crumbs of pottery, some charcoal. Possible feature about halfway down but turned out to be an old rodent burrow."

"That shouldn't be." Jake frowned at the site map. The newly opened units were overlain against definite and possible units dug years earlier. He pointed at a particular set of units. "We must have this group in the wrong spot. I expected them to hit the big garbage midden but it looks like we missed it."

"Could be they misjudged the location during the old dig," Heather said, peering over his shoulder. "They should be hitting tons of stuff if they're over the midden. Maybe they messed up the original map, after Jacklyn Wardell died, in the confusion of trying to close up the excavation afterward."

"The old map has to be off," Scott said. "We hit part of an old unit in our Unit 5, and according to this map the nearest unit was at least four meters away."

Jake nodded. "Makes sense. On the original it does look like three or four people were adding things to the field map at different times, and who knows how accurate they were? All right, make sure Paula and Brooke do a good job drawing the wall profile, and then move them," he scanned the landscape around the students, "over to the west a few meters, near that little rise."

"Gotcha, boss. Even if it doesn't pan out, it'll keep them occupied until the backhoe arrives and we open up a bigger trench."

"Good. And I'll talk about the problems with the old maps during tonight's lecture. Should be a good lesson on keeping detailed records."

"I'm sure Bryant will have dozens of insightful comments to make," Heather said as she rose and strode off in the direction of several frantically waving students at the far end of the site.

CHAPTER EIGHT

The battered pickup truck crept down the dirt road leading to the boat launch, attracting the attention of everyone at the dig. Visitors were fairly common at archaeological excavations. A few were collectors or amateur archaeologists, eager to see the results of kindred spirits interested in the past. Others were drawn in by simple curiosity, wondering what on earth all those unkempt youngsters could be doing grubbing around in the dirt all day long. The majority were pleasant, fortunately, with the disapproving not bothering to waste their time by stopping. Almost inevitably, each visitor thought he or she was the first to come up with the joke, "Digging for buried treasure?" This visitor, however, was a knowledgeable exception.

"Hi, name's Charlie Garath. You folks digging up the Oneota village, huh?" he inquired, extending his hand. Charlie was in his early fifties with thinning hair and a strong, calloused grip.

"You guessed it," Jake said, smiling in return. "I'm Jake Caine, an archaeology professor at Wisconsin State University. We've just started a field school here at Waconah."

"Wow, that's great. No one's been out here in over ten years. Things kind of folded up after the other professor drowned. You know about that, right? Damn shame, she was such a nice gal. Chapman College was out here at the same time, up on the hill to the north. Mostly digging around the mound groups. Not in 'em, though, pretty rare anybody gets to dig up mounds anymore. Some of the old timers 'round here used to dig for

48

pots and stuff when they were kids, but most of what they found is long gone. So you guys finding much?"

His rapid-fire speech left Jake a bit bewildered, at a momentary loss on which statement to address first. He decided to go with the last and the easiest.

"Well, this is only our second week out here but we've recovered a lot of shell-tempered pottery, fair amount of lithic debris, not too much in the way of bone or shell, yet. Couple of pit features, but we won't open them up until we get everything mapped in."

"Is the stone mostly local chert? Most of the guys around here get nothing but that stuff. Really poorly made points, lots of busted tools."

"There's some chert, yeah, but most of the arrow points, scrapers, and other tools are Hixton orthoquartzite, from over in Jackson County. Probably traded for the stone, but they may have made expeditions over there, at least early on. Later, after A.D. 1400, the folks in this part of the state seemed to get cut off from the best stone resources, and had to rely on the local chert."

Charlie scratched at the gray stubble on his chin as he looked around the site. "Seems to me I remember Doc Wardell sayin' something like that, too. Shame about her drowning and all. Bunch of us from NEWAS volunteered on her dig off and on, whenever we could spare the time. That's our local archaeology club, Northeast Wisconsin Archaeology Society. She seemed to really appreciate the help, and was real decent about showin' us stuff, and makin' us feel like part of the team."

"Sounds pretty smart on her part. I've always found that the local collectors are a real treasure-trove of info on area sites. Anybody in particular I should get in touch with?"

As quick as he could, Charlie rattled off a list of names, phone numbers, and descriptions of each person's collection and where they collected. If Jake had been searching for a walking encyclopedia of the local archaeology, he had certainly found one.

"You might want to talk to Al Droessler, too. He's got a good-sized collection and took a lot of photos at the site back during the first dig. Not sure what he's all got, but he was really gung-ho about it back then. Use to come to the NEWAS meetings a lot, but he's got some heart issues and doesn't get around much anymore."

"Thanks, I'll do that," Jake said as he jotted down the names and numbers in his field notebook. A thought struck him. "Say, Charlie, I've been trying to track down some of the grad assistants who were at the site with Professor Wardell, just to get some more info on how their dig went, areas they meant to check, stuff like that, but haven't had much luck. You know any folks from NEWAS who might have kept in touch with any of them?"

Charlie scratched his head, brows furrowed. "Not really. After Wardell drowned and the dig closed up, that was pretty much the end of it. We always hoped we'd get copies of the report, or that one of the students might come up and give a talk. I suppose you could talk to Everett Kojarski. He was the county sheriff at the time and talked to everyone after the accident. Everett's got a decent collection of Archaic notched and stemmed points, too."

Jake smiled, amused but impressed by Charlie's obvious enthusiasm for local archaeology. "Well, my grad assistants and I will definitely try to meet up with these collectors. As long as you're here, how about a tour? I can show you what we've come up with so far, and if you've got the time I'll put you to work on one of the screens."

"Hell, yes! I was kinda hoping you might ask. I run my own landscaping company so I can pretty much set my own schedule, and as long as I keep bringing home the bacon the wife doesn't particularly care if I'm around that much!"

One day later, the first reporter arrived. He was a local, representing the weekly county newspaper (complete with a special insert during the tourist season). His cousin was in the NEWAS group and heard from Charlie Garath about the dig. Thought it would make for a nice piece for their local happenings section.

The next day, the county stringer from the Green Bay paper arrived with a geriatric photographer in tow. Together they used up about three hours of Jake's day, but the reporter was surprisingly well informed about the area and even had some familiarity with archaeology. He knew about the boating accident that had killed Jacklyn Wardell and jokingly asked if the site might be cursed. Jake prayed that tomorrow's *Green Bay Press-Gazette* wouldn't be splashed with the headline "Archaeologists Defy Curse at Haunted Indian Burial Ground!" That kind of publicity he could do without.

Fortunately, when the story ran Friday morning, it was well written and pretty accurate, with only one sentence about Wardell's drowning years earlier. The reporter included some quotes from the students about their finds, where they were from, and how much they enjoyed what they were doing. Despite the photographer's shaky hands, the article even included some nice photos of a decorated rim sherd, a bone awl, and three students pointing to a large biface fortuitously revealed in a dirt-filled screen. The students were all pretty excited. For most, it was the first time they'd ever been interviewed or had their pictures in the paper. After the clamor died down and the students were back at work, Jake called Erin at the field lab and asked her to pick up copies for each student.

Jake's mood sagged by noon when he received a call from the

local CBS affiliate asking to schedule an interview. The reporter talked almost as fast as Charlie Garath and Jake wondered if she might be a relative.

"Yes, Monday afternoon will be fine," Jake said. "Um, how did you get my number, by the way?"

"Oh, the WSU department secretary, Roxanne I think, she gave me the number. She said you'd be thrilled to be interviewed on TV."

"Hmm, yes, thrilled." Heather stood a few feet away, holding her finger like a gun against her forehead.

"So, the film crew and I will be there sometime after lunch, okay? I'll call when we're close so you can direct us to the site."

"Sure. Just take the first road on the left, north of Keeling's Hillside Resort."

Jake closed his phone, stared at it for a moment, and then looked at the rolling waves on Taylor Lake. He glanced at the phone again, and then at the water.

"If you want, boss, I can screen your calls for the rest of the day," Heather said. "Probably not a good idea to toss your phone in the lake. That is what you're thinking, isn't it?"

"Maybe."

"C'mon, hand it over."

Jake took a final look at the lake, and handed her the phone. "Fine. Remind me to kill Rochelle when we get back to campus."

"Sure, sure. Of course," she said with one eyebrow raised. "I would be remiss if I didn't say that I kind of told you this would happen, after Charlie the collector stopped by."

Jake grimaced, mesmerized by the undulating waves on the lake. Why me? Heather found this all devilishly amusing and began to scold Jake further, but he cut her off.

"One more word and I'll black-ball your dissertation proposal, understand?"

Feigning terror, Heather made a quick zip-and-lock motion over her lips, and then scampered off to finish her lunch.

CHAPTER NINE

Jake tried to keep news about the TV crew quiet, so naturally by dinner it was the exclusive topic of conversation among the students. Several students asked if they should take extra time to clean their units for the interview, or even hold back some artifacts so they could be discovered during filming. Erin offered to wash some artifacts for a display and was willing to set up a temporary lab station on site, if necessary. Bryant suggested it might be informative for him to demonstrate stratigraphic profiling on camera, perhaps with some select artifacts placed in the wall profile. Heather whispered a comment in response to that suggestion, resulting in a burst of laughter from the students sitting nearby. Bryant shot her a dirty look, but the chorus of students arguing the merits of their own ideas thwarted any potential fight between the two.

Jake soon tired of the increasingly ridiculous ideas and managed to slip into his room unnoticed. He retrieved his iPod from his battered leather briefcase and let the classic rock and roll of the fifties and sixties drown out the heated voices in the main hall. He spent a few blissful hours updating his field journal and reading before turning in for the night.

Although an early riser by nature, Jake pretended to sleep through breakfast the next morning, hoping to avoid another barrage of questions from would-be TV stars. Once he made his appearance, he was pleased to find that most of the students had driven into town for the day.

Given the size of Donovan, Wisconsin, it hadn't taken long for the students to identify all the best spots in town. Colorful pushpins adorned a map of the town, tacked to a bulletin board near the fridge, noting all points of interest: best bars, cheapest pizza, the sole coffeehouse, the cinema, decent restaurants, and so on. The students were ecstatic when it was discovered that the municipal library had free Internet access and a row of computers available for email, surfing the Web, and blogging. The ancient landline connection at the state park was insufferably slow and most everyone gave up using it soon after.

In the kitchen, Jake grabbed a bagel and an apple from the fridge, poured some coffee, and sat down to enjoy a late breakfast. It was then that he noticed the flyers posted on the doors and walls, and the large sign taped to the empty coffee can in the middle of the table:

BEACH PARTY BLOWOUT!!!
TONIGHT, DUSK 'TIL DAWN
DONATIONS DEMANDED!

Jake rolled his eyes. This wasn't unexpected, of course, but he had hoped this year's students might not come up with the idea so early in the season. Still, it was set for the weekend and as long as it didn't interfere with their work during the week, he was more than willing to let them have some fun. He pulled a twenty from his wallet and slipped it in the donation can, although he knew he would only make a token appearance. The kids would have much more fun if the old man wasn't around to inhibit their carousing.

To Jake's surprise, the crew put a lot of effort into planning their party. Most of the money was spent on beer, wine, and soda (in that order), but there were also plenty of burgers, brats, salads, chips, and even tofu dogs for the vegetarians. Jake ate a slightly charred burger and some watery potato salad, washed down with a bottle of beer. He joked around with the students for an hour or so before retiring to his room. As he left, Jake reminded Scott and Heather to keep an eye on things.

Jake rose early the next morning and enjoyed the blissful silence that permeated the camp. Several hours passed before the first students staggered into the hall, where they sipped coffee and tea in moody silence. Over time, more disheveled and groggy students arrived. Feeling a bit crowded, Jake decided to take a brief hike on one of the nearby nature trails.

As he left the hall, Jake was struck by the minor carnage left from the party. The area between the fire pit and the beach was littered with plastic cups and beer cans. He counted three bikini tops caught on branches in nearby trees and a pair of teal shorts that could belong to either male or female. The debris field faded out as he neared the edge of the woods, with only scattered food wrappers, several mismatched sandals, and a beach towel present to mar the natural scenery.

Jake followed an older trail, partly obscured by vegetation sprouting up in the middle of the path, which curved north and then west. He soon reached a small gravel parking area along the state highway, which he estimated was a few miles north of the main park entrance. Jake backtracked a ways, veered off on a clear, southerly trending path, and within an hour was back at the group campground.

He realized there would be little enthusiasm for the scheduled lecture, so Jake posted a notice cancelling the evening event, provided all evidence of the party was cleaned up before it was supposed to start. He then returned to his room where he busied himself with his field notes, examined some of the pottery recovered during the week, and even added a few pages to an upcoming journal article. The grounds were cleaned shortly after lunch, so Jake gave everyone the night off. The grateful students went into town or loafed around the camp, and were in fine spirits as work resumed Monday morning.

Jake was rereading a battered paperback Monday evening after dinner when his cell phone rang. Recognizing the caller ID, he answered. "Hey, Amanda."

"Hi, Jake. I saw the news report on the dig online, about an hour ago. You looked really good, but it was pretty short."

"Thanks. It was about what I expected. The reporter was here for almost three hours, but I knew they'd only use a few minutes of video on the news. I tried to warn the students but they all thought they would have a starring role."

"Were they disappointed?"

"Actually not that much," Jake said. "Most of them showed up in the background at least, and they thought that was pretty cool. No one was singled out for attention, so I guess they were happy everyone came out the same. Oh, except for Bryant, maybe."

"He's the one that Heather can't stand, right? Kind of a know-it-all?"

"Yeah, that's the one. He kept hovering around the reporter, trying to draw her attention to the feature he was excavating. No artifacts were visible so the reporter didn't show much interest. For whatever reason, Bryant seems to think he should be a supervisor, just because he's a grad student. I've got a couple of undergrads right now who could dig circles around this guy."

"He's Clark Kelley's student, right?" Amanda said. "Maybe Clark told him he would be used as a supervisor or student-leader on the dig."

"It's possible, I suppose. Well, at least he isn't doing too much damage. Heather and Scott have let the students know that they should come to us, not him, if they have any questions."

"So everything is going pretty well otherwise?"

"Yeah. The students are digging better and their notes are improving. Found a fair number of features, mostly storage pits and a few hearths, and some decent artifacts. Having some trouble matching up the old maps with our new grid, but we're doing the best we can."

"When are you bringing in the backhoe to open up a big area?"

"Next week, so we'll have plenty of features to excavate while you're visiting. You wanted video of feature excavations for the museum display, right? And I've got the backhoe reserved again in a few weeks so we can open up additional ground if needed."

"Sounds like a plan. I'll try and get everything I need during the first visit, so I won't get in the way too much during the second half of the season."

"Shouldn't be a problem," Jake said. "The County Highway Department is providing the backhoe and they don't have much use for it this summer. All I need to do is call a day or so before I want them to come out. I'll probably use the backhoe two or three times before we have to start closing things up."

"Don't work yourself too hard, hon," Amanda said. "Or your students. A day off now and then isn't going to hurt."

"Hey, I'm no slave driver. Besides, they just had a big party on Saturday."

"Right, you emailed me about the 'Beach Bash Blowout.' Hope you didn't ruin their fun by standing around taking notes."

"Ha-ha. No, like you suggested I made a token appearance and then made myself scarce. Probably was for the best. Sounds like it got pretty wild later on."

"Oh yeah? And how would you know that, Dr. Caine, unless you were there? Or peeping out the window?"

"Nothing like that. The garbage and clothing scattered around the campsite sort of gave it away, plus Erin filled me in on the highlights afterward."

"Huh. I didn't realize she was such a gossip. Such as?"

"Well," Jake paused for dramatic effect. "Lots of drinking, of course, and some swimming. Apparently the male half of the camp was pushing for skinny-dipping, but the girls weren't going for it unless the boys did it first. A few guys finally got up the nerve to strip down, but Heather made some comments about the cold lake water and something Erin referred to as her 'shrinkage factor theory' and that put an end to that idea. There were a few minor scuffles but sounds like everyone got along for the most part. Some swimsuits ended up in the trees, naturally, but that's it. Things wrapped up about midnight, with a few stalwarts hanging out for a few extra hours."

"Sounds like quite the bacchanal," Amanda said, "on a PG-13 level. Our parties were a lot crazier than that."

"True, but it was their first one. I'm sure they'll reach new levels of debauchery as the season moves on," Jake said. "Speaking of ghosts from the past, I forgot to tell you about our other visitors." Briefly, Jake told Amanda about Charlie Garath's initial visit and how he and other NEWAS members had been volunteering at the dig.

"That's interesting, how some of them were around for Wardell's dig and now show up to help out again. Maybe I can work that in to the History Center display. It's always a plus if we can highlight volunteer efforts. The Center sponsors a quarterly volunteer award and it's a big deal for a lot of our members."

"I'm sure the NEWAS guys would appreciate the recognition," Jake said. "None of them ever heard from the university after Wardell's death, so they always wondered about the results of the dig. They didn't even know about the report that came out afterward."

"That's too bad. I suppose it was such a mess after she died that no one ever thought to wrap up all the loose ends."

"I guess. I'm printing up more copies of the report for them, just to thank them for their help. I was hoping Charlie or some of the other old-timers might be able to help us with our mapping problems, but they really didn't pay much attention to the overall site plan."

"It was a lot of years ago, Jake. Without looking at your notes, you'd probably have trouble remembering specifics about the sites you worked on, too."

"True. I sure wish I could track down Mark Winters. He seemed more involved than anyone else."

"I'll do some Internet searches at work tomorrow and see if I can come up with anything," Amanda said. "But is it worth the effort? He might not remember anything either."

"I suppose, but I hate not knowing for sure. You know me, I don't like to leave any stones unturned."

"I know, but like you said, these are ghosts from the past. Sometimes you need to let sleeping ghosts lie."

CHAPTER TEN

"Jake? Clark Kelley here."

Jake winced, and rolled his eyes as he mouthed Clark's name to Heather and Scott.

"This can't be good," Heather said.

"Oh, hello Clark. What can I do for you?"

"I saw the news broadcast on the dig last evening. You know, you should have informed me. After all, I am the senior North American archaeologist on staff."

Annoyed, Jake cut him off. "Well, Clark, there really wasn't time to call everyone. Lots of work to do and I'm busy enough running the field school."

"Yes, well, always good publicity for the department, you know," he countered, oblivious. "Do you happen to know offhand if any more TV interviews are scheduled?"

Jake realized why Clark had a sudden interest in the field school. "Well, Clark, nothing set up so far but the reports have generated a lot of interest. I certainly can keep you informed if anything comes up."

"That would be excellent. Just so happens that I was planning to drive up for an inspection tour, probably in the next few weeks. I can have the department secretary let you know my itinerary."

"You are certainly welcome to visit my site any time you'd like, Clark. Maybe you can answer a few questions I have, too, since you've been here before."

"Ah, well now, I really wasn't there that much. Professor Wardell was in charge, after all. Anyhow, must be going, there's a student at my door. Goodbye."

That was a little strange, Jake thought. Clark was never one to avoid a conversation where he could toot his own horn, even if he didn't have a clue about the subject under discussion.

"Bad news? You've got a puzzled look on your face," Scott said.

"Yes and no, I guess. Clark's planning to come up in a week or so for an inspection," he stressed the final word and frowned. "He saw the news report and I think he's miffed that he wasn't involved."

"Nothing shocking there. He's more about appearance than results anyway," Heather said. "Did I ever tell you he chewed a bunch of us out last summer because of how we looked when we came in from the field one Friday? 'Clothes make the man, after all.' Do you believe that crap? How clean does he expect us to be after digging test units all week?"

"I know, I know. Like I said the last five times you told me this story, Clark's view of field archaeology is 100 years behind. In his world, real archaeologists sit in lawn chairs sipping gin and tonics while native laborers bring their finds to him for inspection. Of course, they also need servants to fan them, peel grapes, and things like that."

"You try a stunt like that and you and your lawn chair will end up getting tossed off the end of the pier," Heather said, adding a respectful "sir" at the end.

"That's fair enough, I guess. I'm not a big gin-and-tonic drinker anyway." Jake scratched at his goatee and gazed across the site. "No, what's weird is how Clark reacts every time I try to ask him about Wardell's dig. He shuts me off immediately, acts like he never even heard about it. Twice I stopped him in the hallway during exam week to ask him about the field school and he couldn't get away from me fast enough. Usually he falls all over himself trying to latch on to anything that anyone else is involved in, but not with this. Just odd, even for him. Plus since when does he interrupt a phone call to talk to a student?"

"That doesn't make any sense," Heather said. She screwed up her face in disbelief. "It's the intersession period, anyway. How many students are even on campus now?"

The rest of the week passed in relative quiet. As the students gained experience and confidence, their excavating speed increased. The quality of their notes and record keeping lagged slightly behind, however, as they all agreed finding cool artifacts was much more exciting than writing descriptions of subtle shifts in soil color. With the students able to work with less direct supervision, Jake, Heather, and Scott were able to devote more time to evaluating the results and refining their excavation strategy. Unproductive units were closed and new portions of the site were tested.

Midweek, the students working in one of the east-central units encountered a very large, dark stain that extended into the walls of the adjacent unexcavated units. Too large to be a storage pit, Jake ordered them to excavate the adjacent units to the same depth, in order to define the edges and determine what the feature represented. As more of the stain was exposed, Jake suspected it might be a house basin. Some possible post molds were uncovered, too. Given the potential size of the structure, it was decided that a portion of the overlying soil would be removed when the backhoe was brought in next week.

Between the recent news articles and the exciting artifacts now recovered almost daily, enthusiasm was high across the site. The eager students were immune to the heat and dusty conditions, while the NEWAS volunteers greeted every new find as a local treasure. The students appreciated their help, to say nothing of the doughnuts and bagels they brought to the site every morning.

The media coverage had a cascade effect and resulted in a dramatic boost in local interest. During the first week, a few curious locals and tourists stopped by. That number increased tenfold after the television report, with multiple carloads descending on the dig. Some visits were brief, people stopping only to stare quizzically at the odd stains and sharply broken rocks. Other folks stayed for hours asking questions, and in some instances returned with friends or possible artifacts that needed identification. Jake, Heather, and Scott were busier than ever but as each day drew to a close there was a strong sense of accomplishment.

Things were progressing so well that Jake decided to give himself a little break that afternoon and catch up on his field notes, rather than wait until evening. He reached into his cluttered backpack and felt his fingers brush against dry leather. Curious, he pulled out Jacklyn Wardell's journal, a bit surprised he had brought it into the field. He had likely grabbed it along with his regular field items that morning, in the rush to get moving. Jake flipped it open to a random page, startled to see a beautifully detailed drawing of a large Archaic spearpoint.

June 11. OUSTANDING!, as my Dad says when he is extremely pleased with something! Curls found this fantastic corner-notched spearpoint eroding out of the bank on the "Big" island. (Do any of these islands have actual names? Need to check on that.) Looks to be Early Archaic, maybe a Kirk point, based on the style and shape. Could be made from one of those nice cherts from Illinois or Indiana, but nobody seems sure. I'll study it more tonight, once Curls stops showing off to the students (grimace). For the record, I didn't really "walk right by it" as he claims; the painted turtle moving down the beach distracted me. Although I guess that doesn't sound much better.

HEADLINE: Sinister Painted Turtle Distracts Archaeology Professor: Most Important New Site in Wisconsin Saved by Attentive Graduate Student.

Oh, well. I guess I can let Curls have the glory on this one. At least The Dark One has left, so he wasn't around to criticize me. Heaven knows he found enough to complain about during his inspection. Can't wait for the next one; sounds like I'll be seeing him every few days all summer! This is really going to put a damper on the field season. Lady Margaret's late-day visit didn't help, either. She can be an oddball, no two ways about it. One minute she's defending me to The Dark One (thanks, but I can take care of myself), next she's pointing out things for him to yell about (don't need that kind of help, either).

But my island excursion paid off! I knew taking a boat to those islands would be worthwhile, and this point definitely proves it. Course, getting there was a challenge; some slow going against the wind. You'd think a five-horse motor would move an aluminum boat like that a little better; at least it wasn't as tippy this time, with Curls onboard as human ballast (ha-ha). Maybe I'll ask Mr. Powell if I can exchange it, or rent a bigger boat. Be nice to take some of the students over there and give those islands a proper survey. Or maybe I'll go over on my own, so I can get all the glory next time!

CHAPTER ELEVEN

An overcast sky greeted the crew Thursday morning, foreshadowing the rain expected over the weekend. A strong breeze blew across the lake, providing the students with a welcome respite from the flies and mosquitoes. None of the students took notice of the growing whitecaps on Taylor Lake, but for whatever reason Jake found himself entranced. He couldn't stop staring at the choppy water, watching uneasily as the few small boats filled with hardcore anglers drove through the waves and spray.

"Jake? Uh, Jake?"

Jolted from the hypnotic effect of the rising and falling waves, Jake turned to see Scott and Shannon, one of the students, standing a few feet away. "Yeah, sorry. What's up?"

"Shannon found an unusual rim sherd," Scott said. "We thought you might want to take a look at it." Shannon was almost painfully shy around Jake, and he suspected that Scott had brought her over deliberately, as she would never take the initiative on her own.

Shannon gingerly handed Jake the rim sherd. It was as thick as his little finger, about seven inches across, and made from dark brown clay. It had a gritty, almost sandy feel to it, unlike the thinner, smoother Oneota pottery typically found at Waconah. Jake pulled a loupe from his pocket and examined the artifact in more detail.

"Hmm. This is interesting. Grit-tempered, so it must be from the Woodland period. Some decoration above the shoulder, too, maybe cord impressions," he handed the loupe and potsherd back to Shannon. "Right there."

She took the items and peered through the eyepiece. "Oh, yeah. I see them now."

"It's pretty unusual to have Woodland pottery like this on an Oneota site," Jake said as she handed the sherd and loupe to Scott. "It may have come from the Christianson site, or maybe it represents a trade vessel from another village. What unit are you working in?"

"Uh, 16," Shannon said, and she pointed in the general direction of her unit.

"Okay. Scott, let's open up some additional units around this one and see what else pops up," Jake said. He looked past them as a dark blue car appeared at the top of the gravel road. "Shannon, you have a really important find here. Keep up the good work," he added, smiling.

She blushed, then took the rim sherd from Scott and ran back toward her unit.

"Looks like another tourist," Scott said, following Jake's gaze as they watched the car drive down the road to the parking area. "Not too many today. Guess the weather is keeping them away. Want me to take it?"

"No, I've got this one," Jake said. "Spread the word about the Woodland sherd. Maybe some of the other students are finding similar pottery."

The occupant of the car parked at the far end of the lot, away from the lake, and was talking to two students digging a one-by-two-meter unit as Jake approached. The visitor was a heavy-set female with short hair, probably in her late forties. As he neared, Jake dusted himself off, in reaction to her businesslike attire. Compared to most of the site visitors they had so far, she looked more than a bit inconspicuous in her mauve pantsuit and faux leather flats.

"Jacob Caine? I'm Maggie, Maggie Devlin, with the State Transportation Department." The statement was more of an inquiry and it took him a few moments to place the name and face.

"Oh, sure," Jake said, and he shook her hand as he made the connection. "You're with the Environmental Management Office. You reviewed some of the state contract reports WSU worked on."

"That's right. I was in the area, checking on some contract archaeologists that are surveying some highway corridors nearby, when I heard about the dig on the news. I did a lot of research around here before I started working for the state, so I had to stop for a visit while I was close."

"That's great. I'd be happy to give you a tour, if you'd like," he offered, gesturing at some nearby units.

Maggie nodded and followed him cautiously through the paths of matted grass and bare earth. At the first excavation block, he introduced the students and handed her some rim sherds and stone tool fragments to examine. She turned them over nonchalantly, before returning them without comment.

A bit nonplused, Jake pointed out the edge of a small hearth in the wall of the next unit and described some of the bone and shell fragments that had been recovered. Again, Maggie nodded knowingly but did not seem interested in communicating further.

"We've uncovered a possible house structure in the units over there," Jake began, pointing to the west, where Heather, some NEWAS volunteers, and a group of students were busy screening and bagging artifacts.

"What about over there?" she broke in, pointing in the opposite direction where two excavators were working at the far edge of the site. Her voice was tinged with a harshness that Jake didn't particularly appreciate. Maggie strode off in that direction before Jake could even answer.

About halfway across the site she paused by an open unit, breathing heavily. Maggie was perspiring despite the cool breeze off the lake. "So," she huffed, "are you girls finding much?"

"Sure, lots," Katy said. She and her dig partner, Jenny, were juniors who sat together in nearly every class. When the field school began, it seemed natural to team them together at the dig. "We're excavating this refuse pit. It was probably used for food storage first. So far we have some burned bones and charcoal, and some chipping debris."

"Couple of rim sherds, too," Jenny said as she dumped another bucket of dirt into the screen. "This one has some tool decoration on the rim, see?"

Maggie took the proffered sherd and held it up to catch the light. "Ah, yes. Sort of a half-cone impression, probably made with a worked piece of bone or wood."

She returned it with a smile. "I saw a few sherds like this while I was doing research near here, a few years back. Very nice find."

Jake and Maggie continued across the site, pausing to examine open units and peek through screens of excavated fill. Maggie became more talkative, although she repeatedly dabbed a handkerchief on her damp brow. The constant attention created a pronounced cowlick in front, an odd contrast against her short, tightly curled hair. Jake made an effort not to stare at it.

After the pair reached the far north end of the site, Jake summarized what they hoped to accomplish over the next few weeks. Maggie appeared to listen attentively, but all the while she stared past him at the trail and woods bordering the stream.

There was an awkward silence when Jake stopped talking. "Well, thank you for the tour," Maggie said at last. "I really must be getting along. Lots of projects to check up on before I head back to Green Bay."

"Sure, feel free to stop by anytime," Jake said. With that, she made a beeline back to her vehicle with nary a sideways glance. He watched until she reached her vehicle and then sped up the hill toward the highway. As he walked back toward the center of the site, Jake again caught sight of the whitecaps rolling across the turbulent lake. The eerie conditions brought to mind Jacklyn Wardell's last day on earth. Jake paused, perplexed at why anyone would have gone out in a boat in conditions that must have been far, far worse.

CHAPTER TWELVE

The anticipated storm shifted north, resulting in a light shower during the night and clear blue skies on Friday morning. The crew spent a few minutes bailing water out of several units but the damage was minor and everyone was soon hard at work. Charlie Garath and three of his NEWAS cronies—Jeff, Art, and Mark—showed up about a half hour later with several bags of freshly baked bagels.

Jake was down in a two-by-two-meter unit with some students, scraping soil from what looked like a bison scapula hoe, when several shadows fell across his field of view. He assumed it was some students with a question, so he rose and turned, a bit annoyed by the disturbance. He did not expect to see three little old ladies in big sun hats smiling down at him, or the eight grandchildren watching curiously from behind them.

"Good morning," Jake said, surprised that he hadn't heard the approach of their vehicles. "I'm Jacob Caine, an archaeologist with Wisconsin State University. We're—"

"Oh, we read all about your dig in the papers, Professor," the middle one said. "And we just had to come over for a visit. Right, ladies?"

Her companions nodded briskly in agreement. The ice broken, the children let loose with a rapid-fire barrage of questions. Jake did his best to answer, aided by the students, who gave a brief show-and-tell with some flakes and potsherds recovered earlier. Soon, all but the youngest two kids were scampering across the site in search of further discoveries.

Jake glanced toward the parking lot but saw only the university vehicles and Charlie Garath's pickup. "Excuse me, ladies, but how did you get here?" he said, tilting his head toward the parking area.

"Oh, we didn't drive over," their unofficial spokesperson said. "We walked over on the trail from the Hillside Resort." She pointed toward the woods on the south side of the parking lot. Jake could barely discern a slight gap in the trees.

"Hmm. Never noticed that before."

"It comes out right by my cabin," the shortest one said as she pulled a juice box from her purse for her tow-haired grandson. "There are hiking trails all over this area, going to and from the boat launch."

"They used to be in much better condition, though," the third woman said, doffing her hat and using it as a fan. "We should say something to the owner. But the children do so love the little beach."

"Looks like it will be a wonderful weekend," Jake said, making small talk as he labeled a large artifact bag for the now-free bison bone.

"Oh my, yes," their leader said. "We always seem to have good weather on festival weekend."

"Festival? What festival?"

"The Donovan Summer Days Festival, of course," she said, in the same tone reserved for explaining the obvious to her grandchildren. "There's a carnival and some bands, boat races, a flea market tomorrow, and a big parade on Sunday. People flock in from miles around. Quite the event, you know."

As the women walked off to collect their brood, it dawned on Jake that the influx of festival patrons would likely mean more visitors to the site. Saturday and Sunday would be particularly difficult, as they didn't work at Waconah on the weekends. With an audible sigh, Jake waved to Heather and Scott, and the trio made their way over to the excavation block where Charlie Garath was working.

Jake told Heather and Scott about the upcoming event and Charlie filled them in on the details. As the three grandmothers had reported, the festival was a big regional event.

"Yeah, you're talking thousands of folks showing up, way more than the locals and tourists," Charlie said as he dropped some flakes in a paper bag. "NEWAS used to set up a booth on the main square and do artifact IDs and stuff like that, but too many of us were busy workin' other parts of the festival, so we gave it up."

"So we can probably expect a fair number of visitors today," Jake said. He noticed there were already an unusually large number of pleasure boats cruising Taylor Lake.

"I reckon, and probably be even more folks stoppin' by tomorrow, too."

"That's going to be a problem," Heather said. "We can't possibly secure the entire site in less than a day. We don't have enough big tarps, or caution tape, or protective fencing."

"Okay, take it easy," Jake said. "I realize we can't keep everybody out, so we'll do the next best thing. We'll restrict access to select parts of the dig and set up our own open house."

"Gonna be tough for just the three of us to handle that, if we get really big crowds," Scott said.

"We'll ask for student volunteers," Jake said. "If we can get ten or twelve people, we should be fine. And I'll ask Erin to pitch in, too. We'll set up some display tables with artifacts, some copies of the archaeology handout from the university, and open up a few of the large excavation blocks."

"Me and some of the guys can probably help," Charlie said. "At least for a few hours. Can we hand out some of our NEWAS fliers, too?"

"Sure. Any help you can give us would be great."

"I don't know, chief. I don't think many students are going to want to give up their whole weekend for this," Heather said.

"Maybe, but if we can we'll divide up in shifts so they only have to be out here for a few hours. We'll treat it like comp time and let them take a day or half day off later on, whenever they want."

Heather shrugged, still dubious, but pulled out a notebook to start jotting down names. "This is not how I want to spend my weekend, dealing with ignorant tourists. 'What's this?' 'Is this something?' 'Find any dinosaur bones?' 'Find any gold?' "

"It might not be that bad, Heather," Jake said. "Things could be quiet today, and if tomorrow morning is a bust, everyone can wrap up by lunch time."

"I don't think so, Jake," Scott said, pointing toward the top of the hill. Two cars and a large RV had pulled off the highway and were making a slow descent down the gravel road toward the site.

The appearance of the three grandmothers and their progeny opened a veritable floodgate of visitors to Waconah. For most of the morning, the parking lot was filled to capacity as vehicles came and went. Even the battered pier received heavy traffic, as curious jet-skiers and boaters stopped for a closer look. The inquisitive crowds soon overwhelmed Jake, Heather, and Scott, so Bryant, Charlie, and several students were enlisted to help monitor visitors, answer questions, and watch over the hordes of children that seemed to be everywhere.

The crowds slowed around lunchtime and the site was considerably quieter in the early afternoon. Charlie surmised that most of the excitement was now in Donovan, as the afternoon and evening events were getting underway.

Taking advantage of the lull, Jake climbed into a deep linear unit and began to clean the wall with his trowel for a photo. A dense deposit of clamshells near the base required careful scraping, so his attention was fixed on his task. He glanced up only once, as an oversized camper from Indiana disgorged a quartet of screaming kids. A few other vehicles were in the lot, but Heather and the others had everything under control, so he turned back to his troweling.

"Hey, handsome, is this something?"

"Amanda!" Jake said, scrambling out of the trench. Oblivious to the surprised and bemused stares of the students and site visitors, Jake swept her off her feet in a crushing bear hug.

"What are you doing here? I thought you weren't going to arrive until late Sunday."

"Things were pretty quiet at the History Center, so I moved some stuff around and decided to head out early," she said, brushing away red and brown dust from her T-shirt. "Thought I'd beat the traffic so we could spend some time together before tackling the dig."

"Hey, Amanda! How's it going, stranger?"

"Hi, Heather. Long time no see. Surviving grad school? I hear your advisor is a real slave driver."

"Oh, you don't know the half of it," Heather said. "Of course, he'll act all pleasant and helpful as long as you're around, I'm sure."

As the latest group of visitors drove off, Jake introduced Amanda to Scott, the field school students, and the NEWAS volunteers. He then gave her an impromptu tour of the excavation, and they discussed items and students to include in the video documentary for the History Center.

"I think the house feature should be our main focus," Amanda said at the end of their tour. "You only have a portion of it uncovered, too, so we can get some footage of the excavation as it happens. At the Center, we can create replicas of basin and post molds, maybe some digitized field maps highlighting the features, and a painting of a reconstructed longhouse. Oh, how about a life-sized model of a longhouse? Kids could walk inside it, and I'll add some replica pots and stone tools, maybe some deer hides, and—"

"That all sounds good," Jake said, "But let's see how much of the house is there first. We only have one edge so far. It may not be a longhouse after all."

"Well, any kind of structure would be cool. The general public likes artifacts and stuff they can relate to, things that correlate with everyday, modern items. And kids go bonkers for interactive displays. Sterile museum displays are a thing of the past."

"Speaking of displays, I'd better call Erin and ask her to pull some artifacts for the display tomorrow. I forgot to do it earlier."

"What display?" Amanda said as she took some photos of the site with her camera phone.

Jake told her about the Donovan Summer Days Festival and how they had decided to set up an open house as a way of controlling the flow of visitors at the site. He repeated the same information to Erin, who offered to spend as much time as necessary at the dig over the weekend. Jake then turned his attention back to Amanda, with a worried look on his face.

"Sorry, honey," Jake said. "It didn't hit me 'til just now, but this whole weekend is pretty much booked. We aren't going to have much time together."

She shook her head. "No problem, I'll just help out at the site. I can take some photos for the Center, maybe some video, too. A big crowd will just highlight how popular archaeology is with the public."

"A little too popular today, if you ask me," Heather said as she joined them. "Should we start getting organized for the weekend?"

"Sure." Jake waved to Scott, who was helping some students

at the far end of the site. "Let's get Charlie involved, too, so we can pin down his schedule. How many students are willing to come?"

"Nearly all, surprisingly," Heather said as she paged through her notebook. "A few don't want to work in the early morning, if they can help it, and some prefer to have the afternoon off. I marked them as AM or PM so we can keep them separate."

Jake read through the list and counted the number of volunteers. With input from Scott and Charlie, they created a rough schedule for the weekend. Jake and Amanda would work all day Saturday and early Sunday morning, in order to oversee the transfer to Heather and Scott, who would handle the Sunday duties. Charlie arranged to set up the NEWAS table Saturday morning and had members scheduled for two-hour shifts through the weekend. Because so many students had volunteered, none of them would be required to work more than one morning or afternoon shift, either Saturday or Sunday.

Jake, Heather, and Scott spent much of the evening preparing for the weekend open house. After she found out that Amanda had arrived early and would be at the site most of the weekend, Erin offered to work both days. She also took it upon herself to give Amanda a tour of the campground.

When Jake and Amanda turned in for the night, he grudgingly decided they had done as much as humanly possible to get ready for their Festival Day presentation. At least they hadn't put out an official notice, so with luck the turnout would be small and manageable. Jake heard a loon on the lake, its call barely audible over the din from the nearby public camping sites. It reminded him of a sketch in Jacklyn Wardell's journal, with *"Two Real Loons"* written above it. A serene-looking loon floated on one side and on the other was a sketch of Clark Kelley, mouth agape, with flies zooming in and out of his ears. With a chuckle, Jake reminded himself to make a copy to use as his screen saver when he got back to his office.

Chapter Thirteen

The field school crew exited their vehicles only moments before the first visitors arrived on Saturday morning. The students quickly uncovered a few select units, set up their screens, and started working. Jake and Bryant erected the large shade tent while Erin and Amanda put up the tables and laid out the artifacts for display. It was chaotic at first, but soon the university team had a workable system in place and the open house went smoothly.

Following Jake's instruction, the students focused their attention less on digging and more on interacting with the public. They explained what archaeologists do, why they do it, and what they can learn. Much of their time was spent politely correcting common misconceptions about archaeological research and explaining the myriad details of excavation that the students had begun to take for granted. Having to explain why they were doing things a certain way, as opposed to simply following directions, actually made the students much more aware of the importance of proper procedure.

Charlie Garath and his cousin Art arrived around nine and set up the NEWAS display, a card table with club pamphlets and several glass-topped boxes filled with local artifacts. Their display, with some of the showiest artifacts found by the members, received a lot of attention. A number of locals actually left and returned with collections of their own. Jake tried to record as much information as possible on each collection, including a rough location on a county map, in the hopes that they could be assigned official site numbers at some point.

Bubbling with even more enthusiasm than usual, Charlie Garath suggested to every collector that they plan to attend the next NEWAS meeting in autumn. Art proposed making it their semi-annual artifact identification night and asked if Jake and his students could attend. Jake agreed and offered to bring along any students who might be interested.

The field school artifacts, in contrast, consisted primarily of broken stone tools and potsherds, and scraps of animal bone and shell. It was difficult for the casual visitor to see the significance of such finds. By observing the excavation in progress, however, and learning about context and patterns, many folks walked away with a better appreciation for the results of archaeological research.

Several teachers from the local elementary and high school toured the site and Jake was coerced into coming back to Donovan during the fall semester to do a presentation on the results of the Waconah dig. The wife of a member of the town council and tourism board overheard this conversation and promptly insisted that Jake give a presentation at the community center as well. He agreed, inwardly wondering how many additional trips to Donovan lay in his future.

Erin supervised the artifact display, assisted by two students, but during every lull she hurried over to help Amanda and her team as they excavated a large storage pit. Jake offered to monitor the table for her at one point, and Erin nearly tripped over a chair in her rush to get back to Amanda's unit. And so the day went.

On Sunday morning, a trickle of visitors, mostly vacationers with kids or grandkids in tow, enjoyed the Waconah open house. A few locals, busy the previous day with festival events in town, stopped by as well. The day was considerably more overcast than on Saturday, with fewer boats on the lake. Some dark clouds were visible on the horizon, threatening to put an early end to the day's activities.

After getting everyone on the Sunday crew organized, Jake strode over to his usual resting spot on a convenient dirt pile to survey the site. The cool eastward breeze drew his attention toward Taylor Lake. Thinking how quickly the weather was turning, Jake wondered if Jacklyn Wardell had noticed the odd weather patterns, too. Hard to miss. Certainly not the kind of weather you'd want to brave the lake in a small metal boat with a balky motor.

"Erin is all set at the display table," Amanda said as she joined him. "Same plan as yesterday and she printed more handouts."

"Good. Looks like some rain coming in," Jake said, pointing across the lake. "Maybe they can knock off a little early this afternoon."

"Sounds good to me," Amanda said as she rubbed a knot out of her shoulder. "Guess I've been out of the field too long, if a couple hours of screening get my muscles all twisted up like this."

"Might have something to do with sleeping on that broken-down mattress last night, too." He turned and massaged her sore shoulder. On the lake, two speedboats raced past, in the direction of the new boat landing.

"As I recall, Professor Caine," she said, a wry smile on her face, "you didn't exactly let me get that much sleep last night."

"Must be the fresh air. Of course, I do find it hard to keep my hands off you."

"No kidding. The way you were ogling me at dinner I'm surprised you didn't drag me into your room as soon as you finished your coffee."

"Ah, as I recall I didn't hear any complaints from you last night."

"You won't tonight, either, handsome."

They turned quiet for a time, enjoying the scenery as another carload of visitors pulled into the parking lot. Erin gave them a little wave as she headed over to greet the new arrivals.

"It was nice of you to partner Erin with me yesterday. She's really bursting at the seams to get hired at the History Center."

"Yeah, Erin's not the most subtle person on the planet, is she?" Jake said. "She's got a lot of drive and I suppose it just spills over into the rest of her personality."

"Well, I'm doing my best to be positive, but a curator position like she wants is tough to find. I can let her help out with some of the work I need to do for the exhibit, and put in a good word for her with the director, but that's about it."

Jake didn't reply for a moment as he crumbled a clod of dirt between his fingers. Finally, he broke the awkward silence.

"We've been apart too much, haven't we?"

"Yeah, we have," Amanda said. "It's harder than I thought it would be."

"There's just no way around it. You've got a great job at the Center, with so much potential. You can't walk away from something like that. With my class load and research projects, I just can't find the time to visit like I want. And the whole damn fight for tenure . . ."

"I know, I know. And if I come down, you feel obligated to entertain me or at least try not to work 24-7."

"I love you," Jake said, taking Amanda's hand in his own.

"I know, and I love you too," she said firmly, a warm smile pushing through the dust and grime of the dig. "We're going to make it work, don't you worry."

CHAPTER FOURTEEN

From Jacklyn Wardell's journal:

June 16. Not sure why Lady Margaret keeps coming down to visit. She starts out friendly, sort of, and then gets awful snippy. Heck, she gets nasty! Doesn't sound like they've found much at Christianson II, but that's hardly my fault. And certainly no reason to snap at my students and assistants. Maybe working with Professor Snootypants is driving her insane? I can kind of see that, after my troubles with The Dark One. Maybe his precious car will break down on the drive up and I won't have to deal with him tomorrow (please!). Plus, CatWoman pointed out that our NEWAS volunteer numbers drop by half every time The Dark One visits; if he keeps this up I'm definitely going to fall short of my excavation goals for this season.

At least Clicker isn't fazed by The Dark One's visits. Never knew anyone with that much energy and enthusiasm. He must take hundreds of photographs every day, and he's so cheerful that you can't help but smile. Well, his spell doesn't work on everyone, admittedly. Snowman seemed a little put out with Clicker the other day, for some reason, but wouldn't tell me why. And I get the impression from Clicker that he wasn't warmly received at the Christianson II site. Oh, well, their loss is my gain!

Jake jumped as his cell phone rang and almost dropped Jacklyn Wardell's journal. He set the book aside and checked the caller ID. It read Musket Mahler.

"Hey, Doc."

"Hi, Jake. How are things going at Waconah?"

"Good, real good. Finding lots of artifacts and some decent features. Still having a few problems with the old Wardell map, but we're making progress."

"I'm sure you'll figure it out. Might take you a few years, but I've got faith in you."

"Gee, thanks. Your confidence is overwhelming. So, when are you going to come up for a visit? I've got the backhoe scheduled for this week, so we should have lots of features opened up in a few days."

"Here's the thing, Jake," Doc Mahler said. "I'm trying to finish my monograph on the fur trader's cabin site and I managed to track down one of the collectors who dug at the site in the late sixties, before I got out there. Anyway, he's up in Michigan now, but he agreed to let me come up and document the artifacts."

"That's great, Doc."

"Yeah. Thing is, it'll probably take me at least a week to analyze and photograph everything, so I won't be able to come out to Waconah after all."

"No problem, I understand. Sounds like quite a collection."

"Sure is. He and a cousin dug out there for a couple of summers when they were in college. Kept pretty good notes, too, from what I can tell." Doc Mahler coughed, and Jake wondered if he was sneaking a smoke in his office again. "I do feel bad, Jake, about not visiting. My schedule is just nuts this summer. I had more free time back when I was teaching, seems like. But I couldn't turn down his offer, not after finally tracking him down."

"Don't worry about it, Doc. Can't say no when a great collection comes your way. Besides, we're kind of overflowing with visitors anyway lately." Jake told Doc Mahler about the onslaught of visitors following the media reports, and Amanda's recent arrival.

"And speaking of collectors, some members of the NEWAS, the local archaeology group, are helping out at the site. Most of them were here during Wardell's field school. Seem real excited that we're digging here again."

"That's a nice surprise, getting some local help," Doc Mahler said. "You should send them an official thank-you letter, from the university, once you get back."

"Good idea," Jake said. He scribbled a reminder on a scrap of paper. "Oh, and Maggie Devlin stopped by the other day, too."

"Who?"

"Maggie Devlin. She's an environmental coordinator with the State Transportation Department. She had to approve one of our contract projects a few years back. Guess she worked around here at one point."

"She wasn't at Waconah, though, was she?"

"I don't think so. She made it sound like she had worked in the area, that's all."

"Huh. Small world, I guess."

"How's that?"

"Just a weird coincidence. I remember her name on our contracts, but didn't make the connection with Waconah. Margaret Devlin was one of the applicants for the North American archaeologist position, the job Jacklyn Wardell got. I was on the hiring committee back then. Devlin didn't even make the initial cut because she didn't have her Ph.D. at the time. That was the minimum requirement, but she still called and gave us grief about not getting an interview. Not much we could have done, and we had lots of better candidates regardless. I suppose she finished grad school and ended up working for the state."

"I guess. I think she does a lot of traveling now, checking on different projects in her district."

"Speaking of traveling, I should get going," Doc Mahler said. "I want to get on the road early tomorrow and I still need to pack. Good luck out there. And say hi to Amanda for me."

"Sure, Doc. Have fun in Michigan."

Jake put his phone away as Amanda, Heather, and Erin entered the hall.

"How'd the shopping trip go?" Jake asked.

"Fine. Picked up extra memory cards for my video camera, so I should be all set for tomorrow," Amanda said.

"We lucked out," Heather said. "The festival is winding down but Donovan is still mobbed with people. The store looked like a tornado went through."

"Doc Mahler called. He won't be coming out this week after all," Jake said.

"Aw, shoot. Doc's a riot in the field," Heather said. "He'll tell you stories all day and then drink you under the table at night."

"He tracked down a collection he needs for his book, so that takes priority. I'm sure he'll make it out next season."

Heather mumbled something that Jake didn't catch.

"In the meantime, we can drink in his honor," Erin said. She pulled two bottles of wine from the fridge. "Who wants to join me around the campfire?"

"I'm in. Amanda?"

Amanda looked at Jake, who nodded. "Sure, as long as it doesn't get too late. The backhoe will be at the site bright and early tomorrow."

Heather rolled her eyes. "You are so not the Doc. He'd be the last one to turn in and the first one up in the morning. What kind of example are you setting for the archaeologists of the future?"

"Fine. If you agree to make it an early night, I promise to be as exciting and interesting as Doc. When I'm his age."

CHAPTER FIFTEEN

The roar of the backhoe's engine almost drowned out the intermittent coughing of the archaeology crew as the gusting wind blew the diesel exhaust over them. Jake and Heather stood side by side, a few yards clear of the swinging bucket with the smooth-edged blade. Behind them, Scott and the students were busy with trowels and shovels, scraping the floor of the exposed trench. Amanda and two students were positioned at the far end, filming the work in progress and taking photographs of the uncovered features. Appearing first as circular or oval dark stains against the light-colored subsoil, careful cleaning revealed the distinct edges of ancient hearths, storage pits, and other remnants of prehistoric village life.

"So, sounds like Amanda is pretty happy at the History Center," Heather said.

"Yeah. She likes working with the public and they have a good director. He's really big on trying new things, with lots of innovative ideas." Jake trailed off, motioning to the backhoe operator to move back and further enlarge the trench.

"It took her a while to land that job, right?"

"Sort of," Jake said. "She was doing seasonal fieldwork for a number of years, trying to find a museum-based outreach position, but there aren't many around."

"Kind of like every job in archaeology, then."

"I suppose, compared to some other fields. What brings this up?"

"Nothing specific," Heather said. "Just making conversation. So, you got a good turnout on Saturday, huh?"

"It was pretty hectic, but I think it went well. Lots of collectors stopped by, too. I'll probably be traveling up here every other weekend this fall, checking out collections and giving talks. You'll end up with lots of teaching opportunities this semester."

Heather ignored Jake's jibe, and mumbled something under her breath as she knelt down to scrape some soil from a brown, circular stain. When she rose, the left side of her face was smeared with red clay from the subsoil. "Sunday wasn't bad. We had about eighty people, but a lot more casual gawkers."

"Gawkers?"

"You know, people who look but don't come down to the site. Cars stop at the top of the hill, and sometimes the drivers get out. Or boats on the lake that slow down to stare but they don't stop. We call them CBLs, curious but lazy. Some of the students have started a bingo game with them. You know, see a red car that doesn't stop, fill in a square. If a man or woman stands at the top of the hill but doesn't come down, you fill in another square."

"I doubt there's that many people like that," Jake said, putting a pin flag in the ground near an exposed stone knife.

"Well, you have to be creative," Heather said, a bit defensively. "Some of the regulars have nicknames and are worth extra points. There's Mustang Mike, Bill With Binoculars, Mr. Peeper, Captain Cadillac, The Skinny Creep, oh, and Red Truck Santa. He has a bushy white beard and always waves. Mr. Peeper shows up a lot, always by those pine trees. Besides, it's harmless fun and kills time when the dig gets boring."

"Boring? An archaeological dig? That's practically blasphemy."

"Maybe so, but it's true and you know it."

Conversation ceased as the backhoe blade reached the base of the topsoil, and their attention was focused on guiding the operator, Rich Halsey, as he carefully scraped away the last few centimeters of dark soil. A skilled operator could create an even floor with only an inch of variation up or down. Fortunately, Rich had many years of experience and the red-colored subsoil made it easier to note the change in soils. As the next section of trench was exposed, Jake and Heather marked each dark stain with a pin flag.

"We had over 200 people on Saturday," Jake said, continuing their earlier conversation. "Maybe close to 300. I asked Erin to make a rough count, but I think she lost track in the afternoon."

"That's still a lot of visitors, given that we didn't advertise ahead of time."

"True. Most of them were locals and seemed to already know we were here. They probably helped spread the word." Jake turned, checking on the students working behind them. He waved to Amanda, who was busy videotaping the work at the far end of the trench. She gave him a thumbs-up in reply, pleased with the day's results.

"We had some locals on Sunday, but mostly tourists," Heather said. "But the townies all seemed to remember Jacklyn Wardell's old dig."

"Hmm. Same thing on Saturday, now that I think about it," Jake said. "But I suppose it's because of her death. A professor from a big university, all the hubbub of the excavation, and then she dies in a storm. Probably was a big deal in such a small town."

"Some of the people I talked to said it was insane that she was out in a boat at all. Lots of accidents on the lake, even in good weather. Nobody with any sense takes chances like that."

"Mrs. Wardell, her mother, said pretty much the same thing. Hard to know what was going through her head though. But people's memories aren't always that great. Could be the storm didn't seem as bad at the time."

"Everyone I talked to said it was bad," Heather said. "More than a few even said they wondered if it wasn't an accident at all."

An electric shiver passed down Jake's back, his unspoken curiosity now out in the open. "So, what do they think happened?"

"Lots of ideas." Heather shrugged. "Most pretty stupid. Some said the site is cursed, just like Tut's tomb. A couple think the director of the other field school killed her, but I forget why exactly. Some bozo even tried to use her death in some murder mystery he was writing."

"Really?"

"Yeah, a local nerd with delusions about being the next Stephen King. 'Course, everyone said he was notorious for starting projects and never finishing them. Supposedly he was making really good progress on his novel when his cabin went up in flames."

"You're kidding. What happened?"

"Well, he died of course," Heather said cheekily. "The fire department said his do-it-yourself wiring was faulty and that caused the fire. Figures, huh?"

"Weird." Jake paused, lost in thought. "I wonder if he had any of the missing maps we can't locate."

Heather shook her head. "I doubt it. How would someone like him end up with university field notes? Besides, it was all fiction. The guy who told me about him said he turned Wardell's death into a murder. The killer was going to be another archaeologist or a local collector. He didn't know which version the guy decided on."

"Still, it sounds like a lot of folks still don't believe her death was an accident."

"Yeah, and you're one of them, I think."

"Maybe," Jake said, a bit embarrassed. "The pieces just don't fit, for it to be an accident. Maybe this novelist was on to something after all."

"Doubt it," Heather said. "Besides, any notes he had all went up in flames, so it doesn't matter. None of it has anything to do with this field school."

By the close of the day, a large linear trench had been opened, creating a rectangular scar across the west-central portion of the site. Several dozen features had been uncovered and flagged. The crew spread out tarps and sandbags to protect their latest finds until they could be mapped, photographed, and excavated. The results were much greater than Jake had dared hope, more than enough to keep the students busy for several weeks. He thanked the operator for his service and informed him that they wouldn't need him again until later in the season.

Although excited by their discoveries, the students and staff were exhausted. Most had worked one or more shifts during the weekend open house, and chasing to keep up with the backhoe was more strenuous than the slow, methodical feature excavations of the past few weeks. A light rain drifted through as they closed up for the day.

"C'mon Jake, everything's fine!" Amanda yelled, and tapped the car horn once again to get his attention.

Jake waved, and scanned the site one last time as he trod over the piles of topsoil lining the newly dug trench. He glanced at the western sky in a vain attempt to predict how much rain might actually fall in the next twelve hours. Jake paused, thinking that he might add just a few more sandbags in one spot. A harsh horn blast warned him of the dangers in pursuing that line of thought. Instead, he made his way to the parking lot and got in the passenger seat.

"About time, Mr. Worrier." Amanda jammed the car into gear. "Everyone else left ten minutes ago."

"Sorry. Just worried about the rain. I don't want water to get under the tarps and wreck those features."

"It's just a little shower, Jake. See?" she said, jabbing a finger toward the scattered drops on the windshield. "Besides, I'm about ready to collapse here."

"Sorry, honey. Guess it's been a tough couple of days."

"Honestly, it really has been, but in a good way," she said as the vehicle pulled onto the state highway. "I think I have all the material I need to get started on the mock dig for the History Center."

"So you still plan to head back to La Crosse tomorrow?"

"Yeah, I think so. I'm glad we had some time together, but you're busy running the dig and I have other projects to work on. Plus if I save a few days now, I can come back for a longer stretch in a few weeks."

"Sounds like a plan," Jake said as he rested his hand on her knee. "How about a fancy dinner in town to celebrate the success of your visit? Say, with a ruggedly handsome archaeologist for company?"

"That's sounds great, but I'd rather go with you instead."

Chapter Sixteen

Jake and Amanda dined at the High Hat Supper Club, tucked away on a side road off the main highway, about a mile north of the state park. The décor harkened back to the Roaring Twenties, with a vintage neon top hat sign blinking on the roof. Only a few other diners were present, so they decided to sit for a while and enjoy some after-dinner cocktails. It was a pleasant, relaxed evening for them both, one of very few that they had enjoyed together in recent months.

"You're sure you have enough video? I can always ask Scott to get more photos, but the university video camera is pretty dated."

"I should have plenty to start with," Amanda said. "Once I start putting the presentation together I can decide what sections might need extra material. I'll take care of it on my next visit."

"Fine. I promise you'll have a lot less fieldwork next time."

"Good. I don't mind helping out a bit here and there, but it's not my focus anymore."

"No problem. The students are improving rapidly, so I can expect better results out of them. And I can always work Heather and Scott harder. Even Bryant is showing some potential, assuming I can get him to tone down his ego."

"Good luck with that. I think Heather would argue that he's a lost cause."

"Ah, he just rubs her the wrong way, I think."

"I'm not so sure, Jake. I think Heather feels threatened by Bryant."

"Heather? That's hard to believe. She has lots more field and lab experience, and more years of grad school under her belt."

"I realize that, but I think it's more what Bryant represents. I think Heather's tough-and-bluff exterior is all an act. You know, just a shell to hide her real feelings."

"I don't know," Jake said. "Heather's never been shy about expressing her opinions. On any subject."

"But Heather is also at that stage of grad school where the pressure really builds," Amanda said. "Her thesis is done but she has to start developing her dissertation research, which is a much more involved process. Plus, she's expected to write articles, give papers at three or four conferences every year, and secure funding for her own projects. Bryant is in the initial stages, when his advisor takes care of most of that. Or at least he should be."

Jake considered her argument as he sipped his bourbon sour. "Thinking back, I guess there were a lot more drops during my later years in grad school. If people made it through the first year, they were fine until the third or fourth year. Yeah, that's when they realized they couldn't cut it, or all the work wasn't worth it."

"See? Heather's right on that cusp."

"Still, it's hard to see that happening to Heather. She's too rock solid."

"Maybe, but you'd better keep an eye on her." Amanda took a sip of her wine and glanced around the dining room. "So, how did you find out about this place?"

"It's really something, isn't it? Great food, but since it's off the beaten path I think only the locals know about it."

"It is close to the campground, like you said. When you suggested we walk to the restaurant I thought you were nuts."

"Jacklyn Wardell used to walk up here, during her field school," Jake said. "She mentioned it in her journal. She stumbled on it while out running one night after work, stopped in, and fell in love with the place. Sort of kept it to herself and stole up here a few times when she wanted to escape from the students."

Amanda gave him a quizzical look. "You're reading her journal?"

"Well, sure. About half the pages are field notes. Maps, artifact counts from units, stuff like that. I made copies of those pages back at the university, right after Mrs. Wardell dropped off that box. The rest of the journal is filled with little sketches, comments and stories about the students, the locals, and even this restaurant."

"Basically, personal stuff?"

"I guess you could say that. What's the problem?"

"It seems kind of morbid to me, Jake. It's like you're snooping through her diary."

"I see your point," Jake said. "I didn't really think of it that way before. To me, it's just a resource, like a historical account of the site."

"I know historians and archaeologists use old diaries, legal records, all kinds of documents when researching the past. But this sounds like more . . . intimate stuff, and some of the people in them are still around. It could be embarrassing for them."

"I suppose, but there's really not much in the way of intimate thoughts in her journal. I really was just hoping to get a better picture of how she interpreted the site."

"I know, love," Amanda said, and gave him a smile. "I guess it caught me off guard. Besides, it's like you're cheating on me with a dead woman."

"Believe me, I wouldn't trade you for any dead woman in the world," Jake said, grinning. "Well, maybe Marilyn Monroe.

Ooh, or Rita Heyworth. And maybe—"

Amanda lobbed a dinner roll at him, effectively ending that discussion.

A short time later, Jake and Amanda walked hand in hand along the side of the road, enjoying the cool night air. The late-afternoon showers had passed through the area and taken the humidity with them. When they reached the state highway, Jake and Amanda moved on to the wider shoulder. A few cars drove by, most moving toward the centerline as they neared the couple.

The next vehicle to appear had its high beams on, and Jake and Amanda shielded their eyes from the blinding glare. A hundred yards away, the car engine revved as the driver accelerated, drifted onto the shoulder, and drove straight at them. Jake leaned into Amanda and pushed her hard off the shoulder into the ditch, and they both fell into the tall damp grass as the car zoomed past. The car veered back onto the road and sped off.

"Are you hurt? Damn jerk!"

"It's okay, honey, I'm all right," Amanda said as she brushed away wet leaves and twigs and got to her feet. "What the hell was that guy's problem?"

"Probably drunk," Jake said, with more than a touch of heat in his voice. "Or some stupid kid thinking he's funny."

"Well no harm done, so don't let it get under your skin."

Jake let out a long sigh and glared in the direction the vehicle had gone. No taillights were visible. "Yeah, you're right, I suppose. I am going to warn the crew to be extra careful when they walk or run along the highway, though. Last thing I need is to have to rush one of the students to the hospital because some jackass doesn't know how to drive."

Jake wrapped his arm around her and they hurried back to the campsite. "I suppose taking out a field school and not coming back with the same number of students would probably constitute grounds for denying me tenure, wouldn't it?"

CHAPTER SEVENTEEN

"There's another set over here, Professor!"

"Here, too! And it looks like someone pulled up this tarp."

Jake cringed, and shook his head despondently as the crew inspected the site. They had noticed a few odd footprints on Tuesday morning when they started work at Waconah, but chalked it up to a few after-hours visitors or perhaps some embarrassed students walking across the tarps by accident. But with the crew's arrival on Wednesday morning, it was apparent that someone had taken more than a casual interest in the excavation.

"It doesn't look like anything was taken," Scott said as he joined Jake and Heather near the newly dug trench.

"Not yet, anyway," Heather said, wiping some dirt from her hands. "So much for the local goodwill from the open house."

Jake scowled at her, but didn't reply. The students had finished uncovering their features and units, and from all indications none of the deposits had been disturbed and no artifacts were missing.

"It could be some overly curious visitors, I suppose," Jake said. He raised a hand to thwart Heather's imminent objection. "But we don't want it to go any further than just looking. I'll ask Erin to print up some signs, cautioning people not to disturb the excavations, and I'll call the sheriff's office and see if they can help keep an eye on things after work hours."

Heather shrugged, then walked off to help some students

working on a nearby unit.

"Makes sense," Scott said. "Don't want people tearing up the site, looking for treasures. Do you think the mounds over at the Christianson site are in danger?"

"Maybe, but not likely. All of the locals probably already know about the mounds, and there's a good chance they were hit by looters years ago. Mound exploration was a big thing back in the 1920s and 1930s. Waconah is attracting attention now because we're so visible. Hate to admit it, but there are some downsides to public outreach events like the open house."

Scott nodded, before hastening over to help the students who were excavating the house structure. Jake called Bob Jingst, the property manager, and spoke with him about the possible trespasser. He then called the county sheriff's office and left a message with the desk sergeant.

Less than thirty minutes later, a sheriff's patrol car appeared at the top of the hill and drove down to the parking area. Jake walked over and introduced himself.

"Nice to meet you, Professor. I'm Jim Rostlund, County Sheriff. This is one of my deputies, Pam Hauser." Sheriff Rostlund was in his late fifties, with a ruddy complexion and a noticeable spread around his midsection. Deputy Hauser was about Jake's age, with a friendly smile and blonde hair pulled taut in a short ponytail.

"I talked to the property manager about the possible vandalism," Jake said, "but he admitted they don't have the manpower to patrol unoccupied properties. They have to concentrate on the campgrounds and beaches, so he suggested I give you a call. I realize this is probably pretty low priority, but—"

"No, don't you worry about it," the deputy said, patting him on the arm. "The crime rate is low up here and we mostly deal with trespass, burglaries, and stuff like that."

"Personally, I prefer it that way," Sheriff Rostlund said. "During the summer months we get flooded with DWIs, fights, traffic accidents, and all that garbage I hoped to leave behind when I left Green Bay. When the tourists arrive all the peace and tranquility goes right out the damn window."

"I suppose it's a real headache during Summer Days."

"You said it. I had everyone working double shifts and we were still short-handed. Glad that's over."

"We had an open house out here during the festival, and I think that might be part of the reason we're seeing off-hour visitors," Jake said.

"I'll be happy to drive by here a few times during my shift, Professor," Deputy Hauser said. "You folks are staying over at the campground, right? In case I need to get in touch with you," she added, tucking a stray blonde lock behind one ear.

"Sure. We're in the group section, by the old recreation hall," Jake said as he handed the deputy his card. He frowned as Heather coughed loudly from a few feet away. "My cell number is on the card, Officer."

"Please, call me Pam. We're, uh, pretty informal up here."

She reddened, and Jake thought he caught Sheriff Rostlund giving her a curious look. "Okay. I answer to Jake more often than Professor, too. Can I give you two a quick tour of the site?"

They both agreed, so Jake spent the next half hour pointing out the various pit features and hearths the students had found, as well as the possible longhouse structure. He showed them some of the artifacts that had been found that day, and Heather brought out the display case with the showier items from the open house. Deputy Hauser seemed particularly interested, marveling at every potsherd, broken bone, and flake chip.

"My brother and I used to find lots of little arrowheads, like these here, on our granddad's farm when we were kids," Sheriff

Rostlund said, referring to some triangular points in one corner of the case.

"Was that around here?"

"Nah, his place was on the other side of Lake Winnebago."

"Lots of sites in that area. Most of the big camps and village sites in Wisconsin are located on big lakes and rivers."

"You know," the sheriff said, "you ought to get in touch with Everett Kojarski, the former sheriff. Everett had some nice arrowheads in a frame in his office, before he retired. Spent a lot of time out here when the last dig was happening. I mean, before the other professor had her accident."

Jake nodded. "Charlie Garath from NEWAS said the same thing, but we've been so busy I keep forgetting to call him. I'll make a point of it today."

"Don't forget, you have an appointment with that professor from Chapman College on Friday, too," Heather said as she put the display artifacts back in the travel case.

"Right, thanks Heather. Looks like this is going to be another busy week," Jake said. "So, Sheriff, were you here when Dr. Wardell died?"

"Nope, that was a bit before my time. I was working major cases in Oshkosh back then, so I heard about it, but that's all."

"You'll like Everett, he's quite a character," Deputy Hauser said, giving him a big smile, accentuated with dimples on both cheeks. "Once you get him yakking about something it'll be hard to shut him up."

"Well, thanks for the warning. I'll give him a call this afternoon. And thanks again for agreeing to check up on the site from time to time."

As the officers made their way back to their vehicle, Jake pulled out his cell phone and dialed the number given to him by Charlie Garath a few weeks earlier. Mr. Kojarski answered, and after Jake explained who he was and the reason for his call,

Jake was invited over to his home that evening. Jake scribbled his directions on the back of a paper artifact bag and tucked it into his shirt pocket.

"Get in touch with the old sheriff?" Heather said. She held two large decorated rim sherds in her hand.

"Yeah, I'm going to head over there tonight," Jake said. "What did you find?"

"Lisa and Andy pulled these out of Feature 22, one of the storage pits just outside the house. The decoration is pretty intricate; typical Oneota stuff."

"Sure looks like it. If it's contemporary with the house, then the dates would be right on for a longhouse."

Heather took the sherds and returned them to a large bag. "Everything set up with the sheriff?"

"Yes, they'll drive by a few times during the day, and Sheriff Rostlund said he'd have the overnight patrols monitor the area during their shifts. He figures a little extra security will keep most of the uninvited visitors away."

"I suppose Deputy Blondie is taking charge? Is she going to call you nightly with her report?"

"What's that supposed to mean?"

"Oh, come on. She must have said 'interesting' or 'fascinating' to you at least a dozen times. And I saw her touching your arm a few times during the tour. She was obviously playing up to you."

"You're joking, right? I'd have noticed that."

"Right, right," Heather said, rolling her eyes. "Deputy Lovelorn was practically flirting with you. Mark my words, she'll end up calling you for some stupid reason and then casually suggest meeting somewhere for drinks."

"Maybe Pam is just really interested in archaeology," Jake said.

Heather's laugh could be heard across the site. "You'd better be careful, Professor Oblivious. You're just lucky Amanda wasn't here to see all this."

"See all what?"

Heather shook her head in despair, and walked back to the students busily excavating the longhouse structure.

CHAPTER EIGHTEEN

Shortly before six, Jake pulled down the tree-shrouded drive leading to Everett Kojarski's home. Situated on the south edge of town, it was a typical mid-seventies ranch house, showing more than a bit of wear and tear. The crooked pines and overgrown bushes showed years of neglect, giving the property a somewhat foreboding appearance. The weather-beaten but cheerful gnomes scattered along the porch offset the effect, to a degree. As he pulled to a stop, a burly figure pushed open the front door and waved.

"Mr. Kojarski? I'm Jake Caine, from Wisconsin State University."

"Nice to meet you, Jake, and call me Everett. It's always been Everett, or Sheriff, but since I retired that don't fit anymore," he said with a grin, and ushered Jake inside.

"Hope I'm not imposing."

"Hell no. My wife's visiting her ditzy sister and her eight cats down in Stevens Point, so I've been batchin' it for the last week. Happy to have some company."

They passed through the living room into the kitchen, where Everett had his artifact collection spread out on the table. Pulling two bottles of beer from the fridge, he sat down as Jake rolled out a county map with the locations of all the recorded sites marked in red. Together, they went through each artifact. Jake provided information on the point type, its approximate age, and raw material, while Everett pointed out the location at which each item had been found. Most of Everett's spearpoints and tools came from previously known sites, but a few were from other locations so Jake recorded those spots as new sites in his notebook. Once back at the university, he would arrange to have formal archaeological site forms filled out for each area.

After a while, the conversation turned to the recent finds from the field school excavations at Waconah. Jake summarized what the students had found thus far, and how much help Charlie Garath and the NEWAS volunteers were providing.

"Yeah, Charlie really gets into this stuff. Goes on digs, does his own collecting, writes up most of the articles in the group newsletter. Even got something published in the state archaeology journal years back. He was on cloud nine about that! Gave copies to everyone he ran into, dropped 'em off at the school library, everything. I was more into it when I was younger, but after my kids came along and I became sheriff I couldn't find time for it."

"He does seem pretty . . . intense, I guess is the best way to describe it. All in all, the field school is going great. My biggest problem right now is trying to tie in our work with the stuff done by Jacklyn Wardell when she was out here."

"Her drowning was pretty tragic, nice young gal like that. I was out to the site a few times, officially and otherwise, and she was always pleasant and happy as could be, although I don't know how she kept it all together. I mean, bunch of college kids to run herd on, all the paperwork and forms she kept, chasin' from one end of that dig to another. Hell, made me tired just watching her."

"An archaeological dig is a lot of organized chaos, I guess, and some college kids can get a bit rowdy. My group is pretty good, though. A few jokers mixed in, but everybody seems to get along well enough. Plus, I've got a couple of great grad students to help me keep them in line."

"That always helps, to have a good crew to fall back on."

"Speaking of grad students, that's the only other roadblock I've run into with this project. I've been trying to track down some of Wardell's old grad assistants, to see if they can help fill in some of the gaps in the old notes. Naturally the one I most want to find, Mark Winters, seems to have dropped off the face of the earth."

Everett set down his beer and kneaded his fingers together in a calm, deliberate manner. "Mark Winters. Yeah, that name rings a bell."

"He was the senior assistant at the time, and wrote up most of the preliminary report the department put out as a memorial."

Everett nodded without comment. He selected a large notched spearpoint from the table and began to rotate it slowly in his hand.

Without pausing to consider the possible ramifications, Jake voiced the question that had been lurking at the back of his consciousness the entire evening. "Just out of curiosity, Everett, did you ever think that Jacklyn Wardell's death might not have been an accident?"

The retired sheriff made no immediate reply, but stared thoughtfully for a moment. Jake was afraid he had crossed a line.

"You know, it's been a lotta years since I thought about that case," he said, "but since you and your students started digging out there again I have to admit that there were a few things that didn't add up. Maybe it's just an old man's hindsight. Back then it looked pretty clear-cut, but now, I dunno."

"I'd really be interested to hear about it, if you don't mind."

The old man smiled and nodded, rising from the table. "Tell you what, grab us a couple more beers out of the fridge, and I'll get my old case notes."

"You've kept that stuff all of these years? I thought only archaeologists insisted on keeping paperwork for decades."

That brought a snort of laughter as Everett returned to the kitchen. "Well, my wife always said I could never throw anything away, so I probably would have been a damn good archaeologist, then. I hung onto my notebooks after I retired, you know— just in case they'd ever come in handy. Seemed to make sense at the time, 'specially for those dealing with any major crimes or accidents."

"So where does this one fall?" Jake said as he settled himself back at the table.

Everett took a long pull on his beer, eyes scanning the scribbled yellowing pages. "To be honest, although we had our suspicions that there mighta' been some foul play involved, none of the evidence we gathered was concrete enough to suggest it *wasn't* an accident. We finally had to rule it an accidental death, boat accident and drowning, simply because we didn't have enough to conclude there wasn't anything more to it."

"Seems odd that she would have gone out on the lake with a storm approaching. I mean, she could have easily waited a few days to check out the islands she wanted to survey."

"That's true, and I'll admit we considered that at the time," Everett said, shrugging his shoulders. "Course, she may have thought she had more time, or that the storm would move off to the north. It was a lot stronger than anyone expected. Did a lot of damage around town."

The frown on the retired sheriff's face was enough incentive for Jake to prod a little deeper. "If you weren't entirely convinced, I take it you suspected someone?"

"Five someones, actually. Had five folks that had run-ins with the victim prior to her death, or we suspected might be involved 'cause of the way they acted afterward. We kept our inquiries pretty low-key, at first. Didn't want to spook anyone in case it wasn't an accident."

Everett flipped back to the front of his notebook. "First off, we had Mark Winters, your missing archaeologist. He sent up a red flag right off the bat. He was Wardell's assistant, like you know, but it seems he and the victim had a blow-up on the day she disappeared. Wardell had sent the crew back early that day but she and Winters stayed behind. Couple of students had driven back to the site a little while later, looking for a backpack that had been left behind. They found it in the middle of the road, about halfway down the hill. Guess it fell off the top of the car. When they got out to retrieve it, they saw Winters and Wardell arguing, and could make out raised voices. They weren't sure what it was about, but he acted mighty weird when we questioned him after the body was found. He had a couple of drug arrests on his sheet, too, so I thought maybe he was smoking or dealing at the dig and she caught him. But, turned out he was back at the field camp right after the students saw the argument, so he wouldn't have had time to kill Wardell, get her in the boat and out onto the lake, and be back in camp in time for supper. Other students said they saw him there all evening, so he couldn't have gone back out later, either. And he was definitely there when the storm hit, 'cause he ran around checking on folks, making sure they were all safe, stuff like that."

"No one saw him acting strangely, doing anything suspicious?"

"Nope. One or two said he was his usual mopey self, as a matter of fact. Ate dinner with the rest of the crew, then sat out by his tent until dark with his nose in a book."

"Doesn't really sound like something a killer would do, does it?"

Everett grinned. "Not unless he was some kind of cold-blooded serial killer, but I don't suspect that's real likely. I figure he was just nervous 'cause of his drug busts, and maybe he had some stuff on him that he didn't want us to know about.

"We talked to the head of the other field school, from Chapman College, too. Apparently he had in no uncertain terms made it pretty clear that he wasn't too pleased having another dig going on right next door, in 'his' territory. Here's the name, Marv Schumholtz. There were a few run-ins between the two groups of students before the accident, mostly arguments and scuffles in bars. Guys getting too fresh with girls from the other dig, that kind of crap. Professor Schumholtz complained to the Forest Service about Wardell's dig, something about silt in the lake or something, but Wardell had all her permits in order and everything was by the book."

The retired sheriff laughed out loud as he scanned his notes from the interview. "You'd have sworn that this guy was straight out of the 1800s, like women shouldn't be allowed to drive or vote. One of my deputies told me later that she was about ready to shoot him at one point, but just couldn't bear the thought of filling out all the damned paperwork.

"Anyway, Schumholtz was back at his hotel immediately after work ended for the day. The crew and assistant director were all over at the state campground, but not this guy. The hotel manager confirmed it. He rang the front desk a little after five to demand more towels, and ten minutes later called to complain about the lack of hot water. Twenty minutes more and he called room service to order his dinner. Another ten and he was demanding to know where his food was. Made a few out-going calls, then rang the desk again right about ten o'clock, to complain about people 'fornicating' in the next room. The desk clerk didn't know what the hell he was talking about, which is why he remembered it so clearly. Hell, if anybody was gonna get murdered around here back then, my money would have been on Schumholtz, done in by the hotel staff."

"Yeah, sounds like his alibi was pretty solid," Jake said. "I suppose a pest like that really stands out, but I'll bet he's more hot air and noise than anything else."

"You're probably right. Anyway, we could write him off, likewise for most of the students at both sites. Couple of 'em had traffic and underage drinking citations, a few drug arrests, but nothing major. Plus none were anywhere near the boat launch before the storm, near as we could determine. A few were in town, some out jogging, and the rest scattered around the two campsites. Everyone seemed to have been with at least one or two other people."

"So, they were either not involved, or it had to have been a couple of them working together, right?"

"Yeah, right, and it's tough to hide a crime when a couple of people are involved. They all start to suspect each other of turnin' on one another, or their stories don't match, and then out it comes."

"You said you had five possible suspects. Who were the other three?"

Everett sipped his beer and paged forward in his notebook. "The assistant director on Schumholtz's dig couldn't account for her whereabouts the night Wardell disappeared. Said she was doing some follow-up work at their site, fixing some problems with the students' units. Nobody else was out there with her, but when she got back to the state campground a few hours later at least a dozen students remember seeing her all dirtied up, smeared with that reddish clay. That was right about the time the storm hit, I guess. Margaret Devlin, that was her name."

"Maggie Devlin was there?"

Everett nodded. "You know her?"

"Yeah, she's a regional environmental coordinator for the Transportation Department," Jake said. "Oversees a lot of archaeology work for highway projects. Never knew she worked at the Chapman College dig. The work was never written up, but now that I think about it I suppose she could have been there around that time."

"Well, Devlin said she was busy at her site the whole time, for a few hours or so, and never saw or heard anything. Claimed she and Wardell were good friends and seemed pretty upset to hear about her death. She did mention that the victim and another WSU professor, Clark Kelley, were fighting a great deal, and also said she heard rumors about problems between Wardell and one of her grad students, but didn't have anything concrete. I assumed it was Mark Winters, and maybe she heard about their fight on the night of the accident."

"I heard rumors that Jacklyn and Clark Kelley didn't get along," Jake said.

"Well, he was suspect number four, mainly because of what Devlin told me. Professor Schumholtz said something similar, intimating that Kelley and Wardell were having an affair and that's why she was running the dig. But to be honest Kelley didn't seem like the physical type, you know, someone who would get his hands dirty. He didn't have an alibi, either, for the night in question, but claimed he was at his hotel all evening. The desk clerk couldn't confirm or deny it, but a few students thought they saw him driving off in that direction when the day's work was over. A guy in the next room thought he heard someone in Kelley's room, but he said it could have been the TV, too."

"Dr. Kelley still teaches at the university. I had the impression he really wasn't out at the site all that much."

"That's the feeling I got, too. Came out a few times, drove everyone nuts for a while, then left."

"Yeah, that's Clark in a nutshell," Jake said. "And between you and me, he definitely isn't someone who takes to the physical side of the job. Tough route to follow when you're an archaeologist."

"Even without a solid alibi, I didn't put much stock in him as a murderer. And if he and the victim were having an affair, they sure hid it well. She wasn't outspoken about it, but damn near all the students could tell that she really, really disliked that man."

"She wasn't alone. Clark has a tendency to rub people the wrong way."

"Finally, the last person we considered was Herb Keeling, owner of the Hillside Resort south of the site. He was the most vocal of a group of local landowners all worked up about too much development in the area. For some reason they had it in their heads that the archaeologists were there to clear the land for a condo development, or some big resort that would put all the family-owned places out of business."

A sour look crossed Everett's face as he continued. "Herb was, and still is, a real ass with a big mouth and a short fuse. His poor wife, Annie, used to show up in town with all kinds of bruises from her 'accidents.' Tried to get her to press charges on the bastard, but no go. She did divorce him, though, a couple of years after Wardell's death, and moved away. Anyway, we talked to Herb 'cause he had had a few shouting matches with the victim while the field school was out there, but he had an airtight alibi. He was in Minneapolis at a resort trade show the entire week. Seemed as shocked as anyone about her death."

Everett closed the notebook. "That's it. Each suspect had an alibi or no clear motive. The body was pretty badly chewed up from the storm and decomposition. That's pretty common with floaters. So we couldn't find any evidence of foul play. Nothing showed up in the autopsy, neither. So even with a few loose ends, there wasn't enough to go at anybody, and no real reason to suspect anything."

"Well, one person definitely thinks otherwise," Jake said. "Mrs. Linda Wardell."

CHAPTER NINETEEN

Thursday passed quickly. Most of the students were now proficient excavators and could easily handle the daily tasks of digging and screening. Taking detailed notes was still a challenge for some, but all had shown some improvement. The initial thrill associated with finding thousand-year-old artifacts had begun to wane and only the more interesting items drew extra attention. After sorting by type, artifacts were deposited in paper bags, labeled, and set aside for processing in the lab.

The increased student efficiency was a definite boon for Jake, as his mind was elsewhere on Thursday. He mentally retraced his conversation with Everett Kojarski. The retired sheriff's review of the Wardell case had crystallized the thoughts that had brewed beneath the surface of his mind since his meeting with Linda Wardell. Was Jacklyn Wardell's death an accident? Why did Clark act so weird whenever he brought up her name? Were any of Kojarski's suspects somehow involved in her death?

Jake tried to broach the topic with Heather, Scott, and Erin that morning, but only Erin seemed even remotely interested. Her attention disappeared as soon as her lab students started unpacking artifact bags, so Jake was forced to mull things over throughout the morning on his own.

A small number of visitors came down to tour the site, but fewer than in days past. Several vehicles were seen at the top of the hill, which Jake mentioned to Deputy Hauser when she stopped by during her shift. She promised to circle back a few more times in the afternoon, and then drove off with a broad smile and a wave. Heather, standing a few yards away, rolled her eyes and pretended to retch into an empty artifact bag.

Maggie Devlin arrived just after lunch. Jake was helping some students clean and mark some post molds near the structure, but made his way over to greet her as soon as he had finished. Heather and Maggie were looking at some pottery as he approached. When they turned toward him, Jake was a bit startled by Maggie's appearance. The skin on her arms and face was puffy and red, and her short hair matted and tangled.

"Uh, hello Maggie," Jake said, extending his hand. "Nice to see you again. How are you doing?"

"Fine. Just fine. Very busy at work, you know how it is. Ten-hour days, barely enough time to check up on the field projects. And now state budget cuts looming again. So how are things going here?"

"Good. We brought in a backhoe last week and opened up a trench over there. Managed to expose more of the house, and a few dozen new features."

"Humph. Never was all that fond of mechanical stripping, myself. Backhoes really chew up a site and you lose all kinds of artifacts in the topsoil."

"Not necessarily. Feature damage is minimal if the operator is careful and you keep your eyes open for soil changes. And I have the students check the dirt piles every few days for artifacts."

Maggie didn't reply, but from the stern look on her face it was clear she did not agree. Instead, with a curt gesture to the northeast, she asked, "So, what kinds of pottery are you getting over there?"

"We're finding similar Oneota pottery all over the site. Some of the decoration is a bit unusual, so I'm thinking—"

"What about Late Woodland pottery? Are you finding much

115

Woodland material?"

"Some," Jake said, a bit put off by her brusque behavior. "Mostly undecorated body sherds but a few rim pieces, too."

"I could take a look at them, if you want."

"Thanks, but everything is back at the campground lab, being washed and processed. I could arrange to pull some examples if you're interested."

"Well, no, it's not that important," she said sharply. "Besides, I'm too busy overseeing state projects right now anyway."

"Thanks for the offer," Jake said. "I have a meeting tomorrow with Professor Schumholtz from Chapman College. He's supposed to have a ton of unpublished data on local ceramics."

"Well then, you should get all the help you need," Maggie said. She gave her watch a cursory glance. "Look at the time. I must be getting back. Good luck with things here." She turned away before Jake could reply and paced briskly back to her car. She sped back up the hill, reaching the highway just as Heather caught up with Jake.

"What's her deal?"

"Beats me," Jake said. "She bolted out of here after her last visit, too. Guess she feels obligated to visit since we're in her district, but doesn't have time to chat. She said she's really swamped with projects."

"She's hardly here at all," Heather said. "Don't see why she bothers."

"I could do without her visits, to be honest. She's curt to the point of being rude."

"Maybe you did something to piss her off?"

"Nothing I can think of," Jake said, scratching his head. "Not too many of the recent university contract projects were in this part of the state."

"Whatever. Are you still planning to visit that Schumholtz guy tomorrow?"

"Yeah. Erin's pulling some pottery for me to take along, and he's supposed to be the regional expert."

"Okay," Heather said as she looked over her shoulder. The nearest students were several yards away, hunched over a screen full of soil. "Look Jake, can . . . can you make a point of reminding everyone that I'll be in charge tomorrow? I know it sounds stupid, but I think Bryant's going to try and pull something."

"Heather, you don't have anything to worry about. I'll remind everyone again at tonight's meeting, like we talked about Monday."

"I just don't trust that guy. I can see him acting up just to give me grief."

"Try not to think about it. You know this site like the back of your hand, and you know how to run a crew. Scott will have your back, too, and I have complete confidence in you."

"Thanks, boss. That means a lot. Really."

"No problem, since it's the truth," Jake said. He peered at the horizon on the far shore of Taylor Lake. "You may have a short day anyway, if those dark clouds are any indication. If we get a good rain tomorrow, just herd the students into the lab and put them to work for a few hours. Then they can have the rest of the day off and you'll win their hearts for sure."

"I suppose," Heather said with a weak smile. "But you will say something tonight, right? Even if it looks like rain?"

CHAPTER TWENTY

For a change the weather forecast had been dead on. Jake squinted through the rain-spattered windshield, the overworked wipers struggling to maintain visibility in the driving rain. He drove well below the speed limit, cautious of hydroplaning on the slick rural highway and equally worried about missing yet another poorly marked turn. Dr. Schumholtz was courteous when Jake had called two days earlier about some Woodland sherds they had found at Waconah, but his sketchy directions had left much to be desired. Fortunately, only a few other people were foolish enough to be driving on such an unpleasant day and most seemed content to plod along behind him while he blundered around the upscale suburbs outside Wausau.

Once it dawned on him that left meant right and right meant left in the professor's lexicon, Jake made up ground and soon found himself at an imposing brick colonial revival house. While not the largest home in the neighborhood, it dwarfed most of the other residences with its size and manicured landscape. As he pulled in next to the black Lincoln in the driveway, Jake thanked his lucky stars for having the insight to wear a tie and his battered gray sports coat.

Jake's instincts had served him well. By the time the door chime had ceased echoing through the house, the owner had appeared in a velvet smoking jacket and tie, with a well-worn meerschaum pipe jutting out from beneath a neatly trimmed moustache.

"Professor Schumholtz? I hope I'm not late."

"Ah, yes, Dr. Caine, you're right on time." He glanced imperiously down his long nose at a gold pocket watch, before slipping it back into his pocket. "Decidedly foul weather, wouldn't you say? I'll have the housekeeper bring some coffee into the study, while you put aside your overcoat." With a dismissive nod at the coat rack, he shuffled off down the hallway, surprisingly quick for a man of his advanced years.

Professor Schumholtz's study was enormous, lined with walnut-paneled bookshelves and cabinets, and a large oak desk and table dominating the center of the room. The woodwork was stained dark brown and was offset by the overhead track lights and rich auburn-hued hardwood floor. The cut crystal decanters on the sideboard were almost lost in the opulence of the room. The arrival of the matronly housekeeper jarred Jake from his reverie. If Schumholtz designed the room to impress his guests, he had certainly succeeded.

"Here are some of the sherds I mentioned on the phone," Jake said, and he placed the items on the table. "All grit-tempered, but fairly well made with thin walls. The decorated examples display very narrow cord impression. Some of the designs look similar to the few published images I've seen of the Christianson II ceramics, near as I can tell. Only recovered a few rim pieces but again they seem pretty similar to your materials."

Professor Schumholtz leaned forward in his chair and examined each sherd. "Yes, they certainly fit with the Christianson II vessels. The real proof is in the paste characteristics." He tilted the nearby desk lamp to illuminate the specimens. "See here, the denseness of the clay and the inclusion of sand in the mix? Only appears in later Woodland assemblages from this part of the state."

Jake retrieved one of the sherds, and using his 20× loupe

could discern a number of iridescent white grains. "Hmm, yes I see what you mean. I don't recall reading anything about this trait."

"Well, it's taken a few years to finalize all my studies. Thin sections of the ceramics, compositional analyses of the clay, that sort of thing. The manuscript is just about ready to go out for review," Schumholtz said as he handed Jake a thick three-ring binder. "I can have a copy of this draft made for you to read, but I can't let you cite it until after it's been accepted for publication."

Jake nodded and began paging through the manuscript. It was a final, detailed summary of the Chapman College excavations at Christianson II that had come to a close some dozen years before. He skimmed past the short chapters dealing with the history of the site investigations, field and lab methods, and environmental setting. Comments and corrections were penciled in the margins of nearly every page, and to Jake's critical eye it seemed that the report was far from finished.

The pottery section was by far the longest, in itself comprising about half of the report. Black-and-white photos of rims and decorated body sherds were interspersed into the text, along with profile sketches outlining the form and curvature of the larger rim pieces. Nearly all compared favorably with the small fragments found at Waconah. At the end of the pottery chapter, two pages of text and one photo covered the few shell-tempered Oneota sherds recovered at Christianson II.

"These decorated rims are identical to those from the early Oneota component at Waconah," Jake said, sliding the open manuscript back to Professor Schumholtz. Reaching back into his briefcase, Jake pulled out some of the more impressive decorated Oneota rims from the site. Schumholtz picked up each in turn and gave it a cursory inspection. "I've never been all that familiar with Upper Mississippian pottery," he said with some disdain as he brushed the reddish dust from his fingers. "Always too busy trying to make sense of the Woodland cultures, before the Mississippian intrusion. Those studies formed the core of my dissertation, you know, examining why and how some Woodland groups transformed into Oneota and why others did not."

Jake returned his sherds to their plastic bags. Schumholtz's dissertation, while now somewhat dated, had fostered a great deal of subsequent research on the Late Woodland-to-Oneota transformation in the region. It hadn't hurt that the professor had republished various chapters of his Ph.D. manuscript, in slightly modified form, over the years. By volume alone the articles had established him as a recognized expert on the subject. "Yes, I'm familiar with your many publications, Professor. Standard reading for anyone working with late prehistoric assemblages in the state."

Schumholtz beamed, obviously pleased with the compliment. He was less thrilled with Jake's subsequent remarks. "I've referred to a number of them in my own articles, as well as some more recent thoughts on the subject. Based on her research proposal for the original Waconah field school, it looked like Jacklyn Wardell was hoping to test a number of your theories with her work."

Schumholtz scowled. "I remember her proposal, such as it was," he replied haughtily. "Too little background research in my opinion, and not enough contextual information on the site itself to support her proposal. Personally, I'm surprised the other committee members supported it so vigorously."

Jake began to understand why Schumholtz gave Jacklyn such a hard time, and why he had told all those stories to the sheriff after her death. "It seemed pretty thorough to me, but then my focus is on developing a better understanding of the post-transformation development of Oneota culture," Jake said. "Our results so far tend to support a number of Professor Wardell's ideas, but obviously a great deal more research is needed."

Professor Schumholtz harrumphed with some flair, obviously at odds with Jake but not willing to pursue the topic in a lengthy debate. He rubbed his fingers together, apparently musing over how to broach his next topic.

"Not to speak ill of the dead, my boy, but I had heard rumors that all was not aboveboard with Jacklyn Wardell."

"Oh? I'm not sure I understand your meaning, Professor."

"Well at the time, I had it on quite good authority that Ms. Wardell was a bit . . . shall we say, cavalier . . . in her personal relationships, specifically with one of her graduate students." Schumholtz arched one eyebrow with dramatic effect, which was a bit disconcerting given the bushiness of his eyebrows and the contrasting lack of hair atop his head. "It was also bandied about that her appointment as director of that field school was more to do with the influence of a senior professor rather than on any merit on her part."

Jake bristled but managed to keep his voice neutral. "From all the reports I've heard, Dr. Wardell was a highly respected archaeologist and quite a popular member of the faculty. It seems unlikely that she would have enjoyed such a reputation if all these stories were true."

"Perhaps so. As I say, much of it was based on hearsay and it's all water under the bridge regardless." The silence that followed was a bit awkward, and Jake gathered up his sherds and notes. "Hopefully your excavations will prove fruitful," Schumholtz said as he stared at the rain spattering against the window. "Unfortunately, a number of my own graduate students failed to follow in my path, and a great deal of potentially important work has been left undone. Our last season at Christianson II was the year after Dr. Wardell drowned, but by then I was wholly committed to my Wolf River survey, you know. I passed the excavations along to a student whom I thought had some promise but her efforts never proved adequate. A shame, really."

There was a slight break in the rain as Jake dashed out to his vehicle a short time later. Jake had thanked Schumholtz for his assistance and received in return an assurance that a copy of the Christianson II manuscript would be waiting for him in the department office when he returned to WSU in the fall. Once out of the suburbs and back on the state highway, Jake loosened his tie and tried to relax as he drove gingerly through the storm.

Jake wasn't sure why Professor Schumholtz's insinuating comments had annoyed him so. It was not as if he knew Jacklyn Wardell personally, and truth be told he had heard similar rumors from a number of other people. Maybe it was the haughty manner in which he callously dismissed someone's life, their work, and all their contributions to the profession without a second thought. A lot like Clark Kelley. Clark was quick to ridicule anyone who dared disagree with him, but never face-to-face. Having a petty and vindictive supervisor was probably the main reason Jake fretted so about keeping his job. Clark carried just enough seniority to make Jake's life miserable at times, creating just enough waves to put his career track in jeopardy. It certainly could explain why his tenure applications kept getting put on the back burner, Jake concluded grimly.

His musing was abruptly interrupted as Jake jammed on the brakes as a passing sedan cut over into his lane. Jake's car began to fishtail on the rain-slicked highway as he struggled to regain control. Steering in the direction of the skid, Jake forced himself not to brake again. As the car slowed and the steering became responsive, he guided the vehicle carefully onto the soft, wet gravel shoulder. Jake winced as he neared the steel guardrail, bracing for the impact of metal on metal. Braking with more force, Jake brought the car to a lurching stop on a grassy strip just past the rail.

Safely stopped on the side of the highway, Jake started to breath normally again. He leaned his forehead against the steering wheel, his trembling hands still wrapped tightly around the grips. As his heart rate relaxed, Jake looked up and saw the brake lights from a stopped car a few hundred yards ahead. The same jerk that cut him off, he realized, but at least the guy stopped to see if he needed help. Jake opened the door, deciding to at least wave to the other driver to signal that he was unharmed. As Jake stepped onto the soggy grass, the offending car accelerated and raced down the slick roadway.

Muttering some choice curse words under his breath, Jake climbed back into the car. He eased back on to the highway as the spinning tires splattered mud and gravel behind him. Once safe on the pavement, Jake started back to the campsite, eager to see the end of a frustrating afternoon.

CHAPTER TWENTY-ONE

The daylong storm on Friday gave way to a gorgeous sunny and warm weekend. The field school students lounged around the lake, played volleyball, and visited their favorite haunts in nearby Donovan. An impromptu barbecue and brew-fest was held on Saturday night, but the level of debauchery was considerably less than the previous party so Jake felt no desire to rein them in.

Sunday was much like Saturday, albeit a bit quieter around the campground. Several carloads of students had driven into town to see the latest summer blockbuster, starring some celebrity couple that Jake had never heard of. A few students stayed behind but for the most part Jake was left alone. In truth, he preferred it that way.

Ever since his meetings with Sheriff Kojarski and Professor Schumholtz, Jake found his thoughts returning again and again to Jacklyn Wardell's death. Schumholtz's innuendo about Jacklyn's supposed unethical behavior upset him more than he realized, but Jake had to wonder if there was a kernel of truth behind it all. The retired sheriff, even after all these years, still found aspects of her death unsettling. A mystery, perhaps, but not one Jake could fathom unraveling, especially after so many years. Besides, he had a field school to run, students to train, and a very busy semester of teaching and research on the horizon.

After dinner, Jake hid out in his room and made a vain attempt to update some syllabi for two of his fall classes. Unsuccessful with that project, he started working on the student grades for the field school, but his heart wasn't in it. Jake shut down his laptop, moved to his cot, and grabbed something to read from the top of the pile of books stacked haphazardly next to his bed.

Finding he had grabbed Jacklyn Wardell's journal, Jake sighed and sat back to read. A fair rendition of a moose head, poking out of the trees, was drawn in the middle of the page.

June 26. Rained out AGAIN!!! It never rained this much when I was a kid, or at least it never seemed to. 'Cept maybe for that time me and Pops got drenched hiking in the Chequamegon. It was worth it though; never thought I would see a moose in Wisconsin (and never have seen one since)!

Had to remind Curls to check the artifact bags more closely at the end of the day. Blondie 1 and Blondie 2 just can't seem to remember to include quarter-section and level info on their bags, and if he doesn't catch it in the field we might as well toss the artifacts in the lake! Snowman said Curls cuts them more slack because of how little clothing they wear HAHAHA! Might be some truth in that!

Two stick figures with long hair and hourglass-shaped bodies were drawn below that entry, with a curly-haired man standing nearby, panting. Jake laughed out loud, mentally reminding himself to send a copy to Terry Schroeder as soon as he was back on campus.

Thought the recent rain would keep The Dark One at home, but no such luck. He drove up this morning, made some snotty comments about our field results, and then scurried off to his hotel. Took one of my students (Ms. Amethyst) with him, too, to help with some project. Not sure I like the look of this situation;

may have to snoop around and see what is really going on. Hope it isn't what I think it is.

CatWoman earned her pay yesterday, for sure! Couldn't believe how fast that storm blew in, but she stuck in there and helped me get those units covered. Snowman too, but I can always count on him. Need to warn the students to cover their features better, EVERY NIGHT, instead of rushing back to the cars! Gonna be pretty mad if some of those features get washed away 'cause they were afraid of a little rain!

A shiver went down Jake's spine as he looked at the accompanying sketch. Stick-figure students ran madly across the site, while Jacklyn and a few stalwarts struggled with tarps. In the background, hurricane-like cyclones churned up the lake, with fish and boats and people caught up in the storm.

Given how Jacklyn had died, the image was prophetically disturbing. And somewhat surprising, that she would have been out in a boat after having experienced the effects of a sudden, dangerous storm only a few weeks earlier. Jake felt genuinely uncomfortable. He had found himself uneasy when reading Jacklyn's journal, ever since Amanda's comments over dinner the previous weekend, but this was especially pronounced.

Jake's cell phone rang, breaking into the eerie silence of his room. Dropping the journal, he grabbed for his phone and hit the accept button without checking the caller ID. "Hello?"

"Hi, honey," Amanda said. "How are you? I miss you so much."

"Hi, Amanda. Man, this is really eerie."

"What, a call from your girlfriend is suddenly eerie? Nice way to start a conversation."

"No, that's not what I meant. I was lying in my cot, thinking about something you said at the High Hat when my phone rang. Kind of startled me, that's all."

"What were you thinking about?"

"Oh, just your reaction when I said I was reading Jacklyn Wardell's journal," Jake said, a bit embarrassed. "I was paging through it and I came to a day when she was talking about how suddenly a storm blew up."

"Oh, that is creepy. It's not from the day she died, is it?"

"No, a couple weeks before that. But the drawing she made is pretty disturbing," Jake said, and he described the scene.

Amanda was silent for a few moments and Jake thought perhaps the call had been dropped. "Amanda? You still there?"

"Yeah, still here," she whispered. "That is really sad, when you think about it."

"So, what's happening in La Crosse?"

"That's kind of why I called. Have you gotten my last few emails?"

"No, I don't think so. Our Internet service is pretty spotty. I think the last time I got one was Tuesday, or maybe Monday night. I was going to try the Donovan library today, but the students warned me that they've been swamped the last few Sundays. Figured I'd try tomorrow."

"Well, I'll just give you the highlights, then. Looks like I've got plenty of video footage for the exhibit, and the photos I have already are great. I might swap out a few later, once the season is over. Got some ideas on what artifacts to include in the displays, too. Oh, and Dr. Holley approved my idea about building a replica longhouse."

"That's great, hon."

"The exhibit is going to be fantastic. With the extra space I'm getting, the longhouse will be set up right next to a reconstruction of the feature and post molds. Kind of like a mirror image, before and after."

"That does sound impressive," Jake said. "Good way for folks to see how we use archaeology to reconstruct the past. I'll make sure we have really detailed maps for your reconstruction."

"Speaking of construction," Amanda said, "that reminds me of the bad news."

"Uh-oh. What?"

"Because of the additional space we have to redesign the layout area, which means basically scrapping most of the old plans and starting from scratch. So I need to meet with the designers and building staff on a daily basis for the next few weeks. I won't be able to come back out to Waconah, at least for a while."

"Oh. So next week is out?"

"I'm so sorry, honey, really. I wanted to come back out next week, but things are going to be crazy busy around here for a while. Sean offered to help out, so that should speed things up. Maybe, if things go smoothly, I can come out in a couple of weeks."

"Hey, don't worry about it," Jake said. "We both have our career demands right now and we knew stuff like this would happen from time to time. It's not a problem."

"Really? Are you sure?"

"Definitely. It just caught me off guard, that's all. Maybe things will work out and you can come out in two weeks, or three."

"Okay, Jake. I'll keep everyone focused and get done as soon as I can," Amanda said. "So, what have you found lately?"

Jake described some of their latest finds, in an attempt to lighten the pall brought on by Amanda's unfortunate news. After describing some interesting pottery and bone tools, he exaggerated some of the recent antics of the students, and by the end of his story both of them were laughing.

"It hasn't been all fun and games, though," Jake said. "We noticed that someone has been snooping around the site after hours."

"How bad is it? Is someone looting the site?"

"Doesn't look like it, at least not yet. Some of the tarps were disturbed but none of the features were touched, and nothing is missing. I called the sheriff's office and they agreed to send some patrols around, just in case."

"Sounds good. How did your meeting go with Professor . . . Schumann, was it?"

"Schumholtz. Saw him on Friday. The Woodland pottery we found at Waconah is a good match for the material he has from Christianson II. The clay is identical, and he told me about some traits that apparently are only recorded in his unfinished manuscript."

"That's helpful. When is the report going to be published?"

"Not anytime soon, based on the draft he showed me," Jake said. "Some of the chapters looked ready to go, but most are just photos and some text cobbled together. I think he's been puttering with it for years and now it's almost unworkable. Oh, and he had a few nasty comments about Jacklyn Wardell, too."

Jake summarized Schumholtz's comments about Wardell, the irritation he felt evident in his voice. "And to top it all off, on the drive back some moron cut me off on the highway and I nearly ended up in a ditch!"

Jake swore under his breath. He had purposely planned to avoid mentioning that little misadventure, but now it was out in the open.

"Oh my god! Are you all right? What happened?"

"I'm fine, don't worry," Jake said. "The road was slick from the rain, and when the guy passed me I probably got too close to the shoulder and just slid off. It was more of a gradual slope than a ditch, anyway."

"Still, you could have been hurt. Did you call the police?"

"No, there wasn't any damage and nobody got hurt, so there was no point."

"After your accident and that guy who nearly hit us last

weekend, maybe you should complain to the sheriff about the drivers up there."

"It wasn't an accident, just a bad combination of events," Jake lied, hoping to end the discussion. "Say, speaking of sheriffs, I finally met with Everett Kojarski, the retired sheriff, and checked out his collection."

"Anything interesting?"

"Some nice Archaic points and part of a fluted Paleo point. Turns out he was the sheriff when Jacklyn Wardell died. He found his old case notebooks and we ended up talking about it for a while." Jake described his meeting with Sheriff Kojarski, and his thoughts on the five tentative suspects.

"Wow, that's really shocking that they thought it might have been murder, rather than an accidental drowning," Amanda said. "You don't think it's true, do you?"

"I don't know what to think, to be honest. Lots of little inconsistencies with the whole situation, and something about it doesn't feel right."

"Are you sure you're not just being overly influenced by Mrs. Wardell's opinion? She did lose her only child, and obviously is still in a lot of pain after all this time. Besides, you do have a weak spot for older women, you know."

Jake let out a long, audible sigh. Before they began dating, Jake had been involved with an art instructor some eight years his senior. For whatever reason, Amanda took a perverse pleasure in needling him about it whenever the opportunity arose.

"You're never going to let that go, are you? Well, maybe I should just stop calling you until you've aged a few more years."

"Like a fine wine?"

"I was thinking more like an old cheese, smarty."

131

CHAPTER TWENTY-TWO

On Sunday afternoon, Jake posted an order cancelling labwork on Monday so that all the students could be at the site. Work in the trench had uncovered a portion of the possible longhouse structure but much of it remained hidden outside the excavated area. In order to remove the overlying topsoil, they would have to move some of the back-dirt. The backhoe was unavailable due to a mechanical problem and Jake didn't want to wait another week for the part to arrive. The only alternative was old-fashioned hand labor. Since many hands made light the work, as the saying went, Jake insisted that everyone pitch in.

There had been a bit of grumbling when the notice appeared, but most of the students decided it was fair enough since no one would be spared from the drudgery. That evening, the majority drove into Donovan to watch the Fourth of July fireworks.

The sky was overcast on Monday with a cool breeze off the lake, and the work was less arduous than feared. With all the staff and students participating, the imposing pile of earth was soon reduced, relocated, and rebuilt several yards away. A few artifacts were found, including a very finely made bone hairpin. After the dirt was removed, Heather and Scott helped the students set up a grid of nails and string over the exposed area. Jake told Erin she was free to go back to the lab, but since it was almost lunchtime he would keep her helpers at the site for the rest of the day.

About an hour after lunch, Jake's cell phone rang.

"Hello?"

"Jake, someone broke into the lab! They broke the window and got in through the door, and stuff is scattered everywhere." Erin was nearly hysterical and Jake was certain her voice carried over to the students working nearby. "I don't know how this happened—"

"Erin. Erin, listen to me. I want you to go outside the building and wait in your car. Do you understand?"

"Yeah. All right, I'm going outside now. Should I call somebody?"

"No. Just make sure you're safe in your car, with the doors locked, and I'll be right there. I'll take care of the calls, okay?"

Erin sniffled and mumbled something in reply. Jake heard the slam of a car door as the call ended.

Jake spotted Scott about sixty yards away, carrying some artifact bags toward the parking lot. Jake whistled shrilly to get his attention, and then trotted over to meet him.

"What's up?"

"Erin just called. Looks like someone broke into the lab at the campground."

"Oh, damn. Is everything okay?"

"Not sure. I'm heading over there now," Jake said, noting that this was the first time he had ever heard Scott curse in his presence. "Go grab Heather and let her know what's going on. Try and keep it quiet, but I think some of the students overheard. I'll call you guys once I know anything."

Scott nodded and ran across the site toward Heather. Jake sprinted around an open unit and hurried to his vehicle. As he drove up the gravel road, he scanned the numbers programmed into his cell phone. He scrolled through the Ds, found Deputy Pam Hauser, and hit enter. She answered as he reached the top of the hill, so Jake idled there and explained the situation.

Deputy Hauser told him that she was at the far end of her patrol area but would drive over as soon as she could. Jake thanked her, ended the call, and located Bob Jingst's number as he pulled onto the highway. The call went directly to Bob's voice mail, so Jake left a brief message saying that the camp hall had been broken into and that he had notified the sheriff's office.

Jake sped down the road and was soon at the campground entrance. Within minutes he had reached the group campsite. Erin was sitting in her car, her cell phone in one hand and the other gripped tightly on the steering wheel.

"Erin, are you okay?" Jake said as Erin jumped out of her car.

"Yeah, I'm fine," Erin said, her eyes wide. "Jake, I am so sorry! I just stopped in town for supplies, and then I grabbed some lunch, and when I got back . . ."

"Don't worry, everything is fine," Jake said, taking her by the shoulders. "You just stay here for a second, while I take a quick look inside."

She nodded and glanced past him toward the door with its broken window. "Be careful."

Jake recognized the irony of doing the exact opposite of what he had instructed Erin to do, but still could not prevent himself from checking the scene. He stepped carefully through the doorway, the broken glass crunching beneath his boots. He paused, looked around the room, and listened for any sound. Nothing, besides the hum of the refrigerator. The room had been disturbed, but it did not look as if any real damage had been done. He was about to venture further inside when the sound of tires on gravel alerted him to an approaching car. He stepped outside as the squad car came to an abrupt halt.

Deputy Hauser stepped out, adjusted her gun belt and baton, and scanned the area. She waved to Jake and then made a quick call on her radio. Jake assumed she was reporting her arrival at the campground. He stood a respectful distance away, but she waved him over.

"Hi, Jake. You said something about a break-in?" Her demeanor was polite and official, but Jake could discern the hint of a smile at the corners of her mouth. Maybe Heather had been on to something after all.

"Yeah, looks like it." Jake gestured to Erin, who stood a few yards off to one side. "Erin was in Donovan buying supplies and when she came back she found the broken window and the door open."

"I took a couple of steps inside," Erin said. "I saw the place was all tore up, and it hit me that someone had broken in."

"What time was that?" the deputy asked.

"About 1:15, maybe closer to 1:30," Erin said, and looked at her watch. "I called Jake about two minutes later, I guess."

Jake nodded. "It was almost 1:30 when she called me. As soon as I told her to go back to her car, I called you."

"That was smart of you, Jake," Deputy Hauser said. She wrote the time down in her notebook and turned back to Erin. "And what time did you leave the campground?"

"I left with the rest of the crew, a little before eight," Erin said. She looked at Jake for confirmation.

"Yeah, we had everyone out at the site today, to move some dirt piles so we could open up more of the big trench."

"But normally you would be here, correct?"

"Yes, with a couple of students assigned to do labwork."

"It's too bad you had a different schedule today."

Erin looked confused. "Are you saying this is my fault? God, that's all I need! I had to pick up stuff for the office and—"

"Calm down, missy," the deputy said in an icy tone usually reserved for unruly drunks. "That's not what I said. But it's strange that a random break-in would happen on this particular day."

"Sure," Jake said, understanding her point. "Usually you would have been here to keep an eye on things. It's almost like someone was watching, maybe looking for an opportunity to get inside when no one was around. Right, Pam?"

Deputy Hauser favored him with a dimpled smile. "Maybe. Certainly an odd coincidence, to think someone just happened to wander by and break in on the exact day that the building was deserted. Anyway, I'll search the surrounding grounds after I check the interior."

The deputy closed her notebook and led the archaeologists over to the hall entrance. "You two wait here," she said, and then went inside. About five minutes later, she reappeared at the entrance.

"Place is empty. Anyone inside would have heard your vehicle and had plenty of time to take off on foot. 'Course, if they came by car they would have left long before you got back, or you would have seen them on the road."

"So, what do we do now?"

"I'll take some photos of the damage for the report and then I'll check out the trails leading to and from the group campsite," Deputy Hauser said. "Jake, you should probably ask your crew to come back and have them check to see if any of their personal possessions are missing. When I'm done inside, you two can go in and make a record of anything that's missing."

Jake called Heather on his cell phone while Deputy Hauser wrote down Erin's full name and contact information. As he feared, news of the break-in had spread like wildfire and the students were pestering Heather and Scott with questions they couldn't answer. Jake told Heather to make sure the site was secured for the night and then report back to camp.

Deputy Hauser took about two dozen photos and then asked

Jake and Erin to join her inside. "Okay, now try not to touch or step on anything. Just walk through the rooms and let me know what's missing, if anything doesn't belong, and whatever else seems out of place."

The trio walked gingerly through the kitchen area and main hall, trying to avoid the scattered papers, bags, and other items strewn across the floor. After a few minutes, they had completed their inspection.

"So, Jake, can you tell me what's missing in here?" Deputy Hauser said, her notebook open.

"To be honest, Pam, it doesn't look like anything was stolen," Jake said. "It might be because of the mess, but nothing important seems to be missing."

"Maybe they decided nothing was worth taking," Erin said. "The artifact cabinet is still locked, and some of these other boxes weren't touched either."

"Bit odd the culprits didn't grab these cameras, or that laptop," the deputy said as she studied the scene. "What about those items?" she asked, pointing at some large potsherds and a spearpoint lying on a tray. "Do they have any cash value for collectors?"

"Probably," Jake said, "but real hardcore collectors want top-quality, showy items. Broken pot fragments and the odd projectile point don't bring in the real money."

"I think we can assume then that theft wasn't behind this," Deputy Hauser said. "Any alcohol in the building? Something teenagers might be after?"

"Some beer and wine in the kitchen," Erin said, and she opened the fridge. "But none of it is missing."

Deputy Hauser tapped her pen against her notebook as she summed up the situation. "Well, my best guess is that someone, probably kids, broke in just to see what they could find. Nothing caught their interest or they got scared off when Ms. Weiss returned. I doubt they'll come back, but keep the place locked up when no one's around, and maybe lock anything of value in one of these cabinets."

"Can we start cleaning up?" Erin said.

"I suppose. We could dust for prints, but with nothing actually missing it would hardly be worth pursuing. God knows how many people have been in and out of this place in the last six months anyway." The deputy turned her attention back to Jake. "I'm going to check out those trails. Give a yell if you need me."

"Sure. Guess I'll check on my room, see what it's like in there." Jake entered his room and found papers on the floor and one upended file box, but no other apparent damage. He pulled his aluminum laptop case from beneath the cot, turned the numbers for the combination lock, and popped it open. The laptop was unharmed, safely secured by Velcro straps. He found the small picture frame with Amanda's photo under the chair and returned it to the table.

Seeing Amanda's photo reminded him of their weekend conversation and the fact that she wouldn't be visiting next weekend after all. Not exactly the summer together he had envisioned.

Looking at the tabletop, Jake realized Jacklyn Wardell's journal wasn't where he'd left it. He checked under the cot and looked under some scattered papers, curious as to where it had gone. As he heard vehicles approaching, he remembered stuffing it in his backpack that morning.

Jake hustled out the doorway and called the students over to explain the situation. He stressed minor vandalism rather than a burglary and possible theft, and then asked everyone to check on their tents and belongings, and report back to Scott.

As the crowd dispersed, Heather strode up to Jake. "What do you mean, 'minor vandalism'? What's really going on?"

"It's really not much more than that," Jake said. "When Erin got back from town she found the window broken and the door open. The place is messed up but near as we can tell, nothing was taken."

"Weird. Who bothers to smash their way in but doesn't take anything?"

"They might have gotten scared off, or maybe it was just kids goofing around. Pam, I mean Deputy Hauser, is checking the nearby trails now."

"Well, I checked everything twice and nothing is missing," a relieved Erin said as she joined Jake and Heather outside the hall. "Looks like they pawed through some cabinets and boxes but didn't find anything worth taking."

"Must be the world's dumbest criminals," Heather said. "The laptops cost a fortune and even the old digital cameras must be worth something. I thought burglars always took cameras."

Jake shrugged. "Maybe they thought they couldn't pawn them easily because of the university stamps. They rifled through my stuff but didn't get to my laptop. Guess they didn't see it in the case under my cot."

"Jake, none of the kids have anything missing," Scott said as he returned. "Doesn't even look like they bothered with the tents. Couple of the students put twist-ties around the zippers, sort of a crude lock on the flaps, and they weren't disturbed."

"Neat trick. I should try that," Heather said, and she walked past him to check on her own tent.

"It almost seems like they were looking for something, something specific." Jake's voice trailed off as Bob Jingst's pale green pickup rolled into the clearing. "I'd better handle this. Scott, help Erin with the clean-up, would you? And keep the students out of the building until Deputy Hauser comes back and gives us the all clear."

Jake greeted Bob as he clambered out of the truck. Bob

listened intently as Jake brought him up to date.

"Hmm. So nothing was taken at all?" Bob said, perplexed.

Jake shook his head. "Nothing, as near as we can tell. Lots of files scattered around and some boxes turned over, but none of the equipment is missing and all the artifacts are accounted for."

"And no one's personal stuff was disturbed," Heather said as she joined them. "All the tents were left alone. Mine too."

"Could be kids looking for cash, or beer maybe. We had some problems last year with some high school punks breaking in to campers."

Jake shrugged. "Possible, I suppose. Wouldn't they take cameras or laptops, stuff they could sell for some quick cash?"

"These kids were troublemakers, not real criminals. Only took alcohol, cigarettes, dirty magazines, and in one case a .22 handgun. Stuff they couldn't get their hands on otherwise. I doubt they'd even know how to fence any stolen goods."

"Maybe they've started moving up in the world," Heather offered.

"Not these kids," Bob replied. "The oldest one, who took the gun, had a juvie record so he got twenty months in prison. Two of the others dropped out of school and left the area. Rest got scared straight or at least don't come around here anymore."

Deputy Hauser appeared at the north edge of the clearing, near the end of the lakeshore trail. She gestured to the trio and met them near the hall entrance. Bob stooped down to examine the broken window.

"Cheap piece of junk," Bob said as he fiddled with the doorknob. "I'll replace the window this evening and install a new knob and deadbolt tomorrow. I can put clasps and padlocks on some of the cabinets, too, if you want."

"Nothing of consequence on the nearby trails," Deputy Hauser said, brushing some nettles off her uniform. "Plenty of footprints going this way and that, but they could be from anyone."

"Yeah, the students use the trails every day, and campers from the other sites are always going by," Jake said.

"I'll ask around. Maybe a tourist saw somebody suspicious."

"Could be that someone came down the old two-track, from the highway," Bob said. "Every once in a while we get folks trying to sneak into the park so they can camp without paying. Bikers can usually drive all the way in, but cars get bogged down in the ruts. Usually catch 'em in the morning when they don't have a camping ticket."

Deputy Hauser nodded, but didn't seem overly interested. "Like I said, I didn't see anything out that way, but it's possible they came in that way. Probably just kids from one of the other campsites."

"It might not matter, but Paula and Carrie thought they heard someone poking around their tent a few nights ago," Heather said. "They didn't hear a car so they figured it was some of the guys playing a joke."

"It may or may not be related," Deputy Hauser said. "For now, just be cautious and use common sense. Make sure all your valuables are locked up and keep an eye open for strangers. Jake, give me a call if you have any problems."

The mood at dinner that evening was decidedly subdued. After the initial shock and excitement of the break-in was over, an eerie pall settled over the students and staff. Menacing shadows now abounded in the surrounding woods, and everyone stayed close to camp. Many students were jittery and tense, leading to some harsh words and minor arguments. It did not make for a pleasant evening.

CHAPTER TWENTY-THREE

For some unexplained reason, Jake always disliked Tuesday mornings. Mondays weren't all that bad. The start of a new week always held some promise, a chance for new discoveries or to make a fresh start on some held-over problem from the previous week. By the end of the day, of course, things never quite developed as he had hoped, so Tuesdays ended up taking the brunt of Monday's unfulfilled promise.

On this particular Tuesday, Jake felt more than a bit out of sorts. Amanda was gone, not to return for at least another two or three weeks. Everyone was anxious about yesterday's break-in at the lab. Jerry Stiltman, unofficial site klutz, had tripped over the string marking an excavation unit and knocked out two nails and a good-sized portion of an undrawn wall profile. Steve was so busy trying to impress Liz with his muscles that he managed to drop both five-gallon buckets full of soil before he ever reached the screen. Lauren spent more time correcting her pit partner Ray than actually working, ensuring that she would be ready for her third new partner in less than two weeks. To top things off, Andy and Dale had forgotten to refill the water coolers, so everyone was stuck with lukewarm water from Monday. By the lunch hour, Jake had moved from "out of sorts" to "irritable" and was well on his way to "incredibly aggravated."

With his temper simmering at a low boil, the students had taken note and things were pretty quiet for Jake. At least until someone innocently announced, "Hey, he's back."

"Who?"

"Mr. Peeper, see?"

Everyone in the immediate vicinity stopped and looked eastward, and sure enough at the crest of the hill there he stood. Same spot as before, just past the copse of pine trees on the north side of the boat launch road.

"Oh, this just makes my day complete," Jake spat, glaring at the solitary figure that had shadowed their dig for the last two weeks. "You know, I think I've had just about enough of this crap. Heather, keep an eye on things down here."

"What are you going to do?" Heather yelled as Jake stomped through the excavation area toward the north creek trail.

"Public relations!" Jake yelled back, never slowing his pace.

His energy bolstered by his pent-up anger, it took Jake only ten minutes or so to follow the brushy trail up to the highway. As the trees thinned out near the shoulder, he paused to catch his breath and then crept toward the driveway. He made a mental note of the car's license plate. Mr. Peeper was still in his usual spot, about fifty yards ahead of his car, his full attention on the excavations in progress below. Jake drew within a few strides, close enough to intimidate him, but far enough back to defend himself if the need arose.

On the hike up to the road he had tried to think of some witty remark to impress their distant snooper, but in the end could only come up with, "You'd be able to see a lot more if you would just come on down to the site."

Mr. Peeper flung himself forward about three feet, landing on his knees and palms. With a clumsy sideways roll, he came to rest on his backside. Jake had spoken pretty gruffly, but this reaction was still a bit more than he expected. "Did I startle you?" he asked with mock concern.

Eyes wide, Mr. Peeper stared at Jake. "Yeah, man, of course

143

you startled me, jumpin' out like that." He fished a cigarette from the pocket of his grimy T-shirt. His hands shook and he could barely light his cigarette. A couple of drags, and he had regained his composure. With a raspy sigh, Mr. Peeper rose awkwardly to his feet.

"I wasn't doin' nothin' wrong, man. Just checking out the view was all," he explained, scuffing the gravel with his boot.

"I never said you were," Jake said. "But you're up here every few days, and never once come down for a closer look. Or, at least you don't when anyone's around."

If Mr. Peeper realized he was being accused of something, it didn't show in his bloodshot eyes. "No, no. I don't ever go near the lake. It . . . it's not a good place for me, ya know?"

Jake forced himself to not roll his eyes. As far as he could tell, Mr. Peeper's brain was floating around somewhere unsupervised. Despite his earlier irritation, it was pretty obvious that the greasy-haired individual really wasn't a threat to the site.

"We're running an archaeological field school," Jake said as he shifted to his public-speaking mode. "My students are from Wisconsin State University and they're learning excavation techniques. The work they're doing here, and the research we plan to conduct over the winter, will tell us a great deal about the late prehistory of the area. My name's Professor Jacob Caine, by the way."

"Yeah, I know all that, dude," Mr. Peeper said in an irritated tone. "Been down that road myself, once." He let out a long sigh. "I'm Mark Winters."

Still in shock from the encounter, Jake repeated the details of his brief meeting with Mark Winters to Scott and Heather.

"So he never gave any real reason for not coming down to the site?" Heather said, still incredulous as to the true identity of Mr. Peeper.

"Nope. Kept acting like it wasn't safe, or mumbled something like that. To be honest, I'd be surprised if he remembers much about the old field school anyway, given the shape he's in. He did agree to meet me in town tonight so I'll take a chance and see if he can help out at all."

"Didn't the former sheriff mention he had some drug arrests on his record?" Scott said, looking up from the table where he was checking field forms.

"Yeah, he did. Apparently his drug problem has gotten worse over time, or it really messed him up years ago."

"He could be looting from the site, digging up points and potsherds to sell," Heather said. "Maybe it was all an act and he's the one snooping around."

"Technically, we don't know if anyone's actually taking anything from the site," Jake said. "No holes dug in odd places, or disturbed features, or anything like that. Someone's traipsing around the site when we aren't here, for some obscure reason."

"I still think it's him. He probably watches us during the day, trying to figure out where the best stuff is so he can get it after we leave. Come on, Scott, back me up here."

"I don't think so, Heather," Scott said, and he brushed some red dust from the top of a form. "Nothing's been taken, and wouldn't Winters already know where the best artifacts might be? Like Jake said, he's got bad memories of this place and can't make himself come down here."

From the look on her face, Heather still wasn't convinced but decided to let it slide. "So where are you meeting him again?"

"Some bar on Main Street, called Smokey's."

"I heard a couple of students talking about that place," Scott said. "Kind of a dive with a lot of locals in it. It was pretty clear that the regulars weren't too happy when they showed up."

Jake shrugged. "Probably weren't thrilled about seeing a lot of young, loud college kids in their place. I doubt it's anything to worry about. Probably just a local hangout that Mark feels comfortable in."

"Besides," Heather joked, "if you run into any trouble just give us a call and we'll bail you out. Scott, you can take the big scary bikers and I'll deal with any feisty old geezers who get out of line."

CHAPTER TWENTY-FOUR

Smokey's Bar more than lived up to its name. A cloud of stale cigarette smoke surrounded the entrance and the ground was littered with spent butts. Jake felt like a firefighter forcing his way into a burning building and his eyes watered as they adjusted to the dimly lit room. Despite the statewide smoking ban, Jake noticed more than a few patrons furtively dropping or covering lit cigarettes as he entered. A few heavy-set locals at the bar glanced his way as he peered through the haze, but soon lost interest. Most of the crowd stared transfixed at the ball-game playing on TV or conversed good-naturedly with their cronies.

From a corner booth, Mark Winters awkwardly flagged him over. He had gotten an early start on their meeting, based on the quantity of empty bottles on the table. Jake offered to get the next round and took a few empties up to the bar. He suspected that if they waited for tableside service he would probably die of thirst. He soon returned with two ice-cold bottles of beer.

"I appreciate your agreeing to meet, Mark. I'm hoping you can fill in some gaps about the old field school."

"Yeah, okay. Suppose it's the least I can do, man." He gave a weak half-smile, but his heart wasn't in it. Jake decided to keep things light.

Over the next hour, with some gentle prodding, Jake managed to get some additional insight on the Wardell field school

147

dig but took care to avoid mentioning her name. Mark was able to correct some errors on the site maps, and could even recall the location of some probable feature clusters they had noted during shovel testing. He seemed genuinely interested and even started asking detailed questions about the ceramics and ground stone tools Jake's students had recovered.

Mark's beer consumption doubled that of Jake, and before long his replies became shorter, less useful, and even a bit curt. Jake considered calling it a night, convinced he wouldn't get anything else out of Mark. He gathered together the maps and photos scattered across the table.

"Jacks and I were really close, you know," Mark slurred as he traced little paths through the spilled beer on the table. "It really ripped me up inside when she died, man."

Jake wasn't sure how to respond. "From everything I heard she was a really special lady. That memorial report you put out was a nice tribute."

Mark smiled, pleased. "That was my swan song in archaeology, man. Without Jacks around nothin' seemed to matter anymore, so I dropped out and moved on. Life goes on, you know."

An odd sentiment for someone with a life mired in booze and drugs, Jake thought. "That's true, I guess. Doesn't explain why you still hang around Waconah, though."

Mark glared at him, eyes unfocused. "Jus' cause I moved on don't mean you forget."

"I suppose not. Say," Jake said, changing tactics, "I've got a bunch of artifact drawings Jacklyn made. I was thinking of using some of them in the site report."

"She'd have liked that, man. Jacks was a really talented artist."

"Oh, definitely. Really detailed sketches, mixed in a box of her old papers and notebooks. Her mother was kind enough to bring them to me."

Mark paused in midswig. "Linda did that? Huh."

Something had clicked in that beer-soaked brain, Jake decided, even if its owner hadn't fully grasped it. "You know, Linda Wardell doesn't think her daughter's death was an accident."

Mark blanched as his head snapped back against the booth. He swallowed hard, and Jake thought he might throw up. It was as though Jake had tossed a bucket of cold water on him.

"That's crazy, man. She drowned. In the lake."

"You knew her. Do you think she would have taken a boat out on the water with a storm coming? It doesn't make any sense."

"Yeah, well that's what happened!" Mark shouted, and every head in the bar turned their way. "Lots of shit happens that don't make no sense!"

"Calm down, Mark. Just telling you what her mother said, that's all. No need to get so upset."

"Screw you, man. I cared for Jacks a ton, and you come around digging up ghosts from the past. 'Course I'm upset."

Seems like more than that, Jake thought, but he decided not to press the issue. "Okay, take it easy. I'm sure 'Jacks' wouldn't want to see you so torn up. We're just talking, and you were one of the last people to see her alive."

"Yeah? Well, why don't you go give Clark Kelley the third degree? That pompous ass was out there that night, too."

Jake nodded, and rose from the booth. "Thanks for your info on the site. I can tell it wasn't easy for you." He studied the pitiful man slumped drunkenly in the booth. "It's none of my business, but you might be able to put the past behind you if you take that last step and actually come down to the site. It'd probably give you some closure and I bet 'Jacks' would be happy about that."

★　★　★　★　★

Outside, Jake coughed violently for a few moments, expelling the acrid smoke from his lungs. Several hours had passed, so he walked the few blocks to the sub shop he had passed on the drive in. The girl behind the counter wrinkled her nose in disgust at his smoky aroma as he ordered a sandwich, but he was too tired to take offense.

Appetite sated, Jake drove back to the campground. He tried to stay alert for deer and other nocturnal travelers, but he couldn't put Mark's behavior out of his mind. By the time he pulled in next to the university vans, he was certain Winters knew more about the night Jacklyn Wardell died than anyone else.

"Hey, Jake, how'd it go?"

Erin's yell could probably be heard across the lake. Heather visibly winced from her seat on the far side of the fire. Most of the tents were dark, so Jake assumed most of the students were in town and therefore safely out of range.

"Not too bad, I guess. Mark remembered a fair amount about the original dig and managed to clear up some of the map errors and unit discrepancies. He was drinking pretty heavy and got kind of belligerent after a while, especially when we started talking about Jacklyn Wardell. Or 'Jacks,' as he kept calling her."

"Do you think they had a thing going on?" Erin said as she offered her half-empty wine bottle to Jake. He shook his head and settled onto one of the plastic lawn chairs.

"Hard to say for sure. In some ways he acted like they did, but he never really admitted it. I got the impression that he knew some things he didn't want to talk about, though. He seemed upset to hear that I had seen Jacklyn's old field notebooks, too, but I'm not sure why. Nothing suspicious in them, just some personal notes on the crew and visitors."

"In the crime shows on TV," Erin said as she refilled her cup, "there would be an enigmatic 'If I am killed, the murderer is R.B.' in the notes, or something like that."

"If they did have a relationship, it would explain why he was so broken up after her death and maybe why he bailed on archaeology," Heather said.

"When I pressed him about the night she died, he got really defensive," Jake said, replaying their meeting in his head. "What's weird, now that I think about it, was that he seemed really insistent that I grill Clark Kelley about her death. Sheriff Kojarski did say that Clark was in Donovan that night, but Mark acted like he had a specific beef with Clark."

"Maybe he blames Clark for Jacklyn's death, or knows something more than he's telling," Heather said as she pushed another log onto the fire.

"Maybe he found out that Clark and Jacklyn were having an affair," Erin said. "Jake, you told me the sheriff said that the Chapman College folks thought there was something going on between them. Mark could have found out about it, and then killed her in a jealous rage."

Jake shrugged, and pushed his chair back from the heat of the fire. "I suppose it's possible. But why didn't he kill Clark instead? Mark's still enamored with Jacklyn, even after all these years."

"Mark could have just lost it when he confronted her and killed her in the heat of the moment. Maybe he was high. The sheriff told you he had some drug arrests. Afterward, he couldn't deal with the guilt so he blamed Clark for what happened. And he keeps returning to the scene of the crime. They always say criminals will do that."

"What if Mark blames Clark for forcing Jacklyn into taking the boat out that night, despite the storm?" Heather said. "Clark could have badgered her into starting the island survey before she was ready, and that was what led to her accident."

Erin shook her head. "But what could he have done or said to make her do something so stupid?"

"I dunno, but office politics can get pretty nasty," Heather said, giving the silent Jake a sideways glance. "He could have hinted that he'd keep her from getting tenure, or see that her grant funding was pulled unless she followed his orders."

"That might explain why Clark repeatedly denies that he was ever at the site, practically, whenever I've tried to ask him about it," Jake said.

Erin wasn't convinced. "If Mark knew about it, though, why not tell the cops about Clark? Even if he couldn't prove it he would have gotten a lot of satisfaction watching Clark sweat it out under the hot lights in a dingy interrogation room. I think my theory has a lot going for it."

"I think you've seen too many cop shows on TV," Jake said wryly. "Although I do like the mental image of Clark getting smacked around by some angry homicide detectives."

The conversation was cut short as two overloaded cars pulled up the park road to the campsite. The car stereos blasted out two discordant rock songs as the doors opened and the students piled out, the din echoing through the trees. A few individuals headed for their tents or toward the bathroom facility, but most made a beeline for the campfire. A crowd of loud, inebriated future archaeologists engulfed the three and all discussion of the Wardell drowning was put aside.

After a while, Jake bowed out and headed for his room, still wondering how much Mark and Clark really knew about the night Jacklyn Wardell died.

CHAPTER TWENTY-FIVE

Dawn broke on Wednesday to a beautiful sunny day, with white puffy clouds drifting lazily across a rich blue sky. Jake hadn't slept well and was feeling more than a bit sluggish, but the enthusiasm and jovial banter of the students was infectious and within an hour or so he felt much like his old self. About midmorning, a battered silver Ford drove down the gravel road and parked at the far end of the lot. Mark Winters stepped out and Jake's heart sank like a stone.

Jake watched as Mark tried to light a cigarette. As Jake approached, his eyes were drawn to the nervous twitching of the older man's hands. "Mark. Nice to see you."

"Hey, man," Mark said. He took a deep drag and exhaled loudly. "I, uh, thought about what you said. You know, 'bout coming out . . . here." His bloodshot eyes darted back and forth, from the ground to Jake and back again.

"I'm glad you did. I appreciate all the info you gave me last night." Jake spoke in a soothing, level voice. Given his demeanor, Jake suspected Mark would dive back into his car if anything went amiss.

Mark nodded. He looked at Jake for a moment, then quickly shifted his gaze to his right and stared at the tree line separating Waconah and the adjacent Christianson II site.

Jake peeked over his shoulder. No one else was nearby, but behind him the lake dominated the scene. Mark wasn't avoiding him, he was trying to avoid looking at the lake. To put him at ease, Jake moved a few feet to his left so Mark was no longer facing Taylor Lake.

Jake made small talk about the weather, his students, and the site, and received in return noncommittal nods and one-word replies. "How about a tour of the site? We've been finding quite a bit lately," Jake said at last.

Mark froze, but only for a moment. "Sure, man. Came all the way out here, might as well check it all out."

Jake led the way and took Mark to a unit at the northeastern edge of the site. "We were hoping to locate a palisade out here, but no luck. We did find a pretty substantial refuse midden with lots of animal bone and broken pottery."

With a tentative hand, Mark reached out to inspect the bits of bone and ceramics offered by one of the students. He turned each item over slowly, nodding to himself, and soon began pulling artifacts out of the dirt-filled screen. Jake said nothing, and busied himself by reviewing the students' field notes.

"Man, this takes me back, guys," Mark said as he threw some stone flakes into a paper artifact bag. "Forgot how great the artifact finds were. You know, we put in some shovel tests near here, looking for a palisade wall."

"Is that right? Where about?"

"Hmm. I think maybe a couple dozen yards that way," Mark said, pointing to the east. " 'Course, we didn't find anything either, so maybe it was closer in, after all."

"Can you give me a rough idea?" Jake said, and he unfolded a copy of the site map.

Mark glanced at the map for a few seconds before jabbing a dirty finger at a small triangular symbol a few inches from the corner. "Right there. That spot was the southernmost shovel pit, and we dug ten, maybe twelve off of that toward the east."

"How far apart?"

"Two meters. I think Jacks figured we'd hit something, you

know, enough to help us decide where to put some units."

At the mention of Jacklyn Wardell, Mark's face clouded over and he lost interest in screening. Jake decided to push him a little, to keep him interested.

"Great. Well, I'm going to add those shovel tests to the map. Say, want to check out some of the other units?"

"Yeah, sure," Mark replied sullenly, but to Jake's relief at least he hadn't tried to leave. Together they visited students working along the northern edge of the site and gradually made their way to the large trench and the house structure. At each location, Mark became more animated and talkative, and even joked with some of the students.

During the lunch break, Jake and Mark sat with Heather and Scott. They offered him an extra sandwich from the cooler, but Mark ate sparingly as he smoked cigarette after cigarette. As Mark recalled more information about the Wardell dig, Jake added notes to the field map until the margins were nearly full.

"We didn't find much in the way of Woodland pottery," Mark said, in reply to a question posed by Scott. "But Schumholtz made it clear right off that we weren't welcome in his neighborhood. So he wasn't real helpful with the few scraps we did find."

Finally, Heather blurted out a question that she had been aching to ask all morning. "So, Mark. What made you give up archaeology and grad school?"

Mark blanched, but to Jake's surprise he didn't get upset or storm off. Mark let out a long sigh as he rolled a bit of clay between his fingers. "I suppose I can't blame you for being curious," he said, rubbing the reddish-brown clay against his faded jeans. "After the . . . accident, I just had a lot of trouble focusing on school, you know? Didn't seem all that important in the big picture, and I just had it up to here with all the rules, jumping through hoops. I was only a few credits short for my

Ph.D., too. Even had a big head start on my dissertation research. Guess all that crap is stashed away in a box somewhere in the department now, if they even kept it."

Mark fished the battered pack of smokes from his shirt pocket, looked around a bit, and thought better of it. He jammed them back in his pocket. "Well, after that I bummed around for a while, picking up shovel-bum work here and there when I needed some cash. Never could stand it for too long, though, so I ended up splitting before they decided to can me. Even tried teaching some intro-level courses at a two-year college in Minnesota, but bein' back in that academia-bullshit environment just ate at me, so I bailed. My Uncle Mike has a place about an hour west of Donovan, just a trailer in the woods, but enough for me and he doesn't care if I crash there sometimes."

A boat roared by on the lake, and Mark followed its path. "So, that's it in a nutshell, little lady. Found out I just wasn't cut out for the ivory-tower scene, and just moved on. Only reason I heard you guys was here was 'cause I saw the newspaper article."

Heather nodded as he finished, but didn't speak. Jake and Scott were a little surprised she hadn't made anything of the little-lady remark. In the past, a comment like that brought forth a quick, caustic retort.

The shrill ring of Jake's cell phone broke the awkward silence. He took a few steps away from the group, while Heather and Scott started getting the students back to work as the lunch hour ended. Jake joined them a few minutes later, a scowl on his face.

"Uh-oh," Heather said. "This can't be good."

"You've got that right," Jake said. "That was Clark. He's coming up on Friday for an 'inspection,' as he put it."

"Oh, swell. Nice of him to give us so much time to get ready,"

Heather said, as Scott nodded in agreement.

Mark stood a few feet away, smirking. "Talk about déjà vu, man. Clark pulled the same crap on us during our dig. Called once, but after that just showed up out of the blue whenever he felt like it."

"Well, I'm not about to let him disrupt my field school," Jake said adamantly. "Heather, you and Scott spread the word to the crew, but let them all know that everything is business as usual unless we tell them otherwise. We'll clean up a bit here and there but I'm not going to waste time putting on a show for him."

They both nodded and set off across the site. Jake turned his attention to Mark. "Mark, you're welcome to stick around and pitch in if you'd like. To be honest, I really would appreciate any other help you can give us, but no pressure intended."

"Yeah, it's cool, man. Maybe for a few hours. I feel better about bein' here again, you know? But there's no way I'm here when Kelley arrives. I had enough of that prick back then."

"Fair enough. And thanks."

As Mark shuffled toward one of the active units, Jake pulled out his cell phone and called Erin. He told her about Mark's appearance and then about Clark Kelley's imminent visit. "So, I'll need you to pull some of the showier rim sherds, stone tools, and anything else you can think of. I'm not planning any big show, but I'd like to have some nice artifacts on hand."

"I understand. I'll put some stuff in the display case and you can take it with you Friday morning," Erin said. "I'll make sure the lab is organized too, and that everything is shipshape in case Clark needs to inspect the lab, too."

"Good idea. I hadn't thought about that, but I suppose he will. Boy, this is really not something I need right now."

"At least he's not bringing a film crew with him," Erin said. "Or does he have a personal photographer at his beck and call?

On the bright side, Mark Winters did show up today, and you said he remembered more about the old dig."

"I suppose. That reminds me, I need to try and get in touch with Al Droessler, the photographer, again. See you in a few hours."

Jake dialed the number for Al Droessler and as before ended up with an automatic voice mail response. He left a detailed message again, imploring Mr. Droessler to contact him as soon as possible.

Heather approached as Jake put his phone away. "Well, everybody's been told. I tried to sound all blasé but they could probably tell I wasn't thrilled."

"Maybe it won't be so bad. We'll clean up a few units here and there and try to keep Clark from running roughshod over the site. We could hope for rain, too."

"Oh, yeah, that would be great. Stuck in the camp hall listening to Clark ramble on for hours. No thanks. I'll leave that crap for Bryant."

"What did he do this time?"

"Nothing," Heather said, but she glanced in Bryant's direction. "It's just that he actually looked happy to hear that Clark was coming. Did you realize that Bryant and some of Clark's other students are all working together in that group of units? They're getting really cliquey."

"Hmm. I didn't notice that. Are they causing problems? Should I split a few of them off into other teams?"

"Well, no, they aren't doing anything wrong. Yet," Heather said. "I just don't trust them, that's all. Plus, why are they so thrilled that Clark's coming? Do they really think he gives a damn what they think, or cares at all about what they're doing?"

Jake shrugged. "For now, let's just deal with one problem at a time. After Clark's inspection we can decide if something needs to be done with that group."

"Fine," Heather said, throwing up her arms. "But don't say I didn't warn you."

CHAPTER TWENTY-SIX

An eerie stillness permeated the air on Thursday morning. Jake felt it when he woke up early and even more so when he entered the main hall for breakfast. None of the students were acting oddly and yet everything felt off, somehow. Jake busied himself with his morning routine and before long the vehicles were loaded up and everyone was off to the site.

Heather had been irritable and snippy all evening, but most of the crew seemed unaffected by the impending arrival of G. Clark Kelley. Scott and Jake spent a few hours updating the site map with the information obtained from Mark Winters. Jake cancelled the evening lecture, so the students spent a quiet evening watching movies, reading, and hanging out by the bonfire.

Jake wondered when, or even if, he would see Mark again. Mark had disappeared suddenly on Wednesday afternoon, shortly before the end of the workday. Jake was at the north end of the site when he noticed Mark's car driving up the road toward the highway. He asked the students who had been working with him if Mark had said anything before he left, but they said he mumbled something about having had enough for one day, then turned and walked to his car.

The morning clouds burned away by the time the crew arrived at the site and the temperature rose quickly through the morning. The students were enthusiastic despite the heat. More and more artifacts were recovered as pit features, hearths, and midden deposits were troweled, shoveled, and screened. Many of the students cut their midmorning breaks short in order to go back to their units, so only a few were still lounging in the parking lot when Mark Winter's rusty Ford made its way down the gravel drive.

"Hi, Mark," Jake said as Heather and Scott took the last of the crew back to the dig. "Good to see you, uh, again."

Mark gave him a faint smile. "Yeah, man, I'm kinda surprised I'm back here again, too."

"Well, you're always welcome. I'll take any help I can get with this site."

Mark nodded, staring past Jake toward the still, dark blue waters of Taylor Lake. "Coming down here yesterday felt pretty good for me. Brought back a lot of memories. Good ones, mostly. I . . . I'm just gonna bum around the site a bit today, okay?"

Jake agreed, and headed off to rejoin the students in the large excavation block. The crew was exposing a larger portion of the possible longhouse feature, a tedious process as each post mold was cleaned and mapped. As the work progressed, the edges of the house and interior walls were defined. Busy with his task, Jake found little time to check on Mark and soon lost track of him. When Heather grumpily mentioned that it was fifteen minutes past lunchtime, Jake stood up and scanned the site for Mark. He was nowhere in sight.

After retrieving his lunch, Jake found Mark sitting at the edge of the pier, staring out at Taylor Lake.

"Hey, Mark. Hope I'm not intruding. Brought you a sandwich and a Coke."

"It's cool, man. Thanks." Mark took the proffered items and gestured for Jake to join him on the pier.

Jake sat down a few feet away, rinsed some dirt and dust from his hands with his water bottle, and unwrapped a sandwich.

"I never thought I'd say this, man, but coming back here is really doing me some good," Mark said. "All I can think of are the good times. For years, I could never get my head past that last afternoon." He took a bite of his sandwich and chewed it thoughtfully. "God, we all had some great times here, lots of parties, working with the kids, finding cool artifacts. Man, we were so young then. Planned to set the prehistoric world on fire, that was us." Mark chuckled, coughing a bit.

"I think we've all felt that way at times, although the feeling does diminish with age."

Mark nodded, and then sighed. "Time gets us all in the end." He turned back to the lake, apparently mesmerized by the gently rolling waves. Jake had started to rise when Mark spoke again.

"You know man, I can still remember every detail of that day. Runs through my mind like an old filmstrip." Mark paused to light a cigarette, the first Jake had seen him with all day. "I suppose you'd wanna hear the whole story."

"I am curious, I have to admit."

"Well, for a couple of days before . . . it happened . . . Jacks and I had been getting along really well, if you know what I mean. Really comfortable with each other, doing some harmless flirting. On that day, Jacks had me send the crew back to camp a little early, 'cause of the storm coming. She asked me to stick around so we could spot-check some units and review the paperwork. She figured it would be easier without the students around, so we could do an honest assessment without hurtin' anyone's feelings."

Mark dropped his cigarette on the pier and ground it out with his shoe. Jake said nothing, hoping to maintain the mood and keep him talking.

"Jacks was like that. Went out of her way to make folks happy, and always supportive. She had a big heart. Some of it might have been because she was pretty young herself, not too far out

162

of grad school so she remembered what it was like. Anyway, we'd been kind of flirting off and on for a while, pretty low-key stuff, for most of my second year in grad school. I really felt like we had a connection, you know, kindred souls and all that." Mark smiled, lost in the memories. "It never went anywhere on campus, but I figured we—well, she—had to be careful, 'cause I was a student and she was faculty. Hell, she had enough troubles with jerks like Clark Kelley sneakin' around, trying to keep her from getting tenure."

Jake grimaced. Apparently Clark had lots of experience stomping on the dreams of young professors. For some reason this realization filled Jake with dread. Just how far would Clark go to deal with a perceived rival?

"At the field school, Jacks seemed a lot more relaxed, laughing more, and really excited about what we were finding," Mark said. "Man, I suppose this sounds pretty juvenile right now, but I thought she had arranged some time alone for us, so we could get it all out in the open, without anyone finding out.

"Well, I was pretty worked up all morning, so I took a few tokes at lunch just to mellow out. Couple of hours later, the kids wrapped up for the day and everyone headed back to camp. We started inspecting the dig, checking out the units, all business-like. I started cracking a few jokes, like always, and pretty soon we were laughing like a couple of kids."

Mark turned bright red, still haunted by the embarrassment that followed. "I put my hand on her back and pulled her in close and kissed her. She practically recoiled, shoving me back, pretty hard. Man, was she upset! She was all, 'Mark, what the hell?' and stuff like that. I reached for her again, trying to explain how we felt about each other, our chemistry, all of it. Turns out it was just me. Jacks looked really hurt, but she tried to be nice about it, I guess. Went in to the whole student–teacher thing, how she thought I was a great guy, a dear friend, but there was nothin' else beyond that. All the stuff a guy doesn't want to hear when he opens himself up. Huh, and women wonder why guys never want to talk about their feelings."

Mark buried his face in his hands. Jake heard a muffled sob, then Mark regained his composure.

"I suppose that's why I just lost it. Started yelling about the signals she was sending, how I felt, what was I supposed to think? She kept shaking her head, shooting down my arguments, and before you knew it we were standing there screaming at each other in the middle of the site.

"Then she just stopped. Took a lot to get Jacks mad, I mean yelling mad, and she finally said that was enough. Said we would talk about this further, if necessary, when we could be adult and rational about it. Went all boss–employee on me, told me to pack up the field notes and then we covered the open units with tarps and sandbags. She kept looking at the clouds building on the horizon and then would add more sandbags so the tarps wouldn't blow away. Man, I was just steaming mad by that point and couldn't wait to blow out of there."

Mark stared out at the lake. "Got pretty dark by the time we finished. Wind was picking up, but the storm might have held off for a few hours or moved north of us, the way it did sometimes. Well, I could tell Jacks was still ticked off when she told me to head out. Said she was going to secure the boat and take a last look around, and then head back to camp. I said something like 'yeah, whatever' and hopped in my car. Tore outta there, and near the top of the hill saw Clark Kelley standing there. Figured he was going down to talk to Jacks but at the time I really didn't give a damn."

"Clark was just standing there? Why didn't he drive down?"

Mark snorted in disgust. "That S.O.B. never drove his car down that gravel road. Didn't want it to get dinged up or dirty, I guess. Whenever he was at the site he'd leave his ride at the top of the terrace, and someone would chauffer him down to Waconah and then back out again when he wanted to leave."

Mark stopped to light another cigarette. Jake noticed the crew was back at work, guided by Heather and Scott.

"That was the last time I ever saw her," Mark said, wiping away the tears forming at the corners of his eyes. "Back at camp I made myself scarce, so I wouldn't run into her again. Right after dinner the storm hit us and I was busy checking on the kids. It wasn't until the next morning that we realized Jacks never made it back to camp."

Jake let out a long breath, a bit overwhelmed at hearing the whole story. "I can see how being here would be tough, Mark. Your last time together and it ended in a fight. But things would have worked out between you, even if you never had a relationship."

Mark shook his head angrily. "It's more than that, man, a lot more. The way we left it, she was just so damn mad. What if she wasn't thinking clear, and that's why she went out on the lake? That makes it my fault, man! I killed her, don't you see?"

Jake stared at Mark, recognizing for the first time the overwhelming feelings of guilt that had tormented Mark for all those years. It had eaten away at him, a painful abyss that he could never fill, something he tried to block out with booze and drugs and god knows what else. Jake struggled to reply, trying to formulate a response that wouldn't make things worse. The awkward silence was unsettling, and more than Mark could bear.

"I couldn't say nothing to the cops about the fight, either," Mark said. "They might have figured I did something, you know, physical, and they were already givin' me funny looks. You know what I mean?"

"Mark, take it easy," Jake said. "Jacklyn Wardell was a smart woman, right? Angry or not, she doesn't sound like the type who would have made snap judgments about going out in the boat that night." The words sounded thin. He had never met Jacklyn. All he knew about her was secondhand, from her mother, old acquaintances, and reading through her journal.

Mark didn't reply, but he seemed to consider what Jake had said. Jake tried to recreate the scene in his mind, much as he tried to do when reconstructing past activities at archaeological sites. Then it struck him.

"Wait a second. Mark, you said Clark was on the road that night, and you thought he was heading down to the site. He was probably the last person to talk to Jacklyn that night. You could just as easily argue that Clark Kelley was responsible. Hell, we both know how dealing with that jerk gets under your skin."

Mark slowly nodded. "Yeah. Yeah, I suppose you're right. Jacks was already ticked off, and nobody knows what he said or did when he was down there. Kelley could have pushed her over the edge, you know, got her so riled up that she took off in the boat just to get away from him."

Maybe, Jake thought, but she would have had to be pretty mad to chance going out in a storm like that. Unless she had some help getting into that boat. But was Clark capable of murder?

CHAPTER TWENTY-SEVEN

Like a whirlwind, Clark Kelley arrived at the site right after lunch on Friday and within no time proceeded to irritate nearly everyone present. Jake had politely refused to send a vehicle up the hill to collect Clark when he arrived, which undoubtedly contributed to his ill temper. Clark eventually settled his attention on two coeds excavating a feature at the south end of the site. One of them grew uncomfortable enough in his presence to complain to Heather, who in no uncertain terms made Jake aware of the situation. Working in tandem, Jake, Heather, and Scott spent the remainder of the afternoon keeping Clark occupied and ran him from one end of the site to the other. Their efforts were successful, for by the time the students started cleaning up for the day Clark was hot, sweaty, and irritable. Unfortunately, when aggravated his imperious and demanding tendencies multiplied tenfold.

"You really should hire a small plane to take some aerial photos of the excavation, Caine. An experienced photographer should be able to get some nice overview shots of the dig area. Of course, you'll need to clean things up quite a bit. Right now your site looks like a World War I battlefield."

Jake bit his tongue, but it took real effort to keep his voice under control. "I do know of a local photographer who's familiar with the site. I've been trying to get in touch with him."

"Well, be certain he's experienced with this sort of thing. Can't have some amateur mucking things up. Speaking of which, I assume your . . . volunteers aren't walking off with any artifacts?"

"The NEWAS volunteers have been a lot of help. Most have been involved in digs before, and they're experts on local archaeology. They adhere to a strict code of ethics as far as collecting goes and I have no reason to distrust them."

Clark either missed or ignored the rising heat in Jake's replies. "Hmm. I suppose I'd best check out your lab setup, as long as I'm here. Make sure everything's up to snuff."

That was the final straw. "The lab tour can wait, Clark. First, I've got some questions about Jacklyn Wardell's field school."

"I was hardly even here, Caine. That was—"

"That's bullshit and you know it. According to Jacklyn's field notebook, you were here at least once a week for nearly the whole field school," Jake said, closing the distance between them. "Didn't I mention that I got a hold of her journal? Very interesting reading."

Clark paled, the perspiration beading on his forehead. Struck mute, his reaction was enough for Jake to press on.

"Linda Wardell, Jacklyn's mother, was kind enough to bring me the notebook before the field school started. Real nice lady. Did you know that she's convinced her daughter was murdered? And from what I hear she wasn't the only one who thought that."

A gurgling noise escaped from Clark's throat and his wide eyes spoke volumes. Jake went for broke.

"Did you know I met with Mark Winters the other night?" Jake said, his voice low and level. "Very helpful guy. He suggested that I ask *you* about the night Jacklyn Wardell died."

"All right, enough!" Clark glanced about wildly, then lowered his voice. The only students still present were busy loading their gear into a van parked at the south end of the site. "I didn't have anything to do with Jacklyn Wardell's death."

"Then why are you so evasive whenever I mention her field school? You were here the night she died. According to Mark, you were at the site that evening. He passed you on the road, walking toward the site. What are you hiding?"

"I was meeting someone . . . a student. A female student." Clark's eyes narrowed conspiratorially as the words gushed forth. "Can't you see, I couldn't tell the police or anyone that I was seeing Amy. Carol would have left me, my career would have been ruined! You won't say anything, will you?"

"I'm not interested in your problems with your wife," Jake said. "I just want to know about Jacklyn Wardell."

"So Amy could vouch for me, but I couldn't use her as an alibi without people getting suspicious. After the accident, Amy also told me that Jacklyn had spoken to her, in vague terms but obvious enough, about the dangers of getting too involved with her professors. At that time, Jacklyn made it seem like they were just chatting, but it was clear she knew what was going on. Amy was understandably panicky, which is why we met in the woods that night, and then took the north creek trail out to my car."

"So at the time of the accident you were . . . ?"

"At the Pine Tree Lodge up the highway, with Amy," his head hung low, eyes studiously avoiding Jake's.

Jake rubbed his chin, lost in thought. It could be a lie, to cover up his own involvement, but would Clark chance using a lie to cover up murder? Not likely. Too easy, even after all these years, to track down this Amy girl and check his story.

The silence was too much for Clark. "You aren't going to tell anyone, are you?" he blurted out, almost a shriek. "I'll deny it all, damn you, if you try and ruin me! I have seniority in the department, and they'll think you're just out to get me."

"Relax, Clark," Jake snapped, and swatted Clark's wagging finger out of his face. "I don't give a damn about your personal problems, or you for that matter. I'm just trying to figure out what really happened to Jacklyn Wardell."

Clark nodded, a relieved half smile on his lips as he mopped the sweat from his forehead. "Good, good. Amy was so distraught that night, and the next week was hell for both of us. She was getting paranoid. I was afraid she'd snap and go to the police. Hah, she even thought Wardell was behind her on the creek trail when she came to meet me that night."

"That couldn't be possible," Jake said. "You saw Jacklyn and Mark arguing on the boat launch road on your way to meet her. She couldn't have been in both places at once."

"Well, the fool girl was obviously paranoid, as I just said." Clark's imperious tone replaced all the remorsefulness he had shown moments earlier.

Not necessarily, but Jake decided to keep his thoughts to himself for now. But Clark's brusque manner had gotten his dander up. "Well, whatever happened to this 'fool girl' you took advantage of, Kelley?"

His face flushed and the earlier look of apprehension returned, but only for a scant second. "That's none of your business, Caine. Suffice to say, we have moved on to separate paths, period!" With that, he turned abruptly and stormed off toward the parking area.

As Clark's car sped up the gravel road, Jake stood in the growing twilight, the puzzle pieces still a jumble in his mind.

CHAPTER TWENTY-EIGHT

Clark did not come to the campground or lab on Friday evening. Jake kept everyone around the camp for nearly ninety minutes after dinner, just in case, but finally decided there was really no reason for them to be present even if Clark did stop by for his inspection. Dismissed, about half of the students went into Donovan while the rest swam, played volleyball, or lounged around the camp. Bryant and a few of his friends had hung around the hall a little longer than most of the students, but once it was apparent that Dr. Kelley was a no-show they had drifted off. As darkness fell, an impromptu party started around the bonfire. The revelry around the fire, however, did not extend to the dour quartet inside the hall.

Erin fidgeted and fussed about the lab, moving artifact trays and equipment back and forth. She enlisted Scott's help for a while, but he soon found other busywork after Erin had snapped at him for the umpteenth time. Heather settled herself into a corner and typed on her laptop for several hours. Any attempt to make conversation was met with short, curt answers and stony glares.

Jake puttered with the site map and halfheartedly worked on his field notes, but his thoughts were elsewhere. He kept replaying his conversations with Mark and Clark, comparing them, analyzing them, approaching them in the same way he would tackle an archaeological question. But it was no use. Jake had found out more details about Jacklyn Wardell's last night but it only raised more questions in his mind. Jake looked around the room for the hundredth time that evening, but it was obvious that none of his friends were in the mood for conversation. He had tried to email Amanda but the local server was down and Jake didn't think he could deal with a lengthy phone call. All in all, the last two days had been exhausting.

Clark arrived around ten on Saturday morning, after checking out of his hotel. His arrival went largely unnoticed by the students, except for Bryant who trailed behind him like a lost lamb. Clark made some disparaging comments about the amateurish state of the lab facility and needled Erin about allowing the break-in. She reddened, but Jake shot him a harsh look and Clark was quieter after that. The tour ended soon thereafter and Clark was gone, much to the staff's relief.

The rest of the day passed without incident. After the evening meal, Jake settled himself in his room and called Amanda.

"Hey, honey. How's it going?"

"Hi, Jake. It's all right. I miss you."

"Me too. How are things at work? Will you be able to come back soon?"

"Good, real good," Amanda said, a bit subdued. "I'm not sure yet about my schedule. Still a lot to get finished."

Jake's shoulders dropped. It was not the reply he had hoped for. "That's fine. Plenty of time left in the season. So, tell me what's happening."

"I gave an impromptu PowerPoint for Dr. Holley and some of the staff, and they were really impressed with the photos and video I took. I added some rough sketches of the new layout area and I think they were able to get a good idea of how it's going to look when it's finished."

"Any snide remarks from Ann or her cronies?"

"Hah! Seems she couldn't make it to the show. At first I

thought she was just being a bitch, but Kathy told me that Holley was not impressed with the exhibit review she turned in and called her on the carpet about it. She could hear them arguing in his office and I guess Ann was getting the worst of it."

"Wow. Nice to have the boss's assistant on your side, huh?"

"You got that right. The next day Holley told Kathy to amend the upcoming monthly schedules. Ann and some of the other curators have almost nothing assigned except to work on exhibit reviews. They've been excluded from all the staff and budget meetings, workshops, all that stuff until their work is up to snuff."

"I imagine Ann is pretty pissed at you right now, since the exhibit review was your evil suggestion in the first place," Jake said. "Better keep an eye on that cute backside of yours."

"I'll leave that job up to you, honey. Don't worry, though, I'll be fine. So, how are things at Waconah?"

"Good. The students are starting to hit their stride, so we're moving lots of dirt. Finding a lot of pits, especially near the longhouse. I'm probably going to bring the backhoe out again so we can open up a larger area over there. We should have most of it uncovered by the time you get back."

"Sounds like you're making a lot of progress. You have to be pretty happy about that."

"I am, believe me. Did you get my email about Mr. Peeper?"

"Yeah. I can't believe he's Mark Winters. Too bad he wasn't more helpful when you met him later on."

"At the bar, no, but he showed up at the site on Wednesday."

"No! Are you kidding me?"

"I was as shocked as you are," Jake said. "I never thought he would actually come down to the site, after the way he acted Tuesday night. He was pretty skittish at first, but before long he really mellowed out and actually remembered some useful stuff about the original dig."

"That's pretty incredible, considering he wouldn't even drive down to the site before that."

"And then he came again on Thursday. That's when it all came out. I guess he needed to unburden himself, but Mark told me the whole story about the day Jacklyn Wardell died." Jake excitedly related Mark's story about his feelings for Jacks, their fight, how he tore past Clark Kelley as he drove off, and the guilt he felt afterward.

Amanda was silent as he wrapped up the story. "Well, do you believe him, Jake?"

"What do you mean, do I believe him?" Jake was taken aback. "What could he be lying about?"

"Well, that's just it," Amanda said. "He could have made up the whole thing, or twisted the story to cover up his real crime. What if he and Jacklyn did have a big fight, and he hit or killed her and threw her body in the boat? Maybe he attacked her and she tried to escape in the boat and that's why she was out in the storm?"

Jake was thunderstruck. Mark had seemed so upset, so earnest, that it had never occurred to him that he might be lying to cover up his real actions that night. "I don't know, Amanda. You weren't there. It's hard to believe he could be that convincing."

"Honey, you don't know this guy at all. Maybe he's just that twisted and this was his plan all along. Could be that after all those years of drinking and drugs his brain is fried, and he really believes his own story."

"If he was going to lie about it, why bring it up?" Jake said. "It's not like I was pressuring him."

"Maybe not directly," Amanda said cautiously. "But maybe Mark could sense that you were curious, or were hinting around about it."

"It wasn't like that," Jake said. "Besides, I know for a fact that at least some of it is true. Like the part about seeing Clark Kelley on the road."

"How do you know that?"

"Because I asked him."

"Oh, Jake. You didn't call Clark and accuse him of something, did you?"

"What if I did?" Jake said. "It's not like Clark is going to dislike me any more than he already does. And I didn't call him. He was up here on Friday for his 'inspection' and I asked him about it at the end of the day."

Amanda sighed. "So, what did he say?"

"Clark admitted being here that day and that he was waiting at the top of the hill. But he claims he wasn't there to see Jacklyn. He said he was meeting a student named Amy that he was sleeping with."

"Ew! That disgusting slob!"

"No kidding. Anyway, that proves Mark was telling the truth."

"Not necessarily," Amanda said, with growing irritation in her voice. "Mark could have only told you bits and pieces of the actual story, to cover up what he did. If he even did anything! Jake, you still don't know for sure if Jacklyn's death wasn't an accident."

"Well, it seems more and more likely that it wasn't an accident, to me!" Jake said. A few students in the kitchen turned as his voice carried into the hall.

"Jake, don't shout at me!" Amanda said. "I think you're getting way too involved in Wardell's death. It's like an obsession with you. Reading her journal, digging up old gossip, confronting your boss—"

"He's not my boss! He's just an arrogant son-of-a . . . dammit." Jake stopped himself, and got up to close his door. He took a deep breath. "Amanda, honey, I'm sorry. I guess I'm more stressed out than I realized. I'm not obsessed with her death, it just seems to keep coming up."

"Okay. I'm sorry too. But I think your problems with Clark are making you want to believe Mark more than you should."

"Maybe," Jake said, although deep down he still felt like Clark was more involved than it seemed.

"You know, Jake, this may be one of those times when you aren't going to find all the answers."

"I know. You'd think I'd be used to that, being an archaeologist." Jake kept his voice level, but he still felt annoyed.

"I think being apart so much is starting to wear us both down," Amanda said quietly. "It's hard for me, too. Sean said his sister's fiancé is stationed overseas, and they've had all kinds of problems."

Jake wasn't particularly interested in Sean's sister, her fiancé, or his opinion. "I know. I suppose we're going to need to sit down and have some long talks about our future, when this is all over."

It sounded foreboding, but Amanda understood his meaning. The idea of a life together was undercut by their respective careers, with no simple way around it. "We'll deal with it when the time is right," she added lamely.

They spoke for a few more minutes about nothing in particular before saying their goodbyes. Jake tossed his phone on the table and then reached into his suitcase and pulled out a pint bottle of bourbon. He poured a measure into a nearby coffee cup and sat back down on his cot. He took a sip, then another. Relaxing, he leaned back against the wall and picked up Jacklyn Wardell's journal, and started idly paging through it.

CHAPTER TWENTY-NINE

From Jacklyn Wardell's journal:

July 1. That settles it! Next semester I will definitely sponsor a graduate symposium on dealing with the public. I'm going to call it The Good, the Bad, and the Exasperating! Most of them are okay, just ignorant about archaeology. I can understand farmers not wanting to lose their land to highway projects, but can't they realize we're on their side? Bullethead from the Hillside Resort has got to be the WORST, though. How many times do I have to tell him THEY AREN'T BUILDING A SUPER-RESORT HERE before he gets it?

Maybe there's something weird in the water around here; practically everyone seems to be acting out-of-character. I can understand the students getting twitchy, working in the hot sun all day, but how to explain the rest? The Dark One's visits are weekly now but he hardly ever comes out to Waconah; spends most of his time at the hotel, working on his stupid mystery project. Caught Lady Margaret poking around the site early yesterday morning; no explanation, got all defensive when I challenged her about it. I don't see how asking her why she is at MY site before anyone else is "turning on her, too"??? Even Snowman isn't quite himself lately. Seems out of it, like his head is somewhere else. Maybe he's partying too much at night? Hate to be the camp killjoy but I may have to remind everyone that this is a field SCHOOL, not an excuse to party from dusk 'til dawn.

Guess I'm in a funk because of the 'Dear Jane' letter I got from Don. He didn't get moved up to Ass't Prof in the Geology Depart-

ment, so he decided to take that job at Kansas University. Guess I can't blame him, and we were only dating casually (or was it? Seemed pretty hot and heavy to me a few times!) so I had no claim on him. Going to miss those blue eyes, but that's life.

"The boss is in a bit of a mood today, huh?" Scott said as he passed the bucket full of soil to Heather.

"Yeah, that's for sure," she replied, dumping the damp soil into the screen. "Hey, don't fill these so full. I ain't Hercules, you know."

"Sorry. Thought I could get the rest of this feature out, but it looks like it curves underneath."

"Probably another bell-shaped storage pit. Considering we aren't finding many artifacts, it doesn't look like they used this one as a garbage pit."

"Guess not. Oh, well." Scott scraped his trowel along the edge of the darkly stained feature, revealing the red clay subsoil beyond it. "Do you suppose Jake is upset that people are poking around the site again?"

"Well, aren't you?" Heather said as she tossed a piece of pottery into a paper bag. "And now it looks like they're digging into the features, too. Before you know it the whole site will be wrecked."

"At least he called the cops again."

"Yeah, like that will do any good. They haven't done much so far and that blonde deputy is just going to make his other problem worse."

"Huh? What other problem?"

"Crap," Heather said, annoyed with her slip. "Look, Jake and Amanda are having some problems lately. They got into a big fight over the phone on Saturday. A whole bunch of kids heard them." She paused to dump the pebbles and rootlets out of the screen. "It's tough being apart all the time."

"So what does that have to do with the blonde deputy?"

"I think she's got her eye on Jake. He doesn't realize it, of course. He's clueless, like all guys."

"Hey!"

"Deal with it, Scott. It's true and you know it."

Scott mumbled something under his breath, as his attention was drawn toward the road. "Uh oh, another car. Do you suppose it's the sheriff?"

"Not in a car like that, Einstein," Heather said. She watched as the vehicle pulled to a stop and a large woman got out. "Looks like that woman from the Transportation Department again."

"I don't know why she keeps coming back," Scott said. "She hardly talks to anyone, and sure doesn't act like she cares about what we're finding."

"Whatever. Jake's heading over there so he can deal with her."

Like Scott, Jake was a little surprised to see Maggie Devlin again, less than two weeks since her last visit. He was truly shocked, however, by her appearance. Still heavy, her face looked drawn and ashy, and noticeably pale for midsummer. Her clothes were disheveled and didn't look particularly clean. Jake tried to hide his reaction, but the look on her face suggested he hadn't succeeded.

"Hello, Maggie. How are you doing?"

"Oh, not so well, actually," she said, clearing her throat. "Barely able to get out of the office anymore, what with all the projects I'm responsible for. And I'm getting over a cold, too."

"Sorry to hear that."

"If it isn't one thing, it's another," Maggie said. "So, you're certainly opening up quite a large area here."

"Yes. Dozens of features, and we've uncovered part of an

Oneota longhouse in the trench," Jake said as he guided her past the lathe and flagging tape marking the edge of the exposed area.

"Very interesting. Lots of large potsherds, I see," she said, pointing at two students brushing some reddish soil away from a half-buried ceramic vessel.

"Yep. Not much Woodland stuff, though. There's a pretty substantial midden deposit over there, just beyond the house."

"How are you going to finish all this? Your backhoe has opened up a lot of ground."

"We have a few weeks yet, and I wanted to get a good sample from all over the village," Jake said, a bit defensively. "But we'll focus on finishing up what we can now, and if we have to we can put tarps down and start fresh next season."

"You're going to be out here again next year?" Maggie said, her voice rising.

"Well, yes. This was always going to be a multi-year project," Jake said. "Of course, a lot of it depended on the results from this season, but as you can see we have plenty to keep us busy."

Jake's cell phone rang, interrupting their conversation. He excused himself to answer the unrecognized caller. "Hello? Oh, yeah. I've been trying to contact you . . . uh-huh. Right. Sure, that explains it. That would be great, if it's not a problem. No, tomorrow night is full. How about Wednesday? Great. Okay, let me jot down the address."

Jake fished through his pockets for a pen, only to find Maggie holding a pencil a few inches from his face. He had turned away when he answered the phone, but she had apparently remained rooted in place during his conversation.

"Uh, thanks. All right, go ahead. Uh-huh. So that's north of the new boat launch, right? Okay, I know where that is. See you about seven. Thanks again."

"Good news?" Maggie said as Jake handed back her pencil

and put his phone in his pocket.

"Great news. I finally managed to get in touch with a photographer who worked at the site during Jacklyn Wardell's field school," Jake said. "I've been leaving messages for him for weeks, but I guess he had some trouble with his machine. He finally got it working and gave me a call. Said he has tons of photos to show me."

"Really? How fortunate for you. I'm surprised he kept that stuff all these years."

Jake shrugged. "Not sure how useful the photos will be, but considering how little I had to work with, anything is going to be helpful." He paused to answer a question from a student, and then turned back to Maggie. "If you'd like to take a look, we have part of what looks like a circular sweat lodge in that unit over there—"

"I don't have time for that," she snapped. The students working nearby glanced up from their screens. Maggie took note, and lowered her voice. "I mean, I really have to get going. I've spent too much time here already. Well, good-bye."

"Thanks for stopping," Jake said halfheartedly, as Maggie clambered up the steps cut into the side of the trench. Her shoes were caked with red clay but she did not appear to notice as she got into her car and drove away. Halfway up the road, Maggie's car passed a blue and white sheriff's cruiser making its way slowly down to the site.

Chapter Thirty

"Hi, Jake," Deputy Hauser said with a smile as Jake greeted her at the edge of the parking lot. "Heard you had some more uninvited guests."

"Afraid so, Pam. And this time they were a little more destructive than before."

"How so?"

"Someone dug into some features over there, in those units by the lake," Jake said, pointing to the southwest. "It looks like they pulled back the tarp a little bit and then poked around in the fill. Not sure if they found anything. They didn't dig very deep."

"So they gave up pretty quickly?" she said, writing in her notebook.

"I think so. It doesn't look like they had shovels, either. Maybe sticks, or they dug with their hands."

"Not pros, then. And it wasn't planned out ahead of time."

Jake nodded. "Nope. And only six or seven features were disturbed. Commercial looters come prepared, hit sites hard and fast, and then clear out with the best artifacts, stuff they can sell easily."

"Might be dealing with vandals rather than thieves," Deputy Hauser said, tucking a stray blonde hair back into her ponytail. "I wonder if—"

"Jake, we're finished with Feature 48," Heather announced loudly as she and Scott walked up to Jake and the deputy.

Scott's arms were laden with artifact bags and he had a sheep-ish look on his face.

Heather handed her clipboard and notes to Jake, with her back to Deputy Hauser. The deputy took a step back, one eyebrow arched in amusement.

"Okay, thanks," Jake said as he glanced at the paperwork. "This looks fine. Go put it in the binder with the rest, and we'll figure out where to put you guys in a minute."

"Oops. Hey, we forgot to add the bag numbers here," Heather said as she yanked the clipboard out of his hands. "Better get on this, Scott." Grabbing a nearby five-gallon pail, Heather turned it over and plunked herself down only a few feet away from Jake and Deputy Hauser. Scott sat on the ground opposite her and began sorting the bags.

"Sorry about that, Pam," Jake said. "You were saying?"

"I wonder if kids are messing around here. They started dig-ging around and then got scared off."

"Makes sense. Might not even be the same people as before."

"Wonder where they're coming from, though." Deputy Hauser tapped her pen against the leather cover of the notebook. "We had a car parked by the entrance Saturday evening and most of Sunday. Doesn't seem likely that anyone could have driven down."

"Maybe they were in a boat," Scott said. Heather gave him a withering look.

"That's a possibility."

"What about the trail, from the Hillside Resort?" Jake said, remembering the last time unexpected visitors had appeared. "We had some guests hike over from there, just before Summer Days."

"Hmm. That rings a bell." Deputy Hauser paged through her notebook and soon found the entry she sought. "One of our troopers saw some kids down here about a week ago, in the evening. Young teenagers, two girls and a boy. Said they walked over from the Hillside Resort. Didn't look like they were disturbing anything. They had a plastic pail full of shells and rocks from the lakeshore. He told them to be careful then drove off. He was going to call it in, but got interrupted by a traffic accident south of town."

"Maybe all our snoopers are coming from the resort."

"Do you want me to go over there and ask around, find out if anyone has suddenly discovered any points or artifacts?"

Jake considered her proposal. "I don't think that's necessary. Nothing missing that we know of, and except for this last visit there hasn't been any damage. I don't want to cause a fuss if it can be avoided." He cringed inwardly, recalling Wardell's problems with the resort owner. According the Everett Kojarski, Herb Keeling was out of town when Jacklyn died, but that didn't mean that someone else from the resort couldn't have been a witness. "I suppose I could go over and talk to the owners."

Deputy Hauser seemed to sense his reluctance, and found an opening. "If you don't want an official visit, why don't you let me go over there with you after my shift? I'm off at two and I can meet you back here after I change into my civvies. We can hike over there and just have a nice, neighborly chat."

Jake agreed, feeling a bit foolish that he might need a bodyguard just to talk. But it made sense, since as a trained law enforcement officer she would be able to pick up subtleties that Jake might miss.

Ten minutes after two, an older Camaro zipped down the gravel road and screeched to a halt a few yards from the processing table. Heather, entering artifact bag numbers into the site inventory, coughed loudly as a light spray of dust blew over her.

Jake grabbed his backpack and canteen as Deputy Hauser got out of her car. The transformation brought on by her civilian attire was striking, to put it mildly. She was dressed in shorts, cute hiking boots, and a fairly snug tank top. Her long blonde hair, freed from the constraints of the ponytail, draped loosely across her neck and shoulders. Without her standard bulletproof vest, her curvaceous figure was readily apparent. In the distance, Jake heard a couple of guys whistling, uncertain if it was for the deputy or the car. "Hey, Pam. Nice car."

"Thanks," she said with a wide smile. "My brother buys old clunkers and rebuilds 'em, then sells them when he needs cash for his next project. I get the family discount so I always have a pretty sweet ride. Shall we go?"

"Sure," Jake said, and glanced at his watch. "Heather, I'll be back in an hour or two, tops. Give me a call if you need anything." He patted his pocket to make sure his phone was handy.

Jake and Pam talked sparingly as they followed the trail that ran parallel to the edge of Taylor Lake. A few smaller trails branched off the main route in various locations but they soon found themselves on the edge of a large clearing, dotted with cabins and other buildings. Most of the structures were painted pale yellow or orange, trimmed with forest green. A large tavern with an attached house sat on the east side of the road, farther from the lake. Several families were down by the beach and a few senior citizens were fishing off the dock. Jake spotted a young man in a green shirt with "Hillside Resort" stamped on the back, tinkering with an outboard motor, and asked for the owner.

"I think Ma's in the office, doin' paperwork," replied the boy, wiping some grease off his hands. "Just go up to the bar and look in the back."

They thanked him, and walked to the large building on the opposite side of the road. Inside, they found two older men drinking beer at the bar, watching a sports talk show on the overhead TV. Two women sat at a table on the far side of the room, playing cribbage. A woman in her late fifties, wearing a green T-shirt identical to that of the boy outside, was perched on a stool behind the bar, entering receipts into an accounts ledger. Her head snapped up as they entered.

"Hi there, folks. What can I do for you?"

"I'm Jacob Caine and this is Pam Hauser. We're working at the archaeological site up by the old boat launch."

"Oh, sure," she replied cheerfully. "Heard all about it. Saw the pictures in the paper, too. I've been hoping to get up there myself when I can find the time. You're not done yet, are you?"

"No, not yet. Still a few weeks to go," Jake said. "We're actually looking for the owner."

"Well, you found her. I'm Melanie Stevens."

"Oh. Did, uh, was someone named Keeling the owner before that?" Jake said.

"Yeah, Herb Keeling used to own the place. Me and my sons bought the resort after his accident. He was cutting some logs with a chainsaw and gashed his leg. Ended up losing his foot. Anyway, he didn't have any insurance so he had to sell to cover his medical bills." Melanie paused to refill the glasses of the men at the far end of the bar. "I think Herb's in a nursing home in Wausau now. I'm not really sure. Why do you need to see him?"

"We don't, actually," Jake said. "It's . . . uh . . . ."

"More of a social call, Melanie," Pam said, taking a seat at the bar. "Some of your guests have been visiting the site, so we thought we should return the favor."

"That's wonderful! Yes, lots of folks have gone over there, and they just rave about how friendly everyone is. I need to get over there myself, but summers are just crazy around here."

"Well, you're welcome any time," Jake said, and handed her his card. "Feel free to call me, too, if you'd prefer to visit on a weekend, if that's more convenient. I can always meet you out there."

With a smile, Melanie took the card and tucked it in her pocket. "Thank you. I'll see what I can do. Are you going to have any more open houses?"

"Probably not this year. We only have a few more weeks left to finish up. But we'll be here again next season."

"Good, good. I'll be sure to mention it to my annual guests."

"Do you know if people are visiting the site after hours, Melanie?" Pam said. "It's not a big deal, but the police are concerned about vandals."

"Have there been problems? Ooh, I knew those two boys were trouble!"

"Who's that?" Jake said, glancing at Pam.

"A new family, with a couple of teenage boys. You know the type, just old enough to cause major-league mischief," Melanie said, nervously wiping the bar top with a rag. "They spent the week getting into everything they shouldn't. Messing around by the boats, taking candy bars, trying to filch beer from the cooler, stuff like that. On Sunday, the parents ended up checking out late because the boys had disappeared, again. I think they found them up by the boat launch. They were covered with that red mud from up there. Reason I remember it is 'cause the sheets and towels in their cabin were coated with the stuff. I'll probably end up throwing it all in the garbage."

"They checked out yesterday?" Pam said.

"Yes, just before dinner. Our normal checkout time is noon."

"Well, the red mud does sound like our site," Jake said. "Guess that solves this mystery."

"Oh, I'm so sorry," Melanie said. "Did they do any damage?"

Jake assured her that the boys' intrusion had no lasting impact, and that they were simply curious as to who might be responsible. Pam made a big show of minimizing the damage, but Melanie still looked concerned.

"They didn't take anything, did they?"

"Probably not, but there's no way to know for sure," Jake said. "I don't think any harm was done."

"All right. Well, when guests ask about the dig, I'll make sure they know not to touch anything, or even to go over there when you folks aren't around."

"That's fine," Jake said. "Most people are just curious and they don't intend to cause any damage."

"Speaking of curious," Melanie said, pulling a shoebox out from behind the bar. "Lots of our guests find trinkets and curios around the resort. I don't think there's anything from your site, but maybe you want to take a look?" She opened the box to reveal a menagerie of oddly shaped rocks, fish bones, a few fossils, some old dish fragments, and several stone tool fragments. Jake examined the tools closely, taking note of the style and raw material. Bits of black, peaty soil still clung to the largest item, a notched spearpoint.

"I don't think any of this is from Waconah," Jake said. "Looks like Archaic material, so it's probably a few thousand years older than the village site. You might have an important site right here at the resort."

"Really? How exciting! Maybe you can do a dig right here."

Jake grinned. "A big dig takes a lot of planning. But if you're willing, our crew could put in a few test units next season and we'll see what we can find."

"That would be wonderful! Maybe you and your wife could come up this fall and give a talk or something."

"Um, we're not married." Jake stammered, turning crimson. "Just friends. She's . . ."

"I'm a local," Pam said, patting Jake on the back. "Been helping out at the site a bit during my off-hours."

"Oh. Well, you make a cute couple, that's all," Melanie said, turning as a harried-looking couple with three children entered the bar. "Here, have a couple of Cokes while I check in these folks."

Melanie excused herself to greet her latest arrivals. Jake took a sip of his soda and cleared his throat. "Well, somehow I don't think the resort owner is going to cause any trouble for the dig."

"I think you're right there, Watson," Pam said, grabbing a handful of pretzels out of a nearby bowl. "I'll bet this place is the source of most of your after-hours visitors, although it seems pretty quiet. I've never been called out here before. 'Course you might get a few curious strays off the lake, too. But since they're not doing any real damage . . ."

". . . it isn't anything we need to worry about," Jake said, finishing her thought.

"All in all, a nice diversion from my usual routine," she said, raising her glass in a faux toast. "Most police work is pretty boring. Lots of paperwork, too. Nothing like you see on television or in books."

"Sounds like archaeology," Jake said. "Hours and hours spent scraping through soil, pushing dirt through screens, and putting tiny crumbs in plastic bags. And meticulously recording every detail of everything you do. How come I never find gold idols, like the guy with the whip in the movies?"

"You'd probably have fewer students if you threatened them with a whip all the time." Pam gave Jake a playful elbow in the side. At the far end of the bar, Melanie had sent the new arrivals to their cabin and now raved excitedly over a small walleye brought in by another guest.

"Hmm. I was kind of expecting Herb Keeling to still be here," Jake said. "Causing trouble for us the way he did for Jacklyn Wardell."

189

"Couple of old-timers on the force said her death wasn't an accident."

Jake was immediately alert. "Really? What did they say?"

"Nothing much more than that. After the sheriff and I visited you the first time, the topic came up one night after work. A few guys who were around then insisted Wardell wouldn't have gone out in the boat on her own. But, they didn't have anyone they could pin it on, so it got written up as an accident."

"Sheriff Kojarski told me pretty much the same thing. He had some suspects at the time, but nothing tied any of them directly to her death." Jake briefly relayed the information he received from Kojarski, along with their alibis. "Keeling was on his list, too."

"But nothing came of it?"

"He was out of state when she died."

"Perfect alibi."

"Yeah, but I still wanted to ask him about her death, see if he had heard anything from anyone who might have been here that day. Not that he would have been very forthcoming, most likely."

The proud young angler brought his catch over to Jake and Pam, who both agreed that it was the finest fish either of them had seen in years. Melanie gave the fisherman a filleting knife and directed him toward the fish-cleaning house behind the bar. Four more fishermen entered, looking for a late lunch, and Melanie hustled over to take their order.

Pam took another sip of her Coke. "You know, you seem awfully interested in Wardell's death, if you don't mind me saying. Did you know her?"

"No, but the circumstances of her death are curious, and unanswered questions always pick at me. Guess that's why I became an archaeologist."

"Maybe you just like to play in the dirt, like a big kid."

"That too, I suppose," Jake said. He then told her about his meeting with Linda Wardell and the scraps of information he had picked up since then. Finding a receptive audience, he also described Mark's last meeting with Jacklyn and Clark's version of that fateful night.

Pam listened attentively throughout, occasionally nibbling on a pretzel or sipping her drink. She paused, nodding, as he finished. "Wow. That's quite a case you've got there, when you lay it all out like that. If you'd like, I could help out with the detective work. You know, check into the official records, stuff like that. But cold cases are tough. Witnesses are gone or their memories have faded over time. And, just to play devil's advocate, it might not have been a crime in the first place."

"Yeah, it very likely could have been just a tragic accident," Jake said. "But one with a lot of weird circumstances surrounding it. I dunno, maybe I should just stay focused on the site, like my girlfriend said."

Her face fell. "Oh, you have a girlfriend?"

"Yeah, Amanda Rohm. She works at a history museum in La Crosse. She was out at the site a few weeks ago, but hasn't been able to come back yet."

"Hmm." Pam tapped her fingers nervously on the bar. "Well, she's a very lucky girl, Jake."

Jake blushed again. "Thank you, Pam. If it's not out of line, I could say the same about your boyfriend. Or husband?"

"No, nobody like that in the picture right now," she said with a harsh little laugh. "Tough meeting nice guys on the job. Can't really ask a guy out while you're slapping the cuffs on him, after all. And this is a pretty small community, so the dating pool is kind of restricted."

"You know, I'm sorry if I said or did anything . . ."

"No, Jake, it wasn't you. I didn't see a ring, so I assumed you were . . . available."

"Sorry. Still friends?"

Pam smiled. "Sure, I can always use a few more good friends. Heck, maybe I'll quit the force and go into archaeology, until a decent guy comes along."

"I'd say you're just waiting for the right guy. When Mr. Lucky comes along, I'm sure you'll spot him a mile away. And he'll fall for you like a ton of bricks."

"Well thanks, friend. I needed to hear that." Pam glanced at her watch. "We should probably get out of here. It's been over an hour and your assistant will probably have her dogs out looking for you soon."

"You're probably right about that," Jake said, and he tossed a few dollars on the bar.

"Plus, I don't think she likes me too much. Call it cops' intuition."

"Hmm, I hadn't noticed," Jake said jokingly. "Although she did suggest rather strongly that Scott accompany you over here instead of me."

Laughing, Pam and Jake said goodbye to Melanie, promising to stop back again soon. She, in turn, agreed to come over to the site as soon as she could find the time.

About halfway back to the site, they met Scott on the trail. "Hey, Scott. What's up?"

"Heather was starting to wonder where you were, so she sent me to check."

"Why didn't she call?"

"I dunno," Scott said. "I would have asked but she was pretty insistent."

The trio finished the journey back to the boat landing, where Scott left them and returned to his work. Jake walked Pam back to her car.

"Well, Jake, thanks for the date," she said loudly, giving him a wink. "I'll keep checking on the site during my shifts, just in case your snoopers decide to come back with a shovel and pail."

"Uh, thanks," Jake said. "I appreciate it."

Deputy Hauser stood awkwardly for a moment and then gave Jake a quick, friendly hug before getting into her car. Waving, she drove off quickly.

Jake turned to see Heather standing ten yards away, hands on her hips and glaring at him with murder in her eyes. He sighed, half-turning as the throaty roar of the Camaro's engine faded in the distance. "Oh, thank you very much, Pam."

CHAPTER THIRTY-ONE

The summer sun scorched the Waconah field school on Tuesday. The clear blue sky stretched for miles, mirrored in the smooth, still surface of Taylor Lake. With no breeze to cool things off, the students suffered terribly in the hot, humid conditions. Jake and his assistants reminded everyone to drink plenty of water and take frequent breaks under the shade of the canopy tent, but by early afternoon everyone was miserable.

Jake didn't expect many visitors given the oppressive heat, so he was surprised to see a fancy luxury sedan crest the hill and zoom down to the parking area. He walked over to greet them, only to stop short when Clark Kelley emerged.

Clark stomped across the parking lot and stopped a few feet short of Jake. "Well? Where is it?"

"Where's what?" Jake said.

"My flash drive. Look, I don't have time for this, so if you would just hand it over, I'll be on my way."

"Clark, I have no idea what you're talking about. What flash drive?"

"One of my flash drives disappeared the last time I was up here. I thought I left it at the hotel, but they couldn't locate it." Clark snorted. "Yesterday I got a call from one of your assistants and she said you had it out at the site. So where is it?"

"Slow down a second," Jake said. "I don't have your flash drive, and as far as I know, no one has found one at the site. Who did you talk to?"

"I don't know, I didn't catch her name. You know how these kids mumble all the time."

Jake held up his hand and called out to Heather, who joined them. "Heather, did you call Dr. Kelley yesterday about a lost flash drive?"

"Huh? No. What flash drive?"

Clark let out a stream of curses as Jake tried to explain. "He lost a flash drive during his last visit. Someone called him yesterday and said we found it at the site."

"Well, it wasn't me," Heather said. "And nobody found any flash drives that I heard about."

"It was probably that other one," Clark snapped. "The lab girl, the one who doesn't have enough sense to lock up when she wanders away from a building."

"Erin didn't find one either. She would have told Jake right away if she had."

"Okay, Heather, thanks," Jake said. Given their last meeting, Jake doubted that Erin would call Clark herself. "I think I can handle it from here."

Heather strode off, and Jake turned back to Clark. "Let's try this again. Where did you last see your flash drive?"

"This is ridiculous."

"Just humor me. Please."

"Fine. I had it at the hotel when I was up here for my inspection. I couldn't find it when I checked out, so I informed the manager that it was missing. I called a few days later to remind them about it, but it hadn't turned up."

"Where were you staying?"

"The Plymouth Inn, north of here. That's not important. Anyway, yesterday afternoon one of your people called and said they found a flash drive with my name on it. The woman on the phone said you had it."

"You drove all the way up here to get it?"

"No. Well, uh, I was going to be in the area anyway. Just passing through, so I thought I could make a quick stop and pick it up."

"I'm sorry, Clark, but I don't have your flash drive. It almost sounds like someone is playing a practical joke on you."

His face reddened. "That's absurd," Clark said. "Who would do something so stupid? And besides, who even knew the drive was missing?"

Jake shrugged. "I don't know. Did you tell anyone it was lost when you stopped by the campsite, before you left?"

"I didn't, I mean, I don't think I did." Clark fished a handkerchief from his pocket and dabbed his forehead. "God, it's hot out here. Hmm. Look, I may have said something about the drive when I arrived, but only to a few of my students. None of them would do something so crass."

Jake wondered if Erin had heard about the missing drive from a student and decided on a little payback. But it didn't seem like something she would do, and there were enough gaps in the plan that it could easily be traced back to her.

"I can ask around," Jake said. "But I doubt anyone here was trying to prank you. Most likely the drive disappeared at the hotel and ended up in the trash."

Clark frowned, but seemed unable to come up with a counter-argument. At that moment, the passenger door of Clark's car opened and a tall, busty woman stepped out. Her dark designer sunglasses accentuated the platinum blonde color of her hair. The mystery woman glanced at her watch, and then stared at Clark and Jake.

The woman looked vaguely familiar. "Is that . . . Carol?" Jake said. "I thought your wife had curly brown hair."

"As I made it clear last time, Caine, my personal life is none of your business." Clark gave the woman a wave, and checked his own watch. "Since you don't have my flash drive, there's no reason for me to waste my time here. I have to get going. Uh, if my drive turns up—"

"I'll call you right away. If it shows up." Clark turned his back to Jake and hurried back to his car. Jake nodded to the woman, who smiled and waved back.

Clark and his companion drove off in a cloud of dust. "Stop by anytime, Clark," Jake said to himself. "Your visits really make my day."

CHAPTER THIRTY-TWO

From Jacklyn Wardell's journal:

July 15. We're over the hump and the end is in sight for this site (bad pun). Been a good season but the strain is starting to show. I'm feeling burned out (and this sunburn isn't helping—boy, what is with the bad puns today?) and I could use a break. Can always get a fresh start next season. The archaeology is great; I think dealing with certain people and their issues is causing me the most trouble.

I think the heat is getting to Snowman (ouch—no more puns). His mood shifts are making me worried; hope it is just a temporary thing. He's a great kid and has lots of potential. Maybe he needs a little more attention, just to remind him how much I rely on him on this dig.

Starting to think The Dark One and Lady Margaret are conspiring against me. If one of them isn't giving me grief, the other one is waiting in the wings. I'm tempted to ban them both from Waconah. Not sure if I have that kind of authority but I'm tempted to try it out.

The Ms. Amethyst situation has me the most concerned. Asked CatWoman to ask around, discreetly, and what she discovered confirms my suspicions. Now, how best to handle it? Could call WSU Human Resources, but even a "hypothetical" discussion with them is bound to set off some alarms. Maybe I'll speak to Ms. Amethyst myself, confidentially, woman to woman. Don't want her to get hurt, but I can't stand idly by. I suppose I could give Lisa C. a call; she's been in the department a few years, maybe she's dealt with this sort of situation before. In any event, it would be nice to chat with her for a while.

Just a few more weeks left. Can't wait to pop open that bottle of champagne and raise a toast to the first of many successful field seasons!

After Clark's departure, Jake decided to end the day early and let the students regroup before the evening lecture. For many archaeological field schools, exposure to labwork and evening instruction were required. This practice serves to highlight the relationship between fieldwork, lab processing and analysis, and subsequent research and report preparation. During the first week, Jake had asked each student to take some feature notes from another student and describe the feature based on the notes, map, and artifact lists provided. Some did well, others had good maps and poor notes, and vice versa. By the next day, field forms had improved dramatically.

Jake began this session with a brief discussion of understanding feature patterns, with illustrations projected against the wall. "For weeks now, you've been excavating individual features. Focusing all your attention on the storage pits, hearths, cooking fires, and even portions of the longhouse in excruciating detail." That comment brought some laughter. "While that is important, we can't lose sight of how each feature relates to all the other features in the village. Eventually, we'll do a distributional analysis, to look for patterns in the location of certain feature types, and see if we can recognize patterns that indicate how the village was organized."

Using examples from the site map, Jake demonstrated how storage pits were clustered in certain areas, while the midden deposits were along the edges of the village. For the next thirty minutes, he asked the students to analyze and describe the possible activities reflected in various parts of the site. By relating past events with modern behavior, most of the students were able to present cogent arguments.

"All of these are good ideas," Jake said as talk waned. "Often specific evidence is lost or missing in the archaeological record. Remember, we rarely find all the pieces, so we have to reconstruct past human activities based on what we do have. We can't ever prove things definitively, but sometimes the preponderance of information is enough to bolster our interpretations."

Jake glanced toward the doorway, startled to see Pam Hauser leaning against the frame. She was in her sheriff's uniform, but smiling and apparently at ease. There was no obvious urgency in her visit, so Jake thanked the students for their attention and participation before dismissing them for the evening. They filed out quickly, a few saying hello to the deputy as she moved into the hall.

"Evening, Professor," Pam said as Jake approached. She nodded to Scott and Erin, who stood a few feet away. "Enjoyed the talk. Especially the part about recognizing patterns. Kind of like detective work, in a way."

"Is there something wrong at the site?" Jake envisioned the worst.

"No, no problems," Pam said. "Just finishing up a late-day shift and thought I'd swing by. If you have a minute?" She tilted her head toward the door.

"Sure. We just finished up. Sorry I didn't spot you at first."

"No problem. Looked like you were in the zone, so I didn't want to interrupt." They stepped outside and walked over to the deputy's patrol car.

"After our talk yesterday, I pulled the old case file on Wardell's death. You know, just out of curiosity. Nothing official. If you'd like me to pursue it though, I thought I could track down that student, Amy, and see if she can provide some answers."

Jake rubbed his chin and considered her offer. "I have to admit it's tempting, and could shed some light on this whole mystery. But digging into the issue could cause me some problems with Clark Kelley. He has a lot of influence in my department."

"That's the beauty of it, Jake. I'd be the one doing the digging, not you. And if nothing important turns up, he'd never know anything about it."

"That's true. I guess. Okay, let's do it. As long as we can keep it quiet, I don't see the harm."

"Great. I have to say, your story piqued my curiosity. And if we can solve the mystery it'll really show off my detective skills."

"Looking for a promotion?" Jake said, grinning.

"I wouldn't turn one down, that's for sure," Pam said with a chuckle. "Even if I don't plan to stay around here forever. So, what's Amy's last name?"

"Hmm. Not sure I ever heard her last name."

"That's going to make it a little harder, Watson. I'm good, but not that good."

"I should be able to find it in the records from the old field school. Give me a day or two and I should have it."

"Sounds good. You get a name and I'll use the awesome power of the sheriff's office to track her down," Pam said with a mischievous smile. "But it'll cost you, Jake. You owe me a second date but at a restaurant this time. Full meal, drinks, the works. Not just pretzels and Coke."

Jake scuffed the ground with his boot, in mock consideration. "Deal. But this sounds suspiciously like blackmail, Officer Hauser."

"Oh, I don't think so, and I am a police officer," she said as she opened the car door. "Besides, what's a little blackmail between friends?"

Jake waved as she drove off and walked back to his room. Retrieving two plastic boxes, he began sorting through the files in search of Wardell's student list. Most of the paperwork he had received from Mrs. Wardell was locked in his university office, but he'd brought copies of anything he thought might be useful. After twenty minutes, Jake's search was rewarded.

"Ah, shoot! There would have to be two of them. That figures."

"Jake? Something wrong?" Erin said, tapping her beer bottle against the doorframe.

"Oh, hey Erin. Didn't hear you come in."

"Not surprised, with the party in full swing out there." She tilted her head in the general direction of the bonfire. "What are you doing, anyway? Something to do with the sheriff? Is it about the break-in?"

Erin paled, and Jake cringed. He hadn't thought that Pam's sudden appearance at the camp might be cause for alarm. Especially for Erin, who had finally been acting more like her old self.

"No, nothing like that. Deputy Hauser is interested in the Wardell case," Jake said carefully. "I talked with her about it, a bit, and she's going to pursue it. On her own time. Just out of curiosity, to see if her death was really an accident."

"Oh, I get it," Erin said, and took a sip of her beer. "So why are you in here? Did you need to find something for her?"

"Yeah. She wanted to check on some alibis and needed the names of the field school kids."

"Is it Mark Winters?" she asked excitedly. "It's because he's been hanging around again, right? Remember, I said that criminals always return to the scene of their crime."

Jake let out an audible sigh. "No, it's not about Mark. Clark's alibi for the night of the accident was a student named Amy. It's just a minor thing, but you need to keep it to yourself, okay?"

"Sure," Erin said. "The less I have to do with Clark, the better."

"Problem is, there were two girls named Amy. Amy Taubner and Amy Waterman. I didn't think there might be two people to track down."

"Hmm. Well, I'm sure the deputy will be able to figure it out," Erin said. She held the empty bottle up to the light. "I'm heading back out. Are you coming?"

"Sure," Jake said as he returned the files to the storage box. "I guess I could use a night off."

CHAPTER THIRTY-THREE

"Any trouble finding the place?"

The cheerful, expectant voice seemed out of place in the shadowed, heavily wooded lot, as did the smiling, white-haired man waving from the sagging wood porch. A battered sign with "Al Droessler, Photography" hung on the door.

"No problems at all, Mr. Droessler," Jake said, shaking his hand. "I'm Jacob Caine, and these are my assistants, Heather and Scott."

"Nice to meet you. And call me Al." He ushered the trio into his kitchen, which opened up into an expansive living room and photography studio. The cabin was fairly roomy inside. Framed photographs covered nearly every wall, with dozens of boxes and photo albums crowding the shelving units that took up over half the room. Two sturdy worktables, littered with cameras and other photo equipment, divided the main room in half. A recliner, television, and glass-topped coffee table occupied the space on the opposite side of the room.

"Hope we're not too early," Jake said. The oppressive afternoon heat resulted in a second short field day, and they ended up driving over sooner than originally planned.

"Nah. Time don't mean much at my age," Al said. "Now that I'm retired, about the only thing I need a clock for is to remind me when to take my pills."

Jake noted the dozen or so pill bottles and holders lined up on the counter. The kitchen had been cleaned recently, with only a few crumbs and stains peeking out from underneath the coffee maker and microwave. A small stack of newspapers and mail sat on the small kitchen table.

"Well, come on in to my studio-slash-museum," Al said, grinning. "Best photographic history of the north woods right in here. Been taking pictures since I was a kid, and when I got older I started buying up old collections. All kinds of unique items in here."

Al moved over to the table, half covered with a stack of five-by-five-inch prints, a dozen yellowing envelopes, and some narrow photo albums. "Anyway, I dug through my files after you called," he said, gesturing toward the pile. "I know this isn't everything, but it should be most of the shots I took while Professor Wardell was out digging at Waconah."

"This is pretty impressive," Jake said. He and his students sat down and began sorting through the images. Scott unfolded the site map, laying it on the far end of the table. "There's a lot more here than I expected."

"Yeah," Heather said as she shook some large prints from an envelope. "Check this one out. You can see some of the northeastern units, and the lakeshore in the background."

Al peered over her shoulder. "Oh, yeah. I took that one from the north side, just below the tree line. Couple of the students rigged up a scaffold on some ladders, so I could be up high and include more of the units."

Most of the prints were close-ups of the students and unit excavations, with names and unit numbers written on the back. One album contained nothing but artifact photos, taken in the field and back at the camp. The rest consisted of overview shots, taken from a distance, and scenery shots with Taylor Lake and even the islands visible in the distance. Jake recognized several images from copies he found in Jacklyn Wardell's papers. With Al's permission, the archaeologists added notes relating to the current excavation on the back of some prints.

In short order, Jake, Scott, and Heather had most of the photos sorted by subject, with the most attention given to those showing the position of features and units. Nearing the end, Jake leafed idly through some casual, candid shots of people milling about, eating lunch, swimming, or just relaxing around the site. "These are really wonderful, Al. Archaeologists take lots of photos, but they're almost always of wall profiles, features, and artifacts. Pretty sterile stuff. Guess we're not artistic enough, so we end up as scientists."

Jake paused, entranced by a slightly out of focus snapshot of Jacklyn Wardell sitting on a backdirt pile, writing or perhaps doodling in her journal. The same journal that now sat in his room, back at camp. The wispy clouds in the background of the shot provided a striking if somewhat eerie contrast to the white-tipped waves on Taylor Lake.

Al noticed Jake studying the print and nodded his head knowingly. "I really like that one, myself. It was tough balancing the focus on Jacklyn and on the waves in the background, but the soft focus gives it an ethereal effect. I took a few more that are a little sharper, but I like this one the best because of the effect."

"It's beautiful. Really."

"Jacklyn was really nice about me poking around," Al said. "Some folks get touchy with outsiders on their turf, but she was always supportive. Even joked that she was going to have to put me on the university payroll. She wanted to use some of my photos in the site report, too. Course, after she died I guess that was the end of that. They never did write it all up, did they?"

"No, I'm afraid not. Did you ever receive a copy of the memorial volume the grad students wrote?"

"Gee, no, I never heard anything about that."

"I'll have Scott or Heather drop off a copy in a day or so. I made some extra copies for the field school and I'm sure I've got a few left back at the campground."

"That'd be great, thanks," Al said. "I've got a lot of duplicates here, from the old dig. You're welcome to 'em, if you want."

"I appreciate it," Jake said, and he handed some prints to Heather. "If we end up using any of them, I'll make sure you get paid and receive full credit. The university can be a little tight with the money sometimes, but . . ."

"Hell, anything'll be fine. Just getting to see my work published is reward enough."

"And no matter what, I'll make sure he doesn't forget to give you lots of copies of the report, so you can impress your friends and family," Heather said, giving Al a playful wink. "After all, we lowly assistants are actually the ones who get things done."

Al seemed to think that comment was uproariously funny, and they bantered back and forth, each extolling their own contributions as they sorted through the photographs. Jake was about to counter Heather's latest jibe when one of the images caught his attention. One of dozens of weather-related shots over Taylor Lake, it was somehow different from those he had seen earlier. This photo, unlike the others, was centered lower on the horizon, with a good portion of the original excavation present in the foreground. The image was somewhat dark, but at least a few units were discernible, along with some scattered trees and other landmarks.

"Say, Al, this photo might be able to help us out right now. We're trying to relocate some of Jacklyn's old test units, and it looks like nearly all of them appear in this photo," Jake said, handing it across the table. "Must have been taken a few weeks after the field school started. If we compare it with the maps we have, it could help us find some of the missing units."

Al nodded. "Oh, yeah. I remember this one. Don't have too many others like it, and none with all the holes they dug. You're right, this was toward the end of the field school. I took this photo the night Dr. Wardell drowned."

CHAPTER THIRTY-FOUR

On Thursday morning, Rich Halsey arrived with the county backhoe and opened a fifteen-foot-wide trench in the northwestern part of the site. Before long over thirty dark stains were evident and Jake decided to end the trenching.

"I can keep going, if you want," Rich said upon hearing the news. "The supervisor figured I'd be over most of the day."

"No, we have plenty opened up already. It takes a day or more to map and excavate each feature, and we only have a few more weeks left," Jake said. "But we could use some help filling in the old trenches."

"Whatever you need. Just point them out and I'll get busy."

Scott joined Jake at the side of the new trench, and the two compared notes.

"I've got Shannon and Dale working on that group over there," Scott said, pointing to the north. "And Steve and Liz can handle the feature cluster in the center. Sarah can help out both teams for a while, and then head back to her old unit."

"Sounds like a plan. I put Bryant in charge of the other group at the south end, so I think we have everything covered."

"You put Bryant in charge? I mean . . ."

"I know, he's been a bit bossy in the past," Jake said, brushing some dirt from his hands. "But he's settled down quite a bit lately. Besides, his crew knows what to do at this point, so it's unlikely he's going to mess anything up by making some big mistake. Figured I'd give him a chance."

"I suppose you're right. Can't hold it against him forever, I guess. Well, Heather probably will."

"What's the deal with those two, anyway? They've been at each other since the field school started, but lately Heather seems, I don't know, a lot more antagonistic toward him. Did he do something recently to set her off?"

"I guess you didn't hear," Scott said, and he lowered his voice. "Bryant was all wound up about Dr. Kelley coming for his inspection. Figured he would make some points with his advisor, and apparently Bryant told a bunch of people about how close they were. Well, not only did Kelley hardly even talk to him while he was here, he called him Barry, Bryan, and Ryan at different times during the day. And it was in front of a bunch of other students, making it even worse. Heather heard about it a few days later and I think she's been gloating over it ever since."

"Ouch. No wonder Bryant's been moping around like he lost his best friend."

"Yeah, that had to sting. I don't know if Heather has said anything to him, but Bryant has to know she heard about it."

"Hmm. Guess I'll do what I can to keep those two apart for the rest of the season," Jake said with a sigh. "Shouldn't be too hard. I hope."

Scott shrugged his shoulders as an uncomfortable silence filled the air. He glanced at his clipboard, searching for a new topic to discuss. "So, Al Droessler's photos were pretty cool, huh?"

"That's an understatement," Jake said. "I wish every dig had a photographic record like that. Lots of good overview shots, and all those crew photos. That reminds me, we should probably take more photos of the students in action, digging, screening, all that."

"I'll grab the good digital camera this afternoon and get a

bunch," Scott said eagerly. The normally quiet Scott had grown increasingly animated on the drive back to camp after their visit with the elderly photographer, revealing a lifetime interest in photography.

"I wonder how Erin is making out with the photos?" Jake said, voicing the question he had been pondering all morning. In truth, he had spent much of the previous evening wondering what might be hidden in some of Al's photos. And in one certain photo in particular.

"I don't know," Scott said. "She was going to scan in the ones he loaned us, try to blow up the images, but there is only so much you can do with old photos. It all depends on the resolution of the originals."

"I know. I guess I'm still hung up on that one shot, from the night Jacklyn Wardell died. Too bad Al couldn't remember the exact time he was there."

"Yeah, I guess. But he said it was around five, more or less. He was moving around a lot, trying to get different angles of the storm front coming in. Probably wasn't paying much attention to the time."

"What nags at me, though," Jake scratched at his beard, "is that he didn't remember seeing any other cars or people. Both Mark and Dr. Kelley admit being there that evening." Jake had shared some of his concerns about Wardell's mysterious death with all three of his assistants, to little avail. Scott listened politely each time, but it was clear he didn't share Jake's morbid fascination with the subject.

Scott's shoulders dropped, having heard much of this the night before as Jake grilled Al for additional information. "Like Al said, it was pretty dark because of the storm, and his attention was focused on the clouds, not on the site. He was looking up, not down the hill."

"I know, I know," Jake said, not convinced. "But what about

Jacklyn's vehicle? It was parked there all night. It was there when they came to look for her in the morning."

"Yeah, but it was down here, at the bottom of the hill. Unless the lights were on, there's no way you'd notice a car from the top of that hill," Scott said adamantly, pointing to the rise.

At that moment, a sheriff's patrol car appeared on the rise and drove down the gravel road toward the site. Jake and Scott started walking and were almost to the parking area when the car came to a stop. Sheriff Rostlund took a few steps away from the dark blue squad car and surveyed the site briefly before fixing his gaze in Jake's direction.

The sheriff nodded curtly at Jake and Scott. "I'm sorry to say this, Professor Caine, but this isn't a social call. You and a couple of your students were over at Al Droessler's last night, correct?"

"Yeah. Heather, Scott, and I went to see his photos from the old field school dig. Is there a problem?"

The sheriff ignored his question as he wrote Jake's reply in his notebook. "What time did you arrive?"

"About a quarter to seven. We were scheduled for seven, but we left the site early due to the heat."

"What time did you leave?"

"About nine, maybe a little before that. Right, Scott?"

"Yeah," Scott said. "We got back to camp about ten after nine, and it was probably a twenty-minute drive."

"Any . . . problems while you were there?" The sheriff stared directly at Jake. "Notice anything odd on the way out?"

"No, nothing," Jake said, still confused. "He showed us a bunch of photos and let us borrow some to scan for our report." Jake wondered if Al had forgotten that he had given them the photos, and perhaps called the sheriff when he realized they were missing. Al appeared alert and sharp the night before, but Jake knew from personal experience the awful effects of Alzheimer's in the elderly. "Al gave us permission to take the photos, Sheriff. Is that the problem?"

Sheriff Rostlund let out a long, drawn-out sigh. "Professor, there was a break-in at Al's place. Looks like he surprised a burglar, and in the struggle I'm afraid Al's heart gave out. He's dead."

CHAPTER THIRTY-FIVE

"Oh my god," Jake said, stunned. "Al's dead? It can't be."

"Afraid so. At first glance, it looks like someone forced the door to gain entry. Didn't take much to push that small bolt in," the sheriff said sadly. "Al had a doctor's appointment this morning and when he didn't show one of the office assistants took a ride over to check on him. Found the door ajar and Al on the floor."

"You think it was a burglary?" Jake said.

"The assistant called 9-1-1 and one of my deputies was nearby when it came in. He got there right before the ambulance arrived. Noticed the doorframe was splintered around the lock, and the pieces fell into place. Pretty standard for break-ins around here."

"So it must have happened after we left last night. That's why you asked if we noticed anything unusual when we left."

"That's right, Professor. Well, almost." Sheriff Rostlund removed his mirrored sunglasses and Jake saw the dark circles and haunted look in his eyes. It obviously had been a very trying morning. "Breakfast dishes were in the sink and there was a fresh pot of coffee in the kitchen. Looks like it happened sometime early this morning."

"Isn't that unusual? I mean, for a burglary to happen during the day?" Jake said.

"Not necessarily. Smart crooks hit a house when it's empty, in and out quick, no matter the time. People expect to see folks around a house during the daylight hours. Flashlights at night, that's what draws attention. Plus, Al's place is back in the trees, so you'd never see anything from the road anyway."

"I suppose," Jake said. "It's just unbelievable,"

"We're going to need your prints, too, I'm afraid."

"Why?" Scott said. "We didn't do anything."

"Our fingerprints are all over the living room, Scott," Jake said. "On the photo albums, some of the cameras, the chairs. Heather and I both used the bathroom, too. The Sheriff needs our prints to compare with any other unknowns they might find. Right?"

"Exactly so, Professor." Sheriff Rostlund eyed Jake shrewdly. "I was wondering if you and your assistants could come over to the crime scene and take a look around? To be honest, I can't see you folks as being involved, but since you were just over there last night, you might be able to see if anything in particular is missing or out of place."

"Of course, Sheriff," Jake said quickly. "Anything we can do to help."

"Good. The place is kind of a mess, so it's hard to tell what's missing. Al was a packrat anyway, and with his health problems the last few years I don't think he always had the oomph to do much heavy lifting. Besides, in your line of work you guys have an eye for detail."

"That's true. Did you get in touch with Al's family? He mentioned a daughter in Arizona . . ."

"We're already on it. Doctor's office had his emergency contact info. Anyway, our crime-scene guy is going over the cabin right now. He's thorough enough, but between you and me he doesn't have a ton of experience with stuff like this. And our department doesn't have all that fancy equipment like you see on those forensic shows on television. So, hopefully you can pick up some little details that we might have overlooked."

★ ★ ★ ★ ★

Shortly after lunch, Jake and Scott left Waconah and drove to Al Droessler's cabin. Neither had felt much like eating. Scott had been pretty quiet since Sheriff Rostlund's visit, but he agreed to come along and inspect the scene. An awkward silence filled the car.

"Thanks again for coming with me, Scott."

"It's fine. No worries."

"Uh, I imagine the crew will knock off in a few hours, if the heat is anything like yesterday. We'll probably just head back to camp . . . after this."

"Sure, whatever."

"You doing okay with this?" Jake said. "You didn't have to come."

"I know. It's fine, I just felt like somebody should come with you." Scott fiddled with the air conditioner settings for the third time since they left. "It was pretty obvious that Heather wasn't going to ride along."

Upon hearing the news, Heather's mood shifted abruptly. She became morose and aloof, hardly speaking to anyone unless it was necessary. As Jake prepared to leave, her only reply was a quiet "No, I can't," when he asked her to join him and she sloughed off his suggestion that the Sheriff had wanted them all there together.

"I guess she felt like she had to stay around the site," Jake said, although it seemed like there was more to it than that.

Scott exhaled loudly. He grew more nervous as they neared the cabin. "I just never had to deal with anything like this before."

"Yeah, I know. Just focus on the items in the house, like the cameras. Put your attention on the cameras and see if anything is missing. And if at any point you feel like you can't handle it, just go back outside."

Jake turned into the tree-shrouded driveway, noting as he did just how hidden the cabin was from the highway. The sheriff was correct. From the road, the cabin was barely visible even in broad daylight.

Jake parked next to one of the two squad cars. Sheriff Rostlund was leaning against one of them, talking with two deputies he didn't recognize. The sheriff walked over as Jake and Scott got out of their car.

"Afternoon, Professor. Thanks again for coming over."

"Not a problem, Sheriff," Jake said, shaking his hand. He gave Scott a quick glance, but his assistant seemed to be coping with the situation. "Thanks for giving us some time to get things organized at the site. We couldn't leave right away without shutting down the whole site, and I'd prefer to avoid that."

"Well, the crime-scene technician was still finishing up, and I figured you'd be more comfortable driving over in your own vehicle. Your students might not understand if I had just shown up and then drove off with you in the back seat."

"Yeah, you're right about that," Jake said. He could imagine the field day Clark would have had if he heard that the county police had dragged Jake off in the back of a squad car. Of course, Clark would undoubtedly expand on the details until a much different story had spread across campus, with an enraged Jake screaming obscenities through foam-flecked lips as he was cuffed and tased repeatedly, while the students alternately sobbed and cheered, freed at last from their incompetent instructor. Goodbye, tenure. "So, how do you want us to do this?"

"Well, we've finished processing the scene," Sheriff Rostlund said as he led them toward the front entrance. "But it would be best if you didn't touch anything, regardless. You'll need to slip these on, too."

Jake and Scott put on the blue latex gloves and shoe covers

217

as the trio stepped onto the porch. Despite the heat and humidity of the afternoon, a distinct chill permeated the air under the awning.

"Go through the kitchen and main room, and take note of anything missing or out of place from your previous visit." The sheriff stepped to the door and removed the yellow crime-scene tape. "Things are scattered all over, so watch where you step. Above all, take your time. Feel free to mention anything, no matter how small. Let me and my guys decide if it's important or not."

Jake and Scott nodded, then stepped gingerly through the doorway. Jake noticed the freshly splintered wood around the lock, and resisted the urge to reach out and touch it. He took two steps into the kitchen and stopped, scanning the counters and tabletop. As the sheriff had described, the sink was half full of unwashed dishes and a used coffee cup sat on the counter. The little army of pill bottles was in the same location, but it looked to Jake as if a few had switched positions, suggesting that Al had taken his pills that morning. The pile of mail and newspapers had been rearranged, with one section folded open. All in all, nothing in the kitchen seemed out of place.

Jake took a step forward and moved around the table, checking the floor as he did. It was then that the white tape on the dark brown carpet caught his eye. He moved to the edge of the kitchen linoleum, but stopped short of the carpeted living room as he took in the scene. The room was a shambles. Photographs and broken glass were strewn across the floor, intermixed with broken knickknacks and camera parts. One shelving unit was tipped over and its contents partially buried beneath the metal frame and bent shelves. Amidst the chaos, the taped outline that marked the location of Al's frail form stood out like a beacon.

"Damn," Jake whispered. It looked nothing like the room he had visited less than twenty-four hours before. Behind him,

Scott gasped loudly and Jake realized his assistant was uncomfortably close. Moving cautiously, the two archaeologists stepped into the living room, avoiding the taped area and as much debris as they could manage. In low tones, they discussed what they saw, recognized from the night before, and what was missing. They examined the room scientifically and clinically, earnestly avoiding the taped outline that dominated the room. The minutes seemed like hours, but before long they had completed their inspection and joined the sheriff on the porch.

"So, what do you have for me, boys?"

"Well, Scott noticed that some of the older cameras are missing."

"Yeah," Scott said, clearing his throat. "Al had an old Graflex Speed Graphic, worth maybe a hundred bucks. And he had a nice Rolleiflex on the shelf, from the late 1930s."

"How much is something like that worth?" Sheriff Rostlund said, jotting the information in his notepad.

"Maybe a few hundred, depending on the model. I'm not really an expert on antique cameras," Scott said. "But it's kind of weird. There are a couple of old Leica cameras, M2 or M3 models, still in there. They can be worth a lot more."

"How much more, son?"

Scott shrugged. "Couple hundred dollars, maybe, up into the thousands. I just know they are really valuable. My uncle found a Leica lens at a flea market once and later sold it for something like five times what he paid."

"Maybe the thief didn't realize how valuable they were," Jake said. "The other ones looked older, so he grabbed them thinking they were worth more money."

"Could be," the sheriff said. "I don't suspect the intruder was a professional camera thief, regardless. Anything else?"

"One of the photo albums we looked at last night appears to be missing," Jake said.

"Appears to be missing?"

"Well, yes. Al had five photo albums filled with pictures from Wardell's dig, and I could only see three. We took one with us last evening, but the other one is unaccounted for."

"So it could have been taken, or might just be lost?"

"Right. The thing is, Sheriff, most of Al's pictures were in envelopes or loose on the table. The way everything is strewn around in there, it could take hours to figure out what, if anything, is missing."

"But some cameras are definitely gone, correct?"

Scott nodded. He was about to speak when Jake interrupted.

"I'm confident there are some photos missing, Sheriff. Unless Al put some away last night or this morning, there aren't enough scattered on the floor to account for the number of pictures we looked at."

Sheriff Rostlund chewed his lip, lost in thought. "It doesn't seem likely that any thief would be interested in old photos like that. Most likely some got scooped up when he grabbed the cameras and the cash. Rest of them will probably turn up once the place is cleaned out."

"Sheriff, is it possible the break-in has anything to do with Jacklyn Wardell's death?" Jake said. "I mean, all of the photos on the table were from her dig. And there are still some . . . uncertainties about her death."

Sheriff Rostlund frowned. "Deputy Hauser mentioned you were still curious about Wardell's death. You must be pretty convincing, since she's spending her off-hours digging through the old case files. But in this case, I don't think there's any connection."

"So, it's just a coincidence?"

"Looks like, Professor. In addition to the cameras, the DVD player is missing. You can make out the dust pattern where it sat on top of the television. The intruder broke into a metal strongbox in the bedroom and took whatever was inside. Al's wallet was cleaned out, too. Took the cash, left all the credit cards. Keep that to yourself, though."

"Sure," Jake said. "The thing is, though, Al had some photos from the night Dr. Wardell died. We borrowed most of them, so we could examine them in detail. I don't know what we might find, but—"

"Professor," Sheriff Rostlund said, closing his notebook. "This all looks like a burglary gone bad. Pretty unlikely it has anything to do with an old boating accident. But don't worry, we'll take everything relevant into consideration during the investigation. Right now, I need to get back to the office. You think of anything else, give me a call."

CHAPTER THIRTY-SIX

Inside their car, Jake and Scott watched as Sheriff Rostlund and one of the deputies drove off. The other deputy remained behind to secure the crime scene. He waved to the two archaeologists as they drove away from Al's cabin.

"I don't think the sheriff is even going to consider the possibility that this has something to do with Jacklyn Wardell's death," Jake said, shaking his head.

Scott took a long drink from his water bottle. "Do you really think the break-in had something to do with it?"

"I don't know," Jake said after a moment. "Honestly, it just seems like a weird coincidence. We visit Al, look at photos from the old dig, and even find some from the night she died. And then less than a day later someone breaks in and steals some of the photos."

"Yeah, I guess. But like the sheriff said, they took money and a DVD player, and the cameras. They probably grabbed some photos by accident."

"Maybe. I think I should talk to Pam. She's curious about Wardell's death and might give my idea more thought."

"It was a lot of years ago," Scott said. "Why would someone suddenly want the photos after all this time? Al had those pictures for years, and probably everyone around here knew about them. If they were looking for the photos they could have gone after them anytime."

"So, it would have been someone who didn't know they

222

existed, or they just found out, right?" Jake said, excitement in his voice.

"Umm, no, that's not what I meant," Scott said. "Only that everybody around here already knows and didn't particularly care. We're the only ones who just found out about the photos, and we didn't have anything to do with the break-in."

"You, me, and Heather. And Erin has the photos now, back at the lab. Did you tell anyone about our visit?"

"Well, sure. Most of the students heard about it, and I think Heather and some of the NEWAS guys were talking about it this morning, before the backhoe arrived."

"Did anyone show any interest in the photos from the last day? Did it get brought up at all?"

"I don't think so. I really wasn't part of the conversation," Scott said, somewhat annoyed. "Besides, isn't that kind of morbid? After all, you can't see anything important in those photos anyway."

"Not yet, but I wonder what will show up after Erin plays with the images on the computer. She was going to start scanning them in this morning. Maybe I'll call her and find out how she's doing."

They pulled into a gas station. Scott went inside to use the restroom while Jake made his call. He dialed Erin's number, but after four rings it went to voice mail. Jake waited a few moments then tried again but the same thing happened. On a hunch, he called Heather.

"Hey, boss, what's up?"

"Not much. We finished up at Al's place and are heading back. I don't know how much help we were, but the sheriff seemed to appreciate it."

"Was, was it pretty bad?"

"Yeah, kind of. Place was a real mess, so hard to tell what

was missing."

"Everything is under control here," Heather said. "Some of the students are moving pretty slowly because of the heat, so we might knock off a little early."

"That's fine, I'll leave it up to you. Say, is Erin out there by any chance?"

"No. Why would she be here?"

"I don't know. I called her cell but keep getting her voice mail. I thought maybe she was at Waconah and had her phone turned off for some reason."

"Sorry, nope. Probably taking a nap or something back at camp."

"What, and leave the students to run amok in the lab?" Jake said.

"There aren't any students there today, remember? You wanted everyone here to help out with the backhoe scraping. She's on her own today."

A shiver ran down Jake's spine as he remembered the last time Erin was at the campsite alone. "Thanks, Heather. Look, why don't you take care of wrapping up today? I think Scott and I are going to head back to camp."

"We are?" Scott said as her returned from the station with a granola bar and a bottle of iced tea. "Shouldn't we give them a hand?"

"Probably, but Erin is at camp alone and she isn't answering her phone."

"So? Maybe her phone is off or—"

Jake shook his head. "Maybe, but remember the last time Erin ended up at camp by herself? And what happened over at Al's?"

The color drained from Scott's face. "Oh, yeah. I guess we should get over there. Just to be on the safe side."

Jake and Scott raced back to the campground, cursing the intermittent traffic and every apparent delay, no matter how slight. Jake broke one of his cardinal rules and called Erin again while driving only to receive yet another voice mail message. Reaching the campground, they sped down the winding road until they reached their group campsite.

Everything was quiet, deathly still in the late-afternoon heat.

"Erin?" Scott's yell echoed across the clearing. No reply.

"I don't think she's here," Jake said, scanning the area. "Her car is gone. Better check inside."

Jake tried the door, only to find it locked. He fished out his keys and they entered the hall. The room was undisturbed, everything much as it had been when the students left that morning. A few artifact bags were spread out on the back table where Erin had her main workspace.

"Whew." Scott let out a sigh of relief. "Looks like everything is okay here. Erin was checking in bags this morning, I guess."

"Yeah, I suppose," Jake said grimly. "But where the hell is she and why isn't she answering her phone?" He pulled out his phone and punched in Erin's number. No reply.

"It's probably nothing," Scott said. "Maybe she ran into town for supplies, or something else came up."

"That's not the point," Jake said. He continued to look around the room as if some clue to her disappearance would reveal itself. "I don't want the lab left unguarded, what with the break-ins and people snooping around the site. Wait a minute. Where is the box of photos from Al's place?"

"I don't know. It was sitting right here this morning."

"Well, where is it now? Look for it."

Scott and Jake made a quick tour of the building, but the box was nowhere to be found. Jake pulled out his phone, hesitated about calling Erin again, and then shoved the phone back in his

225

pocket. The stress of the day's events had reached a crescendo.

"Should we call the police?" Scott said, sensing and reacting to Jake's mood.

"I don't know. What do I tell them, I can't find my lab manager and a box of pictures no one cares about but me has vanished?"

Scott stared back blankly. "Well, maybe we should—"

They both stopped short as the sound of car tires crunching on the gravel outside carried through an open window. Jake bolted through the door, Scott close behind.

"Oh, hey guys," Erin said as she stepped out of her car.

"Where the hell have you been?" Jake yelled, storming up to her. Erin took a step back, bewildered by his behavior.

"What? I . . . I was just in town."

"What for?"

"To, uh, pick up some supplies."

"What supplies?" Jake peered through the windshield. "I don't see any bags. And you just went in to Donovan a few days ago."

"Well, I had some other things to do, too," Erin said.

"Like what? All kinds of trouble around here and you decide to go off by yourself, leaving the camp unguarded!"

"Jake, stop shouting at me! What's your problem?"

"My problem? My problem? After the day I had, you have to ask me what my problem is?"

"Jake, take it easy," Scott said as he positioned himself between them. "She doesn't know, remember? She wasn't there when we heard."

"Heard what? What happened today?"

Jake exhaled, forcing himself to calm down. "Erin, I'm sorry. All of this must have gotten to me more than I thought."

"Oh god, Jake, tell me what happened!"

"Erin, there was a break-in at Al Droessler's place this morning. He was gone, but came back home for some reason. Must have surprised the burglar, and I guess his heart gave out. The sheriff came by the site to tell us and then he asked us to come over to the crime scene."

"You mean you had to go see the, the body?"

"No, nothing like that," Jake replied quickly. "Sheriff Rostlund knew we were there last night and he wanted us to take a look around, to help figure out what was missing. And he needs our fingerprints, so they can rule out our prints."

"Oh my god, that poor man. How awful," Erin said, and her eyes welled up with tears. "No wonder you were so freaked out."

"I am sorry. I didn't realize how upset it made me."

"Was it pretty bad . . . in there?"

"Yeah, it was," Scott said. "The place was trashed, and a bunch of stuff was missing."

"Like what?"

"Some antique cameras," Scott said. "And a DVD player, and—"

"And some photos, from the original dig!" Jake said as he remembered what had set him off moments before. "Damn! Erin, that box of Al's photos we had in the hall is gone."

"No, I've got it with me," Erin said. "It's in the trunk. I started scanning photos this morning, then brought them with me when I went into town. I figured I could keep working on the inventory while I was, uh, waiting."

"Whew, that's a relief. I don't know why, but I can't help wondering if the break-in had something to do with Wardell's field school."

Scott turned away from Jake and rolled his eyes as he walked past Erin toward the back of the vehicle. "No harm done, then."

"I'm really sorry, Jake," Erin said. "I didn't think it would be a big deal."

"It wasn't, really. If it hadn't been for the break-in we never would have come back this early anyway. I guess I just imagined the worst when I couldn't reach you." Jake turned and stared at Erin. "Say, why didn't you answer your cell phone?"

"Uh, I don't know. Guess I didn't hear it."

"I called a half-dozen times," Jake said, perplexed. "What were you doing in town, anyway?"

"Nothing. I mean, nothing important. Oh, thanks for grabbing that box, Scott. Should we head inside?"

"Just a minute," Jake said, his suspicions raised. "What were you doing in town?"

"Like I said, nothing important." Erin's eyes darted between Jake and Scott. "Does it really matter?"

Jake studied her for a moment. "Yeah, I think it does matter. You left the camp unguarded . . ."

"Everything was locked up. It—"

". . . and then you didn't answer your phone, and now I can't get a straight answer about your trip into town. To be honest, I think I have a right to know," Jake said. "Scott, take that box inside, will you please?"

"Sure, I guess," Scott said. He gave Erin an encouraging smile as he walked away.

"Erin, between the break-in here and at Al's cabin and trespassers at the site, we've seen more than our share of trouble during this field school. Nothing major, until now at least. But I am concerned and I don't want any more secrets."

Jake raised his hand, cutting off her protest. "I'm not accusing you of anything. We've been friends for years, and I'd like to think you trust me. If it's something personal, you know I'll keep it to myself. But I need to know the truth."

Erin stared in silence at the ground. "You're right," she said at last. "The camp Internet connection was acting up again, and I needed to have a secure connection. So I went to the library in town."

"What was so important?"

"I, I had a job interview," Erin said. "It's for a Senior Curator position at a museum in Vermont. I couldn't afford to fly out there, so they agreed to do an online interview through Skype. I knew if the connection was bad it would be just another strike against me, so I reserved a time at the library."

"Why didn't you just tell me?"

"I didn't want the word to get out that I was looking, you know, actively looking for another job. You don't know what it's like for nonacademic staff. Word gets around that you might be leaving and suddenly your hours get cut back, or they don't want to give you new projects, or they won't give you good assignments 'cause they don't think you'll be around to finish them."

"I didn't realize it was like that."

"You don't know the half of it, Jake. Things can get really cutthroat, especially when annual reviews are looming. A couple of complaints from the wrong people and suddenly you're wondering if you're going to have a job the next month."

"I'm sorry," Jake said. He suddenly felt very uncomfortable. "I knew you were looking for something better, but I didn't know how bad it was."

"It's all right," Erin said, wiping a tear from the corner of her eye. "I would have told you, but you learn fast to keep this stuff to yourself."

"So, how did it go? If you need me for a reference or anything . . ."

"Thanks, yeah. You're on my list, but they'll only call if I make it to the next round," Erin said, her face brightening. "The interview went well, I think. It was hard to hear them once or twice, but I nailed most of the questions. I had my résumé in front of me and I wrote out answers to some of the more typical questions last night. You know, where do you see yourself in five years, what are your strengths and weaknesses, et cetera."

"Good. If I can help out at all, just say the word."

"Sure." Erin looked past him as Scott cautiously poked his head through the doorway. "For now, just keep all this to yourself, all right?"

"No problem," Jake said. He turned to Scott and gave him a slight wave. "If Scott or anyone says anything, I'll just say it was personal, no big deal."

"Thanks. I'm sorry about taking the photos with me, too. I didn't know you'd get so upset about them."

"Scott thinks I'm reading too much into it, but I couldn't help wondering if there might be a connection between the break-in at Al's and his old photos from Wardell's field school. Then when I saw that the box was gone, it just seemed to fall together."

"Sorry, they were safe with me the whole time. I doubt anyone besides us would be interested in these pictures anyway."

"I guess so," Jake said. "So, have you seen anything, I don't know, interesting in the photos yet?"

"No, not really," Erin said. "But I've only just started. I might have the scanning done tomorrow, if you want me to put a rush on it."

"No, don't let it interfere with your other lab stuff," Jake said. "Hmm. I wonder, though, what will become of the photos now that Al's dead. I suppose I'll have to ask his family about using the images."

"They probably won't mind," she said. "But I wouldn't bring it up right away. Awkward, you know?"

"Yeah. Guess I'd better keep my mind on getting this field school done, too, without any more surprises."

As if on cue, several vehicles full of hot and tired students pulled into the parking area. Heather and Bryant emerged from separate vehicles and both made a beeline for Jake, eager to relate their version of their latest dispute. Behind them, the students scattered loudly toward the showers, kitchen, and tents.

Jake shuddered and mumbled to himself as Erin went to retrieve the day's artifact bags. "Please, no more surprises."

CHAPTER THIRTY-SEVEN

"It's like a sauna out here," Scott said as he grabbed his daypack from the back of the vehicle. The students milled around him in the humid, still air, gradually shaking off the lethargy that seemed to affect everyone that morning.

"I'll say." Jake wiped the perspiration from his brow with the back of his hand. Despite the early hour, it appeared that the weather Friday would be even more unpleasant than Thursday. "Heather, did all the water jugs get refilled this morning?"

"Yes, yes. Quit worrying," Heather snapped. "It's all taken care of."

The unyielding heat wave made it difficult to sleep and more than a few students outdid themselves in surliness each morning. Lately, Heather had emerged as the leader of this little group.

Jake had left four students behind to help Erin, in part to atone for his behavior the day before. Usually, their absence was offset by the presence of the NEWAS volunteers, but only Charlie Garath and his cousin Art were at the site today.

"We probably want to cut these up during the morning break," Art said, smiling broadly as he hefted two large watermelons. "Pulled these out of the garden last night. Figured the kids would appreciate 'em."

"Definitely," Jake said. "Thanks, Art."

Art and Charlie walked toward the equipment area to retrieve their dig kits and paperwork before joining the students already at work. Jake pulled his cell phone from his pocket, checking for messages. He had called Amanda the night before, hoping to patch things up since their shouting match on Saturday, but she didn't answer so he left a brief, awkward message. Since they had started dating, he couldn't recall any time in which they hadn't spoken by phone or email at least once or twice a week, even when fighting. No new messages were recorded.

The morning crept along as the students struggled through the rising heat and unbearable humidity. As noon approached, Jake noticed more and more students taking extended water breaks or staring wistfully toward Taylor Lake, now crowded with boats and jet skis. He checked the time and then called to Heather and Scott. He spotted Bryant standing not too far away, so he waved him over as well.

"Let's call it an early day," Jake said as the trio reached him. "It's miserable out here and someone's probably going to collapse if we try and push through this afternoon."

"Fine by me," Heather said, glancing at Bryant. "Want me and Scott to get everyone wrapped up?"

"Please. Have them get to a good stopping point and then we'll pull out the tarps. I want everything secured for the weekend. Bryant, I'll need you to take the crew back to camp today."

"Why him?"

"Heather, the three of us need to stop by the sheriff's office so they can take our fingerprints, while they investigate the break-in at Al Droessler's house," Jake said. "It's no big deal, but we might as well take care of it now."

Heather spun around and walked off, and Scott and Bryant followed a short distance behind. Twenty minutes later, the site was secured and the students were loading the vehicles. Jake waved to Charlie and Art as they drove off and then joined

Scott and Heather in the car.

"This shouldn't take too long," Jake said as they drove up the gravel road. "Sheriff Rostlund said to stop by anytime and they'd move us through right away. Just a formality."

"Right," Scott said.

Silence from the back seat, as Heather scribbled in her field notebook. Jake and Scott left her alone on the drive over, exchanging idle small talk to break the silence.

Arriving at the police station, the archaeologists found that neither Sheriff Rostlund nor Deputy Hauser was present, but the desk sergeant knew who they were and had been expecting them. He passed them along to another officer who ushered them quickly through the fingerprinting process and before long they were on the way back to the campground.

Despite the friendliness of the officers, the brief ordeal left them all feeling uncomfortable. The ride back was even quieter than the ride in.

Once at camp, Heather and Scott turned in their paperwork and bag logs and retired to their tents. Jake listened politely to Bryant's report on the safe return of the crew before heading into the hall. Erin sat at the main table, checking in artifact bags, while two students busied themselves in the kitchen.

Erin reached for her nearby laptop. "I finished scanning the last of Al Droessler's photos today."

"Really? I thought it would take longer."

"Normally it might, but with the extra students today I had less to do, so I thought I'd just finish the job. Besides, I figured if Al's family wants the photos back for any reason, we'd still have all the scans to work with."

"How did they turn out?"

"Great. I scanned each one and then added a note with all the info included with the photo. Names, dates, and stuff like that. Then I sorted them into these folders based on subject matter, so you have people, artifacts, features, and units all grouped together."

"That's great. Should help a lot when we use them to fix the old site map, and when I pull images for the report." Jake scanned the folder icons on the screen. "Just out of curiosity, did you manage to enhance that photo from the night Jacklyn Wardell died?"

Erin's face fell. "Sorry, Jake, I didn't. I only had time to scan them, nothing else. Plus, we don't have any image-enhancing software on the laptops. I'm afraid it will have to wait until we're back at the university."

"Oh. Well, no big deal, I guess. I was just curious."

"If you want, I could try and download some programs, and see what I can do. But it's not my area, so . . ."

"No, it really isn't important," Jake said. "Amanda said I should put all that stuff behind me and just focus on getting this field school wrapped up. After what happened to Al, I can't imagine the sheriff's department wants to waste time with Wardell's death either."

Erin looked puzzled. "I wouldn't call a cold case a waste of time. I can see why you might want to follow up on it, in all honesty. In fact, I did get a little info on Amy Taubner and Amy Waterman."

"Really? When did you manage that?"

"Yesterday. I did a little Web searching while I was in town. I meant to tell you yesterday, but . . ."

"But I was too busy being the world's greatest jerk, right?" Jake said. "I am sorry, you know."

"It's okay. Water under the bridge," Erin said. She flipped opened a notebook. "Anyway, here's what I found. Amy Waterman is now Amy Barnes, married with three kids. She lives in northern California and works in human resources at some engineering firm. Found a couple of women named Amy

Taubner who have connections to archaeology. One works for the Forest Service in Oregon and another teaches in the Sociology Department at a private college in Virginia. The third one used to live in Wisconsin but moved to Ohio at some point. I was just starting to check on her when my interview started."

"Impressive. How did you find all that out so easily?"

"It's frightening how much general information can be found on the Internet. Names, ages, locations, interests, you name it. And so many people post stuff on social media sites, it's like they're advertising their personal histories for anyone willing to snoop through it."

"Scary. Guess it's a good thing I never got into that stuff."

"You said it. I'm going to be more careful about what I post from now on," Erin said. "So, do you think this will help track down the right Amy?"

Jake read through the notes and then let out an exaggerated sigh. "It certainly could. I don't know, though. Maybe it would be best to just let the whole thing drop. Amanda thinks I should let it go, or at least she did the last time we talked. Scott and Heather seem to think I'm wasting my time, too. Maybe they're right."

"Well, it's up to you," Erin said, shrugging her shoulders. "But you might want to pass this info along to Deputy Hauser, as long as I got it. Couldn't hurt."

"I suppose. All right, I'll give her a call after I clean up. But then that's it. Time to put Jacklyn Wardell's death behind me for good."

CHAPTER THIRTY-EIGHT

Jake awoke with a start to the blare of rock music and laughter coming from the parking lot. Peering through his small window, he found the party already underway. Several grills were in use and a huge bonfire was lit. A glance at his alarm clock revealed that several hours had passed.

"Hey, Jake, you awake in there?" Erin said, rapping on the door.

"Yeah, I am now. Wow, I must be really out of it, to drop off in the middle of the day like that."

"After your swim, you said you were going to read for a while. I stuck my head in the door about an hour later and you were out cold. Figured it wouldn't hurt to let you rest."

"Thanks. I guess I needed it." Jake reached down to retrieve Jacklyn Wardell's journal from the floor next to the bed. He recalled paging through it before he dozed off.

"Want to join the party? You slept through lunch, so you must be starved."

Jake caught the aroma of burgers and brats and was suddenly ravenous. "Sounds great. Aren't they starting a little early though?"

"Not really," Erin said, stepping out of the room as Jake slipped on his boots. "Besides, it looks like this rain festival idea is working. There are dark clouds to the west and the wind has been picking up all afternoon."

Jake looked skeptical but followed her through the hall and

out into the parking lot. A gust of cool wind caressed his face. "I'll be damned," he said, staring in astonishment at the gray cloudbank covering the western sky.

"I tell you, the crew is really on the mark this time," Erin said. "Only about half of the kids have tossed their sacrifices in the fire, and this is the result."

"What's gone into the fire so far?"

"Some worn-out gloves, a few hats, a sports bra, couple of candy bars, and a pair of shorts."

"Those are the kinds of things that appeal to the storm gods?"

"I guess. Can't argue with the results. Just wait until everybody has thrown something in."

"Could be the storm to end all storms. Heck, I may join in, if it puts an end to this heat wave. But I need something to eat first."

Jake and Erin were halfway to the tables when a police car pulled around the corner and into the lot. "Uh oh," they said in unison.

"Want me to take it?"

"No, thanks anyway," Jake said, walking toward the car. "If I pass out from shock, though, tell everyone it was from lack of food."

"Hi, Jake," Pam said. She removed her sunglasses and slipped them in her pocket. "Looks like we're finally going to get some rain. About time, too."

"Yeah, definitely. Is this, uh, an official visit or . . . ?" he asked, gesturing at her mismatched clothing, consisting of a white T-shirt, uniform trousers, and battered running shoes.

"What? Oh, no. Do you know how hot ballistic armor can get? I took it off as soon as my shift ended and just slipped on my runners. I only have the squad car because I have to drop it off in Donovan for one of the guys working the night shift."

"Sorry, didn't mean to be paranoid. With everything going on lately, guess I just assumed the worst."

"No problem," she said with a smile, leaning against the car. "I am here on a somewhat crime-related errand, though."

"Which is?"

"The Wardell case, partner. Got your message about Amy Taubner and Amy Waterman. I'll start tracking them down next week and then we can decide how to proceed from there."

"To be honest, Pam, I'm not sure we should pursue it."

"Why not? You convinced me there might be more to the story than the official version. Why give up now?"

"Main reason? Al Droessler's death."

She placed her hand on his shoulder. "The sheriff mentioned he had you and your assistant out the other day to inspect the crime scene. Must have been rough. Even if you've seen them before, you never get used to it."

"I don't know how much help we were, but I felt like we needed to do something. He seemed like a really nice guy."

"Yeah, Al was pretty special. He was the photographer for all the school events when I was in high school, and took most of the senior portraits for years. I imagine there will be a big turnout at the funeral."

"Do you know when that will be? I didn't think to ask, but I'd like to attend."

"Haven't heard, but probably not for a few days, at least. Al's daughter is flying in tomorrow, but I think they are having trouble tracking down his son. He's out at some field station or something. Could be another week before all the arrangements are finalized. I'll give you a call when I hear something."

"Thanks."

"Sure. I understand you're shook up about Al's death, but why give up on the Wardell investigation?"

"I just thought the sheriff's office would be busy enough

investigating his death. Why waste time dealing with an old cold case?"

"But you asked the sheriff if he thought the two cases might be related, right?" Pam said, moving closer. "So it must have crossed your mind that maybe it wasn't so cold after all?"

"Maybe at first," Jake said. "But it was mostly because it seemed like an odd coincidence. Like the sheriff said, it was just a burglary with a tragic outcome. The two events don't have anything to do with one another."

Pam pressed her fingertips together, gathering her thoughts. "Since the break-in at Al's, I started to wonder something. Do you suppose he was somehow involved in Jacklyn Wardell's death?"

"That doesn't seem likely," Jake said, puzzled. "He was never a suspect to begin with. What motive would he have? Jacklyn was happy to have him around and she was going to see about getting his site photos published."

"So he said, but do we know that for sure? Have you found any paperwork or a contract in Wardell's files, or anything to indicate they had an arrangement in place?"

"No, but—"

"Wait, hear me out. You told Sheriff Rostlund that Al had some photos from the night Wardell died. That proves he was at the scene near the time she went into the boat. He claimed no one else was around and that he didn't see anything. Doesn't that strike you as suspicious?"

Jake paused, not pleased with the direction the conversation was heading. "I guess it does. I said the same thing afterward, but Scott came up with lots of reasons why he might not have seen anything. Plus, why would Al want to hurt Jacklyn?"

Pam held up her hand. "I know, on the surface it doesn't make sense. But let's just suppose that they did have an arrangement in place for the site photos, like Al said. Maybe he spoke with Wardell that night, or maybe a few days before, and she backed out of the deal. Al got upset, there was a confrontation, and she ended up in the boat. Maybe it was an accident. Who knows? Al took a few photos as cover to explain why he was there, in case anyone saw him. According to the case file, he has no other alibi for the rest of that evening."

Jake shook his head. "I don't buy it. Like my dad used to say, that dog won't hunt. There's no paperwork about an agreement, so doesn't that also remove support for your proposed motive? And would he kill someone over publishing photos in an archaeology report?"

"You never know what people are capable of, Jake, or what they'll do for even the smallest of reasons. Someone broke into an old man's cabin and caused his death, and for what? A couple of old cameras and a handful of cash."

"I suppose. But I think you're reaching on this."

"Maybe," she said, not conceding the point but unwilling to pursue it further. "Then consider this. Al was at the site, taking photos after most everyone else was gone. Suppose Mark Winters found out about it and he came to the same conclusion that I did. Mark could have gone over to Al's place to confront him about Wardell's death, and things got out of hand."

That was a scenario Jake hadn't considered. He couldn't picture Mark robbing an old man to support a drinking or drug problem, but if Jacks were involved? Hard to predict what he might do, even so many years after her death.

"Winters could have kicked the door in afterward and messed the place up so it looked like a home intrusion. Makes some sense, doesn't it?" Pam said, taking Jake's silence as a tacit endorsement of her theory. "Might also explain why he's been off the radar lately."

"You've been looking for him?" Jake thought back to Mark's last day at the site, right before Clark Kelley's visit. Although nothing was said at the time, Jake had assumed Mark would return once Clark was gone. He hadn't.

"Not me personally, but Sheriff Rostlund has. Winters is on his list, along with some other local burglary suspects."

"Why Mark, specifically?"

"Guy has a record, substance abuse issues, and no visible means of support. Plus he shows up in the area about the same time we get an increase in trespassing reports and break-ins. He does fit the profile."

"But you can't find him."

"Not yet, but he'll turn up, unless he left the state entirely. If he has, it might be a whole lot easier to put this crime on him."

"I don't know. It just doesn't seem like something he would do."

"To be honest, Jake, you don't know this guy at all." Pam's comment echoed that made by Amanda a week earlier. A wave of guilt washed over Jake. He had waited too long to contact Amanda and now he couldn't reach her at all. Thinking back, his messages probably came across as terse and angry. All in all, he had really made a mess of things.

"I guess we'll have to wait and see," Jake said.

Pam missed the challenge in his reply, or chose to ignore it. "In the meantime, I plan to keep reviewing the Wardell case notes. Might not hurt to talk to Charlie and the NEWAS guys too, see if they recall anything from the last few days before Wardell's death."

"Feel free to pursue it if you want, but I'm probably not going to be much help," Jake said. He noticed the increasing shadows as evening fell, and felt weary. "The field school will be wrapping up soon and I really need to focus on getting everything in order."

Pam looked disappointed, but then covered it with a sly smile. "I understand. Of course, you might just be saying that so you don't have to take me out to dinner when I crack the case."

In the distance, the low rumble of thunder resulted in a raucous cheer from the inebriated students gathered around the bonfire. Jake and Pam watched as one coed clambered onto a picnic table, removed her bikini top, and tossed it into the flames. Another cheer rose from the group.

"So, what's all this about, Professor?" Pam said, one eyebrow arched in mock concern. "Some sort of secret archaeology ritual I'm not supposed to see?"

Jake scanned the crowd in the hopes that one of his assistants would take charge and keep things from progressing any further. "Ah, well, the crew decided to hold a little rain festival, to deal with the heat. Sorry, I must sound like a moron. They decided to throw personal items in the fire, to appease the rain gods. It's really just an excuse to blow off steam and have a party."

"Well, it does seem to be working. That's one big storm cloud they've called in. If your kids can do this on a regular basis, I have an uncle down in Iowa who'd pay top dollar for rainmakers on his farm." She laughed, before sliding even closer to Jake, a mischievous twinkle in her blue eyes. "Maybe we should help them out. What do you say, Jake? I'll take my top off and toss it in the fire, if you'll do the same."

Jake's eyes widened. As he struggled to reply, Pam placed her hand playfully over his. Stammering, Jake's reply died in his mouth as a figure stepped out from the shadows and stopped a few feet away.

"Jake?"

CHAPTER THIRTY-NINE

"Amanda! What are you doing here?"

"I was going to ask you the same thing," Amanda said icily, staring at Pam.

Jake yanked his hand out from under Pam's and bolted upright. "Pam, I mean, Deputy Hauser and I were just talking—"

"I'm afraid to ask about what." Amanda sniffled, but continued to glare at him.

"You must be Amanda," Pam said with a smile. She extended her hand. "I'm Pam Hauser. It's so nice to finally meet you. Jake does nothing but rave about you."

"Really? That's nice of you," Amanda said. "I'm afraid he hasn't mentioned you, for some reason."

"That's understandable. I only stop by when work requires. Trespassers at the site, the break-in here at the camp, that's all."

"Oh? Did someone break into the building again?" Amanda shifted her gaze from Pam to Jake, waiting for a reply.

"No, not here," Jake said as he recovered his voice. "There was a burglary at Al Droessler's home, and—"

"Who?"

"Al Droessler, the photographer who worked at the old field school," Jake said. "I finally got in touch with him, and there was a break-in the day after we met him."

"What does a break-in there have to do with you? I don't understand."

"Jake and his assistants were helping with the investigation," Pam said. She turned to Jake. "You haven't told her, have you?"

"We, ah, haven't been in touch for a few days," Amanda said. Jake nodded, unsure how else to reply.

Pam sensed the awkward tension in the air. A roar of approval came from the crowd around the bonfire as another rumble of thunder, much closer than before, echoed through the clearing. "Well, I'm sure you two have lots to catch up on, then. Besides, I should probably get moving before things get too rowdy at the party." She turned to Jake. "Thanks again for your input with the Droessler case. I'll let you know what, um, develops."

"Sure, no problem. Thanks."

"Nice meeting you, Pam."

"You too. Bye."

The police car had barely turned around before Jake shifted his attention to Amanda. "What are you doing here? I didn't expect you back until, well, I didn't know when you'd return."

"I put in extra hours every night and moved some things around on my schedule so I could come back. With my vacation time, I was hoping to spend the last few weeks of the field school with you," Amanda said, watching the fading taillights of the police car. "Now, I'm not sure that was such a good idea."

Jake rolled his eyes. "Honey, I'm thrilled you're here. Just surprised, that's all."

Amanda's reply was interrupted by the arrival of Erin, carrying a plate of food and a can of beer. "Hey, Jake, you didn't make it over so I thought I'd provide home delivery," Erin said, and then noticed Amanda. "Amanda! Hey, I didn't know you were coming this weekend." Erin shoved the plate of food into Jake's hands and gave Amanda a hug.

"Jake didn't know either. Thought I'd surprise him, but he decided to line up a new girlfriend in the meantime."

"Huh? You mean Deputy Hauser? Nah, Jake isn't like that. The cops are around because of the break-in."

"At the photographer's, right?"

"Yeah. Didn't Jake tell you?"

"No, he didn't. Apparently I've missed quite a bit of gossip." She shot Jake a cool look, but not as harsh as earlier.

Jake took another bite of burger, trying to calm his unsettled stomach. "I did call, but I kept getting your voice mail. And we've been having a lot of Internet problems."

"I was putting in ten- and twelve-hour days," Amanda snapped. "So my phone was turned off most of the time. I only got two garbled messages about your being busy and to call back. You hung up every other time."

Erin took a step back. "Say, Amanda, why don't I go get you a beer?"

"Thanks. I think I need one. It was a long drive."

Amanda waited a few moments until Erin was out of earshot. "So, care to explain why you were snuggling up to Officer Big-chest?"

"Cripes, Amanda, nothing happened. We were just talking. Honey, I—"

"Eat your food, Jake. I need a minute."

Jake chewed slowly, hoping Amanda's mood would improve with time. Erin returned with a beer in each hand. She gave one to Amanda.

"So, you just got in?"

"A little bit ago," Amanda said, and took a sip. "Quite the party over there."

"Isn't it wild? Are you going to make a sacrifice?"

"Huh?"

"Oh, right, you haven't heard." Erin explained the reason for the party and pointed to the darkening skies as proof of their results. "So, if we all make a donation, we'll be guaranteed good weather for the rest of the field school."

"It does seem like a good cause," Amanda said, laughing. "Maybe later. Jake and I need to catch up. Don't we, Jake?"

Jake nodded, his mouth full of chips.

Erin caught their meaning. "Sure, sure. But come on over in a little bit and have some fun."

Jake handed his empty plate to Erin, who headed off to rejoin the party. He gingerly reached out to Amanda.

"I'm not sure how mad to be at you," she said, and took a step back.

Jake dropped his arms, but gave her a little grin. "How about not at all?"

She frowned, but it didn't last.

"I am really glad to see you," Jake said. He took a step toward her. She didn't retreat this time. "You will not believe the week I had."

CHAPTER FORTY

Back in Jake's room, Amanda kicked off her shoes and settled onto the bed with her legs tucked beneath her. Jake took a sip of his beer and sat down on the chair, facing her. She smacked his pillow twice, waiting for him to speak.

"Let's see, where to begin?" Jake said. He started slowly, but eventually reached the point of the story where Maggie Devlin stopped by again.

"Who?"

"Maggie Devlin, the Environmental Coordinator for the Transportation Department. She came by right after the site got mentioned in the news. I told you about her at dinner at the High Hat."

"Oh, right. You said she worked around here at one time."

"Yeah, but I didn't know where, at first. Turns out she was at Christianson II during the Chapman College field school, same time Wardell was at Waconah."

"Small world. Is she still doing fieldwork?"

"Doubt it. She's kind of overweight, and I think she spends most of her time in the office arranging contracts. She's been out to the site a few times and each time she's ruder than before."

"That's odd," Amanda said. "Why does she bother to visit?"

"Beats me. She's always complaining how busy she is, but we're not working on a highway-salvage project so it's not anything she has to deal with. Maybe she's just brusque by nature."

"I'll bet she misses doing fieldwork and that keeps her coming back. But then she gets depressed seeing what she's missing, and starts snapping at people."

"I suppose," Jake said. "Anyway, while Maggie was there I finally heard back from Al Droessler, the photographer. We made an appointment to meet on Wednesday night. Heather and Scott came along."

Jake choked up, remembering the spry old man who joked with them while showing off his photos like a proud grandfather. The memory stood in sharp contrast to the image of the mess they saw the following day, and the taped-off silhouette marking where the body was found.

"On Thursday morning, Sheriff Rostlund arrived. Someone broke into Al's cabin that morning, while he was out. Al came back, and must have had a heart attack. He was dead. The sheriff asked us to go over and check out the crime scene, to help see what might have been stolen."

Amanda picked up the bed pillow and hugged it. "Wow. You weren't kidding when you said you had a rough week. It probably didn't help that we couldn't talk. You know, to let off some steam."

"Probably. It was pretty frustrating. The heat and humidity has been making everyone edgy, too."

"This storm should take care of that, at least," Amanda said, setting the pillow aside. "Listen to that wind."

They sat in silence of a moment, taking in the sounds of the howling wind, the rumbling thunder, and the music and yelling at the party. Amanda noticed Wardell's notebook on the table, picked it up, and thumbed through it.

"You know, you haven't mentioned Jacklyn Wardell's death at all."

"Haven't I?"

"No. The old field school and the photos, but nothing to do with her death."

Jake tilted his head, lost in thought. He left his chair and sat next to Amanda on the bed. "I think I'm over it. Since Al Droessler's death, it just seems like a foolish thing to waste my time on. Al did have some photos from the night she died, but you can't see anything except the storm." He decided not to bring up Pam Hauser's interest in the case, assuming any mention of the deputy would aggravate Amanda. "I need to focus my attention on the field school, period."

Amanda nodded with a relieved smile. "Good. That makes a lot of sense." She set the book aside.

Jake smiled in return and put his arm over her shoulders. "I'm sorry I didn't call more, or leave better messages."

"Me, too," Amanda said, and she leaned against him. "You and Pam were sitting pretty close together, you know."

"We were just talking. I think she was just, um, trying to be funny," Jake said. "I think she likes putting people off guard, you know, making them feel uncomfortable."

"Really? How many other times has she made you uncomfortable, Jake?"

He let out a sigh. "Honey, nothing happened. I think she just likes having someone new to talk with. It is a pretty small community, not much excitement."

"All right, you're forgiven. I guess. Shouldn't matter anyway now that I'm here to keep an eye on you. And her."

"Amanda, nothing is—"

"I'm just kidding, grumpy," she said, and gave him a playful shove. "Come on, let's head out and join the party. Besides, we need to throw something in the fire if we want smooth sailing for the rest of the field school."

CHAPTER FORTY-ONE

"I think you may have overdone it last night," Jake said as he surveyed the damage caused by the storm.

"Yeah, you could be right," Erin said, and took another sip of her coffee. Amanda and Scott stood nearby, the latter rubbing his forehead in a futile attempt to ease his hangover.

"Biggest storm I've ever seen," Amanda said. "And that wind! It was like a tornado."

The long-anticipated rain arrived around nine and grew in intensity over the next few hours. Jake and Amanda turned in soon after the rain started and within a short time most of the others had retreated to their tents. Only a few stalwarts remained around the bonfire. Before long, they too were driven to seek shelter as the icy rain lashed down, whipped along by the driving winds.

Around midnight, Jake and Amanda were awakened as several students trudged into the building, seeking refuge from the storm. A few more stumbled in, including Erin, until soon over a dozen people stood shivering in the hall, complaining of flooded tents and soaked sleeping bags. Jake found some extra blankets in a cabinet and passed them out. With Amanda's help, they set up makeshift sleeping areas and everyone was soon settled in for the night. Those still outside decided to tough it out or were too inebriated to notice.

By morning's light, it was easy to see why so many had moved into the building. Fallen branches, some fairly large, were everywhere. Several empty tents had collapsed, and clothing and garbage were strewn across the campsite.

"Any sign of Heather?"

"Uh-uh," Erin said. "I tried to wake her when I left the tent to come inside but she was out cold."

"Well, see if you can rouse her, and then we'd better do a tent-by-tent check, make sure everyone is accounted for," Jake said. "Scott, you start over there, and I'll take these."

"I'll take care of the kids in the building. Most of them are already awake."

"Thanks, Amanda. Meet you back here in a little bit."

The group made their rounds, joined by a reluctant, bleary-eyed Heather. Some of the students were less than thrilled to be disturbed, but before long the instructors had completed their task. They joined Jake and Amanda at a picnic table near the hall entrance.

"Well, it's official, one of the worst storms to hit Taylor Lake in the last decade," Jake said as he slipped his phone into his pocket. "Just got off the phone with Bob Jingst. They've got trees and power lines down all over the park, so it will probably be a while before they get over here. He said to just clean up what we can and he should have a crew out here to deal with the big stuff later today. Everyone accounted for? No injuries?"

They all nodded, sipping the coffee Amanda had retrieved from the kitchen. A few students were now moving about, heading into the kitchen or toward the bathrooms.

"Some of the tents are soaked pretty bad," Scott said. "Couple of them might need a day or two to dry out."

"We can string some more lines between the trees to dry out bedding," Erin said. "That should help."

"If necessary, some of the students can sleep in the building again until their stuff dries out." Jake scanned the campsite, counting the number of damaged tents. "Hey Scott, did you check that tent, near the tree line? You were closer to it than me."

"Uh, yeah, but nobody was using it last night."

"What do you mean?"

"That's the, um, couple's tent," Scott said. "After the tents were set up and everyone had picked theirs, we had one extra. Heather and I thought we could use it for overnight visitors, or if somebody got sick. Didn't pay any attention to it after that."

"A few weeks later I caught two people coming out of it one morning," Heather said. "They told me the students worked out an arrangement for couples to use the tent when they wanted some alone time. That way they didn't have to force anybody out of their own tents."

"Nice set-up," Erin said with a laugh. "Amanda, maybe you can add a couple's tent to the archaeology exhibit at the History Center."

"Ah, no, I don't think so. My boss is big on new ideas, but that might be going too far," Amanda said. "Out of curiosity, how did they schedule time in the tent? Did they reserve it, or . . . ?"

"Oh, that was easy," Scott said. "If the tent was in use, red flagging tape was tied on top of the door flap."

"Well, that explains why we're running out of red flagging tape," Jake said.

"It worked really well," Scott said. "Everyone respected the arrangement, more or less."

"More or less?"

"Once in a while you'd get someone who'd hang around outside, or wander by again and again. Nobody will own up to it, though."

"Hmm." Jake was curious. "Could it have been someone from another campsite? That tent isn't too far from the trail that leads to the highway."

"I suppose," Scott said. "But why would they be over here?"

"Cause they're perverts, that's why," Heather said, massaging her forehead. "Are we about done here? I want to go back to bed for a while."

"Sure. I'll put up some signs asking everyone to pitch in later this morning to help clean up. Other than that, you are all on your own today."

CHAPTER FORTY-TWO

Puffy white clouds drifted across a blue sky on Monday morning, as the Waconah field school began one of its last few weeks. The weekend storm had done minimal damage to the site. Most of the tarps held puddled water and two trench walls had collapsed where running water had seeped between the protective sandbags. The reddish-brown clay on the trench floors was slick with moisture and a few students lost their footing and ended up with stained backsides. After helping with the morning prep work and informing the crew of the new, laid-back plans for the last few weeks, Jake perched on one of the back-dirt piles and caught up on his field notes. After an hour, Bryant wandered over.

"Hey, Bryant. What's up?"

"Not much. We're almost to the bottom of that storage pit near the longhouse. Should be done this afternoon."

"Good. I'll figure out where to put you guys after lunch."

"Okay, sure," Bryant said. "Uh, do you have a second, or are you busy?"

"No, not really," Jake said, setting his notebook aside. "What can I do for you?"

"Well, I was wondering if you'd be willing to serve as my advisor, starting next semester."

"Wow, that's not what I expected," Jake said. "Isn't Professor Kelley your advisor?"

"He was, I mean he is, now. I'm just thinking about my options, but I'm starting to think that I'd get a lot more out of this project. I mean, if you have room for me."

"Well, what does he have set up for your thesis project?"

"Nothing yet, at least nothing specific. I was talking to Scott over the weekend, and I realized I should really be moving forward faster if I want to get my master's degree before long. I'm already getting buried in student loan debt."

"Doesn't your graduate assistantship help with that?"

"Uh, I only got a small stipend during the fall semester. Dr. Kelley said he didn't get budget approval to continue it after that, and he only had limited funds for all his grad students."

Jake frowned, recalling that Clark only had two or three grad students working in the archaeology lab during the past school year. Even with budget limitations, he should have been able to hire twice as many people.

"And, to be honest, I think I could benefit from more field experience," Bryant said with a nervous laugh. He looked around the site. "I'm learning a lot here, a lot more than I thought I would."

"Doesn't Clark, I mean Dr. Kelley, have some fieldwork planned for next summer? He was talking about a project at one of our long-term planning sessions."

"Maybe. I don't know for sure. I've tried to get in touch with him but I haven't heard back."

"Maybe the email never went through. The Internet access at the campsite is pretty bad."

"I know," Bryant said. "But I've sent messages from the library too, and all my other email messages are going through. And I must have called him a dozen times in the last few weeks."

"You called him?"

"Yeah, at his office, but I always get voice mail. I tried the department secretary too, but she wasn't very helpful. Just said she'd leave a message, but never said if he got it or not."

"Hmm. Let me try later today and see what I can find out," Jake said. "In any event, you'll have to get his signature on changing advisors before we can arrange anything. I'd be happy to be your advisor, but have you thought about any of the other faculty? Maybe Dr. Chang?"

Bryant shook his head. "I talked to some of the other students and they all think you're a great advisor. Helpful, good listener, always there when they need you. Never too busy to answer questions."

Jake smiled, but couldn't help wondering how he could keep Heather and Bryant apart in a crowded lab setting. Bryant took a step away before turning back to Jake.

"I had an appointment with Dr. Kelley last semester, to see if he had finalized the field project he mentioned. He told me I could be his field assistant, you know, a salaried position. His door was closed when I got there, so I knocked. Nothing. Knocked again, because, you know, we had a meeting scheduled. He whipped open the door and I asked if he was busy. He sort of glared at me and said 'I'm always busy!' I felt bad, figured I messed up the time or something, but looking back on it, I think I got the raw end of the deal."

Jake nodded. "Okay. Let me make some calls and we'll pursue this when we get back to campus."

Bryant walked back to his feature and Jake pulled out his phone. He dialed Clark's office number, only to be directed to his voice mail account. Curious, he called the Anthropology and Archaeology Department office number.

"Hi, Rochelle. It's Jake Caine."

"Oh, hello Jake. How are things in the great north woods?"

"Fine, just fine. Had a big storm over the weekend but we managed to stay dry. Say, I was wondering if Clark Kelley was in today?"

"Did you try his office number?"

"Yeah, but it went right to voice mail."

"Well, he's not in according to the big board," she said, referring to the magnetic in/out board used to track departmental staff. "Hang on a second."

Her voice faded and Jake pictured her leaning away from her desk. "There's a post-it note by his name, says 'vacation' but no date or anything."

"That's it?"

"That's all. Hold on, Janice just walked in. Let me ask her."

Jake took a sip of water from his canteen and looked across the site. He spotted Amanda, who gave him a wave. He smiled and waved in return.

"Jake? Janice says Clark took some vacation time last week, but she thought he was supposed to be back today. Actually, near as we can determine, he's been out of the office for at least a week, maybe ten days."

"That's odd. No wonder I can't get in touch with him."

"Yes, Janice, I'll tell him. Janice says she thought Clark was helping you on your dig."

"He was up here a few weeks ago, but only for a couple of days. And he stopped by briefly last Tuesday, but just for a few minutes. He said he was in a hurry to leave. I assumed he was heading back to campus."

"Hmm. Well, I don't know what else to tell you," Rochelle said. "Do you want to talk to Dr. Chang? She's in her office. And Musket is back from Michigan. I saw him this morning in the coffee room, if you need him."

"No, thanks. I guess it can wait. Not that important, anyway."

"All right. See you in a few weeks."

Jake closed his phone, wondering where Clark had gone after leaving Waconah. As much as he disliked Clark, not knowing his whereabouts was somewhat disquieting. The last thing Jake needed at this point was for Clark to return unexpectedly and disrupt the last few weeks of the field school.

By early afternoon, Jake had convinced himself that Clark's disappearance had nothing to do with him, and the field school would be spared. Neither Amanda nor Heather saw anything sinister in his absence and both agreed there was little chance he would return. Jake moved about the site, helping out where needed and chatting with the students. With the end of the field school in sight, the pressure was off and he was able to enjoy himself for a change. Jake was sharing an amusing story from his own field school with some students when a police car appeared at the top of the ridge.

"It's probably nothing," Jake said to no one in particular as he walked toward the parking lot. A few students took notice, but most showed no interest, as the sheriff's vehicles had become a common occurrence at the site. Jake reached the lot as Deputy Hauser stepped out of her vehicle.

"Hi, Jake. You survived the storm, I see."

"Hey, Pam. Yeah, couple of soaked tents and some branches down, but otherwise no problems."

"Good, but I was referring to the reunion with your girlfriend," Pam said. She searched the area and spotted Amanda, watching from a trench. Pam waved and Amanda responded in kind. "Sorry if I got you in trouble."

"No, everything worked out fine. Eventually."

"Glad to hear it. I'll try and behave myself from now on," she said with a devilish grin. "I do have some news, though, if you have a minute."

"Sure, what's up?"

"Well, we finally located Mark Winters."

"Really? Did he have anything to do with—"

Pam shook her head. "He got picked up for drunk and

disorderly in Crandon, last Wednesday. He's been drying out in a holding cell ever since, so he has an iron-clad alibi for Al's murder."

"Wow. That's a relief, I guess. Wait a minute. You said murder, right?"

"Yes, it's classified as a homicide. There was evidence of a struggle and some bruising on the body. Winters has an alibi, but we might have more to go on now as far as Wardell's death."

Jake's heart sank. He thought this was all behind him.

"Before we located Winters, Sheriff Rostlund tracked down Mark's uncle, you know, the one who owns the trailer where he crashes. The uncle is in an assisted-living facility in Milwaukee and it turns out his daughter has his power of attorney. Let's just say she isn't too fond of her cousin Mark. Anyway, she gave us permission to search the place, but the sheriff waited until this morning so he could get a court order, just to cover all the legal issues. Anyway, about the same time the boys in Crandon realized they had the guy we were looking for."

"If Mark was locked up all week, why did you bother to search his place?"

"The exact timeline wasn't clear right away, so the sheriff decided to go ahead with the search. And I think it's a good thing he did."

"So what did you find?"

"The place was a dump. Trash everywhere. Fast-food containers, dirty clothes, and a ton of beer cans. Bunch of old books and papers, too. But in the back room, that's where it got weird."

"Pam, you're killing me here. Are you going to tell me or not?"

"Okay, okay. Winters has a damn shrine set up for Professor Wardell. There are pictures tacked to the wall, behind a table covered with candles. Freaking fire hazard. I'm surprised he hadn't burned the place down already."

"Are any of the photos from Al Droessler's place?"

"No. All of Al's prints have 'Droessler' stamped on the back. These are just ordinary photos from Wardell's field school. But we also found an old bandana, a trowel with 'JW' carved on the handle, a couple of arrowheads, and a little clay snowman made out of that red mud you get around here."

"Wow. It's like something out of a horror movie," Jake said. The depth of Mark's twisted guilt and devotion to Jacklyn Wardell's memory was staggering.

"You said it. Pretty creepy stuff. I'm sure Winters was definitely involved in Wardell's death."

"We're not going down this road again, are we?" Jake said. "I told you, I think it would be best if I steer clear of your investigations."

"I know, I remember what you said. But come on, this could be a big break. Once Al's case is solved, I plan to thoroughly investigate the Wardell case."

"Do you really think Mark is involved? Besides, even if he was, why would he come clean now?"

Pam shrugged. "We also found a cigar box full of weed stashed in one of the bookcases. So, we've got him regardless. If it turns out he was dealing the stuff, its just more leverage to use against him."

Jake felt relieved that Mark had nothing to do with the break-in at Al's cabin, but that didn't mean he was in the clear for Jacklyn Wardell's death. "The shrine in his trailer could just be his way of remembering someone important," Jake argued. "I'm not saying I understand how his mind works, but it does seem like something he would do. I think memories, good and bad, are a big deal to him."

"Even if Mark wasn't involved, which I doubt," Pam said, "he still may know something important about Wardell's death, even if he doesn't realize it. And we have a whole parcel of suspects. Everyone on Sheriff Kojarski's list, except Herb Keeling, unless he hired someone else to do his dirty work. And what about the girl, Amy? We know she was there that night, but we don't have any specifics on her movements. She's Clark Kelley's alibi and he's her alibi. Convenient, don't you think? C'mon Jake, you can't tell me you're not still curious."

That was something he hadn't considered. Could Amy be involved, in a more direct way than just meeting Clark? Deep down, Jake was tempted. He looked around and watched his students digging, screening, and mastering the fine art of archaeological site excavation.

"All right, I admit it, you've got me hooked. Count me in," Jake said. "But, for now I need to focus on finishing up the field school."

"That's fine. I'm not really going to do much until we have Al's killer behind bars."

"Okay. I will tell you this, though, since it might relate to the break-in." Jake sighed, anticipating the trouble this might bring in the future. "Clark Kelley has been out of the office, on vacation, since he visited here the Saturday before last. No one at the department knows where he is. The last thing Clark told them was that he was going to be working here, at Waconah."

"So Professor Kelley is unaccounted for and may have been in the area during the break-in. Is that what you're telling me?" Pam pulled her notebook out of her pocket and began taking notes.

"Yeah, I guess. You know, this may only be significant if Al's murder and Wardell's death are related."

"I know. Officially, there's nothing to tie them together."

Jake paused, wondering how much idle gossip he dared spread about his departmental nemesis. "One of my colleagues told me that after Wardell's death, a female student erupted during class and got into a shouting match with Clark."

"Over Wardell's death?"

"Yes. The department hushed it up, so I don't know any details. Heck, now that I think about it, I don't even know the student's name."

"Sounds like a long shot, as far as the break-in," Pam said as she closed her notebook. "But I'll run it by Sheriff Rostlund and he can decide whether or not to pursue it. But I think I'll want that girl's name once I start investigating the Wardell case full time."

"I'll try and get the name for you, once I get back to the university. But no more until then, all right?"

"Sure, partner," Pam said as she opened the car door. "You know, you don't have enough enthusiasm to be a great Dr. Watson, but we could make a pretty good team. I have detective-level police training and you have an analytical, scientific background. Working a crime scene is a lot like archaeology. You try to reconstruct events based on minimal or contrary evidence."

"I suppose. But for now, I'm keeping my analytical skills focused on a thousand-year-old Oneota village, where they belong."

CHAPTER FORTY-THREE

Jake rolled over in his cot, rubbed his eyes, and silently cursed the low-level chatter coming from the kitchen. A morning person by nature, he could not seem to rouse himself. He turned again, trying to shake the uncomfortable feeling that he was forgetting something. Something important. The more he tried to focus his thoughts, the less clear it became. As Amanda nudged open the door with a cup of coffee in each hand, Jake pushed himself into a sitting position.

"Better get a move-on, hon," she said, handing him a cup. "You're running late this morning."

He nodded and took a sip of the hazelnut java. A few of the students had decided to improve on his bulk purchase of inexpensive, generic coffee and experimented each morning with a variety of flavor additives. He was forced to veto their suggestion of Irish coffee Fridays, however.

"One of the perks of being the boss," Jake said, "is that I am free to be late if I want." It came across more grouchy than funny.

"Are you feeling all right this morning? You were tossing and turning a lot last night."

"Yeah. Guess I didn't sleep real well. Had some weird dreams."

"Ooh, tell me!" Amanda made a hobby of interpreting people's dreams, a habit she picked up from an elderly aunt who read tea leaves and dabbled with runes. "Unless it was one of *those* dreams. Deputy Hauser wasn't in it, was she?"

"No, nothing like that. Probably came from what I heard yesterday, and what we were talking about last night. Clark and Mark Winters were chasing me around the site and I kept falling into open units. Then, uh, Heather dropped a pot and there was blood everywhere. I think Al Droessler was in the background, too, taking pictures of everyone."

"I think a lot of this is on a subconscious level. Maybe your brain is trying to clean itself out. Your mind is grappling with the two different stories you heard from Mark and Clark Kelley about Jacklyn's last night. Hmm. The open units could be your concern about the site and finishing the field school in a few weeks. Al was there because of his association with the site, and the blood might symbolize his murder."

She had such a studious expression that Jake gulped the coffee to hide his smirk. He had learned long ago not to make fun of her no matter what conclusions she reached. "What about Heather?"

"Well, you told me a few weeks ago that you were concerned about her finishing her Ph.D. proposal on time. Maybe the broken pot represents her dissertation." She frowned, not satisfied with her interpretation. "Of course, it has been a long field school and you've been pushing yourself a lot lately. You probably just need a break."

By the time they reached Waconah, Jake felt more like himself. He was soon busy organizing students and answering questions, and the shadows of the previous night vanished. Charlie Garath, Art, and three more NEWAS volunteers arrived midmorning. They brought two boxes of doughnuts that were devoured by the hungry students.

As the midafternoon sun high overhead began to drop westward, Jake occupied his usual perch on the large dirt pile next to the trench containing the longhouse. From his vantage point, he could view the entire excavation with the rolling waters of Taylor Lake in the background. Jotting down the results of the day's work in his thick notebook, he paused to flip back and review some old entries. His thoughts were interrupted as Heather and Amanda clambered up the hill and joined him.

"Hey, boss. Paula and Michelle finished their wall profile, so I told them to start two units over the midden north of the house, okay?"

"Yeah, that's fine," Jake said. "With luck they can expose enough of it so we can tie it to the house basin before we close down."

"Feeling any better since this morning?" Amanda asked, and Heather gave her a curious look as she started to explain Jake's rough night and weird dreams.

"I'm fine," Jake said, hoping to cut Amanda off before she got into a lengthy discussion of dream interpretation. He also didn't care to antagonize Heather by airing any concerns about her dissertation research. "I was just thinking about how much we accomplished this season, compared to Wardell's field school. We've got a great bunch of students. Some of them will be fine archaeologists one day."

"They are a good bunch of kids," Amanda said. "Of course, you have to consider that Wardell's field school was shorter. Everything came to an end when she died."

Heather, correcting notes on a feature form, stopped abruptly and brushed some reddish soil off the page. "I think it's kind of eerie how aspects of her death popped up now. Who would have thought that Mark Winters would show up here, after all these years? And a burglar kills Al Droessler, the old photographer. What are the odds of that happening in a desolate place like this? Poor old guy."

"According to the sheriff, lots of isolated cabins and houses are easy targets up here. Not a lot of neighbors around to keep watch, and thieves keep track of when people are gone for extended periods. Al came back at the wrong time."

A few moments of grim silence passed. "As for Jacklyn Wardell," Jake said, "I suppose it was inevitable that her work, and her death, kind of intruded into our field school. It all ended here for her. Excavating Waconah would have bolstered her career. Probably would have made her a lock for a tenured professorship."

"Instead, a stupid boating accident ended it all. All that work, struggling to get her degree, teaching, and all of it was for nothing." Heather stared out across the lake. Without another word, she rose and rushed down the dirt pile and joined some students at a nearby screen.

Jake and Amanda watched her leave. "Guess this whole business bothered her more than I thought," Jake said.

"She's feeling the pressure, just like you," Amanda said. "Heather might not let much slip through that tough, flippant exterior, but I'll bet she's as worried about finishing her dissertation and starting a career as the next student. She just hides it well. It's just discouraging to think about Jacklyn Wardell's ambitions coming to such a drastic end at a pretty young age."

"I suppose our—all right, *my*—playing amateur detective hasn't helped things either. I guess Linda Wardell got to me more than I thought when she brought me those papers. Jacklyn's death obviously hit her pretty hard, and still does. I suppose getting to the bottom of this was just wishful thinking. My nosing around hasn't accomplished anything, has it?"

Amanda gave him a supportive, one-armed hug. "I wouldn't say that. You managed to track down Mark Winters, and he may have gotten some closure out of this."

"You think so? Even after getting arrested in Crandon and

facing drug charges?"

"It could help him in the long run. You know, hitting rock bottom and getting scared straight. Maybe he needed to get over Jacklyn in order to get the rest of his life in order."

"I suppose time will tell."

"It's like you tell your students, Jake. In archaeology you never have all the answers. You collect the data, make your interpretations, and draw conclusions. But no matter how much you think you know about the past, deep down there are always mysteries that you can never fully understand."

Chapter Forty-Four

With the field school winding down, Jake announced that the lecture that evening would be the last for the season. He excused Heather, arguing that he wanted Scott to get more experience speaking before a crowd. She didn't argue, so Jake knew she was happy to have some time to herself.

Scott led a lively discussion on some of the more significant pottery found during the field school, and how the information from Waconah could be used to address research questions on the late prehistoric period in the region. Jake prodded them along as talk ebbed and added comments as he thought necessary. After a half hour, they opened things up for a question-and-answer session and general discussion. The conversation turned to a comparison of the pottery from the Waconah and Christianson II sites. Erin pulled some partially reconstructed vessels and large rim sherds from the collection to illustrate differences in form, decoration, and manufacture.

"Now, as we discussed weeks ago, the Christianson II site is almost exclusively Late Woodland," Scott said as Jake and Erin distributed sample sherds to the students. "The conical and animal-shaped mounds on the upper terrace, and the large mound just northeast of Waconah, were built by Woodland peoples. All of this took place prior to the occupation at Waconah by later Oneota groups."

"The Woodland pottery recovered during the Chapman College dig at Christianson is typical," Jake said. "The pottery is tempered with grit or crushed stone, the exterior surfaces are marked with cord impressions, and decoration consists of single cord marks and tool impressions. The Waconah vessels," he said, raising a medium-sized jar in the air, "in contrast, have crushed mussel shell for temper, thin smoothed walls, and the pots constrict toward the opening with everted or flaring rims. Decoration is more common on later Oneota vessels, generally as trailed, curved, or angled lines."

A timid hand rose in the back row. "Professor Caine, uh, this might be a dumb question but, um, why are the pot sherds from the two sites different colors?" Michelle said. "Does that relate to how they were fired?"

"In some cases the method of firing can affect the final color of a vessel, but in this instance the coloration is from different sources of clay. The Waconah potters used the dense, fine red clay we found in the subsoil at the site. The Woodland folks at Christianson II used a poor-quality clay from some other location, probably from the terrace or a creek bed to the north or east." Jake held up two sherds, one from each site. Following his cue, Erin passed additional examples to the students.

Another hand popped up. "But if the red clay is so much better, why didn't the Woodland people use that stuff too?"

Jake considered the question for a moment, absently wiping clay dust on the front of his gray T-shirt. "Well, the Christianson II people may not have been aware of the good red clay at our site. Keep in mind that we only encounter it when we dig deep into the subsoil, like we did in the big trench and in the bottom of some of our excavation units. Until the Oneota set up housekeeping and started digging their deep storage pits, they might not have known it was there, either. Once they did find it, their potters probably were thrilled. Red is a powerful color in Native American cosmology, too."

A smattering of laughter broke out as the sherds traveled

around the room. Some of the Waconah sherds had been poorly fired in antiquity and red blemishes began to appear on the hands, arms, and clothing of the students.

"So, the Waconah site held a great deal of value for the Oneota," Jake said. "Easy access to water and abundant aquatic plants and animals for food. The higher ground east of the site has a nice loamy soil that would have been good for growing corn, squash, and beans. Could be one reason the later inhabitants decided to fortify the village rather than move to a more defensible location. Lots of resources, and also the only place to find the fine . . . red . . . clay . . ."

The words stalled as he spoke them and Jake stared agape at the students, most of who were stained with red clay. Images from the past few weeks flashed through his mind: of students smeared with the newly exposed red clay, red marks on the paperwork and artifact bags, and crimson-tinted water draining like blood across the floor of the camp shower. The only place one could get covered in red clay.

"She lied," he mumbled. "She lied."

Amanda, Scott, and Erin were the first to notice the sudden change in Jake's demeanor. As he continued to stare open-mouthed at no one in particular, more and more students took note and grew concerned.

"Jake, are you feeling all right? Jake!"

Amanda gave him a gentle shove, and Jake came out of his stupor. Glancing about, he regained his composure. He told Scott to wrap up the lecture and asked Erin to collect the artifacts, and then led Amanda past the students and into the cool evening air outside.

"Are you okay? What's the matter with you?" Amanda said.

Jake brushed at the red stain on his shirt, holding his smeared hand in front of her face. "She lied," he repeated. Amanda shook her head, apparently failing to understand.

"She lied, Amanda. Maggie Devlin lied! Remember what Sheriff Kojarski told me about her alibi? The night of Jacklyn's death, Maggie said she'd been working at Christianson II in the evening, correcting mistakes made by some students. No one was with her, but they all remembered her showing up at their campsite smeared with red clay. The only way she could have gotten covered with red clay was if she was at Waconah that night!"

Amanda visibly shivered. "Geez, Jake, I don't know. It doesn't mean she had anything to do with Jacklyn's death. There could be some other explanation."

"Such as?"

"I don't know. Maybe she was having an affair with Clark, too," she said with a half smile.

Jake stared at her for a few seconds, then let out a short laugh when he realized what she was doing. Her joke broke the tension, if only for a moment. "Ugh. What do you women see in him, anyway?"

"Hey, don't include me in that group. I only fall for rugged, outdoorsy types with sexy goatees." Amanda draped her arms across his broad shoulders and kissed him.

"And here I thought you loved me for my mind. All this time I'm nothing but a trophy boyfriend."

Their repartee was interrupted as the students began exiting the hall. Jake smiled and nodded as they passed, assuring them he was fine, just tired. A few expressed their concern, but most of the talk centered on plans for the rest of the evening and ideas for an end of the field school party.

Moving from the entryway, Jake and Amanda sat down at the picnic table. "Still, Amanda, how would Maggie have gotten all that red clay on her if she hadn't been somewhere at Waconah that night? And unless she was a totally different person back then, I don't see her as someone who would do fieldwork, solo, after hours. She reminds me of Clark that way. He avoids physical labor like the plague."

"Maybe," Amanda said, starting to come around to Jake's line of thought. "If Maggie was like Clark, she would have dragged the offending students out to the site and barked orders at them until the work was done to her satisfaction, no matter how long it took."

"We need to look into this further," Jake said. He looked at his watch. "If Maggie was there and is lying about it, she must know something about that night. I'm going to call her in the morning and see if I can't get her to come down for another visit."

CHAPTER FORTY-FIVE

As always, the best-laid plans oft times go awry. After calling Maggie Devlin's office every half hour that morning, Jake was heartily sick of hearing her voice mail message.

The sour taste in his mouth deepened as Jake started to put his phone away. He halted abruptly as another idea came to him. A quick search through the directory and he had the number he needed.

"Transportation Department District 4, Engineering. Gary Marquardt here."

"Gary, this is Jake Caine, from Wisconsin State University. Professor Mahler and I surveyed a highway corridor for you a few years back."

"Oh, yeah, hey how's it going? Construction crews are going to break ground on the new route next spring." He paused and Jake could hear the shuffling of papers in the background. "There's not some problem with one of the sites on that route, is there? I thought we had that all cleared."

"No, nothing like that. All your compliance paperwork is in order, so you're good to go. The reason I'm calling—"

"Hey, since I've got you on the line," Gary said, "When do you think you'll be done with Maggie Devlin? Personally," his voice lowered, "I think she's a royal pain in the backside, but there's a huge pile of project reports on her desk that need to be cleared. A couple of them are priority rush, too."

"What are you talking about?" Jake said. "Sure, Maggie was

down here a few times to see the dig, but I haven't seen her in over a week."

"Huh. Well, her last email said you guys were having all kinds of problems, and since she's the district archaeologist it was urgent that she be there," Gary said. "She calls or emails about every other day and keeps telling me she needs a little more time."

"Do you know where she's staying? There must be some mix-up here."

"Yeah, just a sec. Here we go. She's over at the Plymouth Inn. State has a contract with them for lodging."

"All right, thanks Gary. Let me look into this and I'll get back to you."

"Fine, do that. Look, Jake, you're an okay guy and I don't know what kind of crap Devlin's trying to pull, but you find her, tell her that she'd better be in the office on Monday or there's going to be hell to pay."

The beep ending the call barely registered in Jake's ear.

CHAPTER FORTY-SIX

"Jake, slow down! You can hardly see the road."

The approaching storm had reached the area by late afternoon and heavy rain continued to fall as Jake and Amanda drove to the Plymouth Inn.

"I really wish you would have stayed at the camp, Amanda."

She let out an impatient sigh, not wishing to continue the argument. "Look, Jake, there's something very weird going on here, and while I don't think Maggie Devlin is a murderer, I certainly don't want you confronting her all by yourself."

"Well, she does have some explaining to do, you have to admit that."

"I do, honey. That's why I'm here."

Jake scowled, feeling that he had been outflanked in the conversation as he struggled to follow the rain-slicked highway. "Nothing bad is going to happen. I just want to talk to her."

"I know."

"Besides, I left a message with Pam . . . uh, Deputy Hauser. She can follow up with Maggie if she feels like it's necessary." After convincing Amanda that he needed to talk to Maggie Devlin face-to-face, she had countered with the proposal that he turn all his information over to his *other girlfriend,* the police officer. To placate Amanda, Jake called Pam and left a voice-mail message describing the lie in Maggie's original alibi, the confusion over her recent whereabouts, and their plan to visit her hotel and get more information.

Reaching the Plymouth Inn, Jake and Amanda found a parking spot near the entrance and made a quick dash into the lobby. The bored teenager behind the counter barely glanced in their direction as they entered. She managed to tear her attention away from the latest reality show debacle on the jumbo TV long enough to give them Maggie Devlin's room number, without even asking who they were.

"Hotel security must not be part of the regular service here," Jake quipped as they climbed the stairs to the second floor.

Amanda nodded and studied the faded plastic signs in the hallway until she found their destination. "Well, now what?" she whispered.

"I guess we just knock," Jake said. He leaned toward the door and heard the muted sounds of the television.

"Wait. What are you going to say?"

"I guess let's use the story I called her about. You know, unusual sherds at Waconah and we're wondering if they could be from Christianson II."

Amanda gave a noncommittal shrug and Jake rapped on the door. He heard the creak of bedsprings and some rustling. "Just a minute."

A drawer slammed shut, and Jake noticed the squeak of the floorboards on the opposite side of the door. "Yes?"

Jake sensed her eyeing him through the peephole. "Maggie? Maggie, it's Jake Caine, from the dig. I, uh, we had some questions about some pottery we found, and . . ."

His words were cut off by a loud clank as the security bolt was unlocked. The door swung open and Maggie, silhouetted in the dark entryway, stepped back and gestured them in. "Oh, right, right. I got your message, but I'm just so busy now. Didn't have a chance to return your call." She turned her back to them and shuffled into the room.

"Sorry to drop by unannounced," Jake said, trailing a few

feet behind her as Amanda closed the door. "One of your co-workers told us where to find you and since it was so close I . . ."

Jake stopped short, taken aback by the condition of the room. Clothes were scattered over half the bed and parts of the floor, with a few articles sticking out of drawer tops like little flags. A small garbage can was overflowing with fast-food bags and crushed soda cans. A half-empty wine bottle sat precariously near the edge of a small table on the far side of the queen-sized bed. The tops of the desk and dresser were covered with papers, file folders, and large highway construction maps. A laptop sat on the desk, buried beneath a folded newspaper and an empty pizza box. A stale, pungent odor permeated the room, as if it had not been cleaned in weeks.

The state of the room was mirrored in Maggie's appearance. She stood on the far side of the bed, near the table, wearing faded sweatpants and an ill-fitting purple T-shirt decorated with food crumbs and condiment stains. Deep, dark bags hung under her eyes and her hair was matted down in the back and on one side, as if she had been sleeping on it. Her exposed skin was blotchy and her hand trembled as she reached down to retrieve a large brown purse. She pushed the wine bottle aside and set the purse on the table.

Jake noticed Maggie watching him, waiting for him to continue. "Oh, this is Amanda Rohm, my girlfriend. She works at the Mississippi Valley History Center and has been helping out at the site. They're interested in setting up an Oneota exhibit."

Maggie nodded with a halfhearted wave. Amanda smiled. "It's, uh, nice to finally meet you. Sorry to barge in like this. We probably should have called here first."

Maggie looked around the room. "Well, as you can see I wasn't expecting anyone. Not that I mind, but how did you find me, again?"

The look in her eyes suggested she did mind, but Jake tried to make light of it. "I was talking to one of the Transportation Department engineers, uh, about an old site we cleared for him. Your name came up and he mentioned you were staying here. While you're doing field inspections."

"Oh, I see. That's fine, then. You said something about pottery?"

"Yeah. We've got a feature, toward the north end of the site. Been pulling out lots of Woodland ceramics. The clay has a very sandy paste, which is unusual. Most of the Woodland stuff we've found so far is, well, just typical, general Woodland pottery. Nothing special."

"The material from Christianson II is fairly unique," Maggie said, folding her arms. "Sand inclusions are a distinguishing trait, too, but since that material hasn't been properly reported, not too many people know about it."

Jake caught her reference to Professor Schumholtz and his unfinished manuscript. "This does sound like we're on the right trail, then."

"Can I see them?"

"See what?"

"The sherds," Maggie said, frowning. "I assume you brought them with you?"

Jake's eyes widened. "Uh, sure." He turned to Amanda. "Amanda, do you have that box of sherds?"

"I thought you had them," Amanda said. "Did we leave them in the car?"

"No, I thought you grabbed them. I'll bet they're still sitting on the table back at the lab," Jake said, turning his attention back to Maggie. "Man, this is embarrassing. We drive all this way, through the storm, and we forgot the damn sherds." He gave her a foolish grin and tapped his forehead as a joke.

"Huh. Guess you drove all this way for nothing, then." Maggie wasn't smiling.

"Not necessarily," Jake said. "From what you told me about the sand, I think they definitely could be Christianson II ceramics. Maybe the next time you're nearby, you could stop by the site and I can show you then."

"I don't think so," Maggie snapped, unfolding her arms. "I am terribly busy right now. Dozens of projects to deal with, you know." She gestured at the mounds of paperwork littering her room.

"Yeah, sure, I can see that." Jake took a step around the bed to inspect the cluttered forms more closely. "Must be a lot of highway projects around here. Kind of surprising, I didn't think they were doing that much in this area."

"Well, they are. It's easier for me to stay on the road sometimes, rather than drive back to the office every other day."

"That makes sense. Say, this project looks familiar," Jake said as he picked up a thick bundle of papers from the desk.

"Don't touch those! I mean, you'll mess up my files. I, I have a system."

"Sorry," he said. "Didn't mean any harm."

Jake set the file down. As he did, the corner of a large black-and-white photograph caught his eye. Curious, he pulled it out to find an image of Jacklyn Wardell screening alongside two young students. He turned it over and saw "Droessler" stamped on the back.

"This is one of Al Droessler's prints."

Jake turned as Maggie reached into her oversized purse. She pulled out a small revolver and pointed it at his chest.

CHAPTER FORTY-SEVEN

"Just put that photo down, right now. And you, missy, you just stay nice and still."

Jake gingerly placed the photo down on the top of the pile, eyes never leaving the gleaming end of the gun. "Amanda . . ."

"Shut up. I'll do the talking now. You," Maggie said to Amanda, "walk over to the door, real slow, and lock the dead-bolt. Then you come right back over here. Try anything and your boyfriend will have a big hole where his heart used to be."

Amanda whimpered once and sniffled, but crept to the door and locked it as instructed. She walked back to where Jake stood. He took a protective step in front of her, half-blocking her from Maggie.

"I suppose you think you have all the answers, don't you, Professor Caine? Big-shot at WSU, so you can come around here and stir up trouble? Dig up a few old ghosts and make everyone miserable?"

Jake stared at her, uncertain how to reply or even if he should. He saw the wild look in her eyes and didn't want to antagonize her further. The short barrel of her gun jerked and bobbed as she spoke.

"All you ivory-tower academics are the same," Maggie said. "Get the world handed to you, never have to slave and suffer like I did at the Christianson site. You just dig here and then there, making your students do all the work."

Jake's mind raced. It was obvious that Maggie was more than

capable of antagonizing herself, based on the increasing hysteria in her voice. He estimated the distance between them, wondering if he should try to subdue her before things escalated further.

"But I couldn't go back to Christianson. Even after that old fool Schumholtz gave up on it, off to loot another site that he would never write up. Oh, and god forbid he let anyone else do anything with *his* data! All my dissertation committee could talk about was how I had to go back out in the field, dig more units, find more artifacts. Easy for them to say, sitting behind their big oak desks, not caring one bit about students like me. The illustrious Dr. Schumholtz never even made it to my last proposal defense. 'Something came up,' he said, as if my future wasn't important. All those years I suffered under that pompous ass, all for nothing since I couldn't go back to those sites, not after what happened!"

Jake shuffled forward slightly, hoping to close the distance between him and Maggie. But then what? He could only get so close before she would notice, and then react. And what would Amanda do? Would she break for the door and get help, or freeze and be in even greater danger?

"So the renowned, student-friendly Chapman College let me go. Reassigned my teaching assistantship and I was left to fend for myself. Nice treatment after all I gave them. I managed to snag some teaching jobs, though, without any help from any of them."

Maggie paused, breathing hard. Her eyes narrowed as she glared at Jake, and he suspected she noticed his slight movement. Amanda placed her hand on the small of Jake's back, as if to warn him not to try anything.

"And I couldn't apply for the archaeology position at WSU, when it opened after her death," Maggie said, resuming her diatribe. "It was absurd, a job I was more than qualified for, after all. But I couldn't apply, because of what had happened.

What if they started asking questions? I should have gotten that job before Jackie anyway, but she had finished her dissertation, as if it makes a difference. Ha! I could have been done years before her if I had gotten a little support."

Jake forced himself to remain calm as he evaluated the situation. As crazy as she seemed, he didn't think Maggie would try to shoot them, at least not in a crowded hotel. That might be the key. Stall for time, keep them in the hotel, until . . . what? Talk her out of it? Bluff their way out?

"Then I got my job with the Transportation Department," Maggie said with pride. Her voice relaxed, but she was still breathing heavily, her face flushed. "From there, I knew I was safe. They couldn't get at me and I could keep an eye on them. One word from me and the government shuts down their projects. No more highway work, no more free money. I knew, I knew that people would forget about Jackie's death as time passed. Forget all about Waconah, about Christianson. Plenty of other sites out there. And maybe in time I'd finish my dissertation, and then lots of offers for teaching jobs would come my way."

"Maggie, I don't—"

"Shut up. I'm running things now, not you. This is all your fault anyway." She leveled the handgun at Jake's chest. "You had to come along and stick your nose in my business, digging up that damned site. You didn't think I'd notice, but I did. I'm not stupid!"

Maggie was raving now, her voice louder by the minute. Jake kicked himself for not signing up for that introductory Krav Maga course when it was offered at the university, after a rash of muggings on campus. His eyes darted around the room, searching for something to use as a weapon.

"I saw that newspaper article," Maggie said. "And if that weren't enough, then you show up on TV. You tried to play it down when I came for my inspection, but I wasn't fooled. For a while I thought it might be a coincidence, but I was too sharp for you. I stayed nearby and kept my eye on you."

Maggie stopped talking as the sounds of voices in the corridor filtered through the door. Jake debated yelling for help, but was unsure of how Maggie might react. The glare in her eyes suggested it would not be a good idea.

"First you met up with those annoying collectors. Most of them are nothing more than looters, stealing points and pots so they can decorate their dumpy houses or sell them on the Internet. Then you went to the sheriff. That's when I knew for sure you were snooping around in things better left alone."

Maggie took a step closer, waving the gun at them. "Pretty soon you didn't even try to hide what you were doing. You got all chummy with that pothead, Winters. He's nothing but trash! You found that old fart, Schumholtz. Bet he told you all kind of lies about me, too."

Maggie was yelling at this point and Jake was certain her voice could be heard in the hall and adjoining rooms. With luck, someone would call the desk to complain, and that might give him and Amanda a chance to get out of there. It was only a matter of time.

"But you wouldn't stop. You had to track down Al Droessler, too. Do you know what he was really like back then? Always hanging around our sites, pestering everyone, sucking up to Jackie about his damn photos. Every time you'd turn around, he was stalking you with his stupid camera. Sleazy old pervert, I knew he was sneaking shots of the girls, trying to get racy photos for his sick thrills. Oh, I kept him away from Christianson, but he was always camped out on the top of that damn hill, taking pictures of Waconah from the road. Who knows what he saw? I couldn't take any chances, not after that. I had to be sure, I did. Had to find out. Oh, why the hell did you have to come back here? It was all forgotten until you came back. Your fault, all your fault!"

A muffled thud at the door caught their attention, and for a split second Maggie pointed the revolver at the door. Jake thought about making a grab for the gun, but she turned the muzzle back at him and the moment was lost.

The trio stood in silence. The seconds passed like hours, before Maggie regained her voice. "You did everything but break down my door and accuse me, you bastard," she snarled. "I suppose you want to know the whole story, don't you? Well, I suppose it can't hurt to tell you, before we go for . . . a little ride." Her smile was as cold as ice.

That was it then, thought Jake. When she tried to move them from the hotel room, he would take advantage of the situation and overpower her. Once Amanda was in the clear, he would make his move. Jake wasn't a fighter, but he had been in a few scraps in his day. Maggie was a large woman, but he doubted she had much physical strength. If he focused on getting the gun away from her, Jake was certain he could give Amanda sufficient time to escape.

"I was there that night, hiding along the north trail by the big burial mound. Saw that stupid girl, Amy, chewing her nails and waiting for Clark Kelley. She kept looking around, but she never saw me. Kept waiting for her to leave, so I could go down and, um, and sabotage Jackie's boat. Yeah, just wanted to do that. Get her out of my hair for a while, and make her look like the fool for once.

"I saw the silly little bitch meet up with Clark, and from the way they carried on it was pretty obvious what was going on. They left, heading up the trail to the highway. I could have turned him in, later, but I had to be careful. I didn't know how much he knew, or what he might have seen. Oh, I spread the word later through some students that Clark was sleeping with a student, but I couldn't nail the bastard like I wanted to. Don't you see, they all would have wondered why I hadn't come forward right away, and what else I might be hiding. I didn't dare."

"Clark is a piece of garbage, that's for sure," Jake said, keeping his voice quiet and level.

"Yeah." Maggie's arm drooped a bit, pulled down by the weight of the gun. Jake's legs were stiff from standing and he knew she must be getting tired.

"So, what happened when you found Jacklyn?"

"Hmm?" Maggie looked confused. "Um, I only went to talk to her, like I said, about what she was finding. We just talked."

Jake couldn't help himself. "And she ended up in the boat?"

Maggie frowned, then scowled at him. "That was an accident. She must have hit her head. After I left."

Jake stared hard at Maggie. Amanda pressed on his back again. Another warning, one he chose to ignore.

"Big storm coming and you stopped by to chat? And Jacklyn ends up dead. If all this happened after you left, how do you know it was an accident?"

Maggie blanched. "You think you're so damn smart. Yeah, I snuck over there that night, thought I'd mess up the site a bit. Heard the boat banging against the pier and figured I'd set it loose. Get her in trouble, cause her some grief for a change. Jackie pops up out of nowhere and starts screaming at me. She was really steamed. She came at me, so I fought back. Swung at her, and she fell backward into the boat. Blood everywhere. Had to get rid of her, so I got the boat going and off it went into the darkness."

Jake's blood went cold. There it was. Maggie killed Jacklyn. And Al Droessler, too. There was no question what she planned to do with him and Amanda.

"That's the story, all of it," Maggie said. "And now I think it's time to go."

A sharp knock at the door broke the tension. "Maintenance," a female voice said. "There's a water leak next door and we need to get at the pipes."

Maggie turned and Jake lunged at her, screaming "Door!" to Amanda. He grabbed Maggie's arm with both hands, twisting the gun toward the floor as he slammed his shoulder into her chest. Maggie crashed backward against the wall and they tumbled to the floor. Amanda tore open the bolt and Deputy Hauser burst into the room, gun drawn.

CHAPTER FORTY-EIGHT

One week later, Jake sat in his usual spot on the back-dirt pile, overseeing the final days of the Waconah field school. The late-summer showers had left the area and the warm sun shone down on the busy students, tempered by a cool breeze blowing off Taylor Lake. More than half of the students were excavating different parts of the midden, a complex mix of discarded shell, pottery sherds, animal bone, and broken stone tools. The deposit required slow digging and extensive notes but produced enough interesting artifacts to keep them enthused.

Jake had kept to himself over the last few days, dealing with the mental and emotional stress of the encounter and scuffle with Maggie Devlin, and then explaining the entire story again and again to Sheriff Rostlund and the County District Attorney. It seemed like the ordeal would never end, but Jake and Amanda realized it was necessary.

Jake took it upon himself to contact all those invested in Jacklyn Wardell's death, starting with Mark Winters and some of her other former students. Jake couldn't provide them with specific details, but all were told that the mystery surrounding Jacklyn's death had been solved at last. Mark's phone calls were restricted, but his lawyer passed along Jake's message and reported back that Mark seemed happy that Jacks was finally at peace.

Calling Linda Wardell caused him the most anxiety, but she took the news in an almost eerie calm. She knew it all along, even if she hadn't known the details. For her, the specifics were irrelevant.

A few reporters got wind of the story through their police contacts and a couple called requesting interviews. Feigning a hectic schedule as the field school came to a close, Jake managed to direct most of them to the sheriff and district attorney's offices. Sheriff Rostlund posted an officer at the entrance to the site, restricting access, and Jake and the students were able to continue their work in relative peace.

Nevertheless, the media onslaught caught them all by surprise. Amanda was worried about possible repercussions for the History Center and left as soon as the police and district attorney had her statement. Her meeting with Dr. Holley went well, though, and she was assured that the Center would suffer no ill effects from what had happened. Other projects had built up during her absence, so Amanda decided it would be best if she stayed in La Crosse rather than return. Jake agreed, although he would miss her presence as the field school came to an end.

Jake, too, grew concerned about negative publicity for the university. After talking to the sheriff, he had contacted Dr. Chang, the current head of the Anthropology and Archaeology Department, and explained the situation and his concerns. She was sympathetic and agreed to contact him the next day. Five days had passed and Jake began to wonder if he should start getting ready to look for a new job. His phone rang, and Jake recognized the department number. "Hello?"

"Hi, Jake. Lisa Chang here. Sorry I didn't get back to you sooner."

"Not a problem. I hadn't noticed."

"Wanted to get the final word from WSU legal, and then Public Relations had to chime in. Anyway, we're solid. None of this will reflect badly on the department or the university. Just refer any questions to the local authorities and the university will handle any media inquiries down here. Okay?"

"Yeah, that's fine. Load off my mind, really."

"Don't you worry about it, Jake. You did a really good thing, to be honest," Dr. Chang said. "Jacklyn and I were good friends, and it means a lot that you were able to set things straight."

"Thank you. I appreciate that."

"My pleasure. On an unrelated note, we'll be discussing tenure-track appointments at the next senior faculty meeting. Your name will definitely be on that list. The official word might not come through right away, but you know how hectic things are in the fall. I don't anticipate any problems, especially after the productive summer you had at Waconah. Everything look good for another season?"

"Definitely. Also have an Archaic site nearby that we can test, if we get enough students."

"Fine, fine. Should be plenty of students available, since Clark backed out of his field project."

"Oh? That's a surprise."

"Humph. Maybe he could get something accomplished if he spent more time in the office. Did you know he disappeared for three weeks? Took his wife on a second honeymoon, just like that with no notice at all. I was about ready to send the campus police over to his house to look for his body."

That explained Clark's recent disappearance and Jake suspected the reason behind it. "Wow, that is unusual. Well, I'm sure he had a wonderful time."

"I suppose. I wouldn't want to spend three weeks with Clark. I heard Carol had all kinds of work done, too. Hair, chest, face-lift, the whole package. No wonder he's been sniffing around for a salary increase."

"Maybe he's having a midlife crisis."

"Ha! My husband pulled that once. Came home with a motorcycle one Friday. It went right back to the dealer on

Saturday and that was the end of that foolishness," Dr. Chang said. "Enough office gossip, then. See you in a few weeks, Jake."

Jake slipped the phone into his pocket as Heather approached.

"Hey, Jake, got a minute?"

"Sure, Heather. What do you need?"

"There's no easy way to say this but I'm taking a semester off," she blurted out, and her eyes welled up. "I'm going to send in the paperwork once the field school is over, but I wanted to tell you first."

Jake paused, and let out a long sigh. "I hope all this stuff with Wardell and Al's death isn't behind this. I'll understand if it was, but . . ."

"No, no, not really. I've been stressed out a lot lately, and the last two semesters burned me out. Being up here, sort of isolated from everything else, has just given me more time to think," Heather said. She stared out across the lake. "I need some time to breathe and figure out where I'm going in life. I hate leaving you short-handed and all . . ."

"Hey, don't think twice about that," Jake said. "First and foremost you've got to take care of yourself. If that means taking some time off, that's what you do."

"Scott should be able to pick up some of the slack. I've managed to whip him into shape for you, but it wasn't easy."

Jake smiled. It was good to hear the old Heather again. "Thanks. You know, if you want I can arrange for you to stay on as a part-time researcher, so you can maintain your health insurance. And it won't be as if you're getting paid for nothing. I suspect I'll have to contact you from time to time as I try to decipher your handwriting."

CHAPTER FORTY-NINE

In the afternoon, a second squad car appeared at the top of the hill, and after a brief pause continued down to the parking lot. Jake was a bit surprised to see Pam Hauser step out of the vehicle.

"Hi, Pam. Is it okay for you to be here like this?"

"Officially, I'm only here to inquire about your health, following your traumatic experience with Maggie Devlin. The sheriff's office takes victim counseling quite seriously. We're not discussing any aspect of the Devlin case, as it relates to Wardell or Al Droessler." She winked at him. "Understand?"

"Perfectly, Officer."

"Do you want to see our trauma counselor? I can schedule an appointment for you."

"Uh, no thanks. I'm fine."

"Good. That guy is all touchy-feely and creeps me out. So, partner, you doing all right?"

"Yeah, getting through it," Jake said. "By the way, thanks again for saving our lives."

"You're welcome, but like I told you before, that's what partners are for. I'm glad I listened to my inner voice and drove over there after I heard your message. Anyway, it looked like you had things well in hand when I arrived."

"I guess. I probably wouldn't have tried anything if I hadn't recognized your voice at the door."

"Don't let your girlfriend hear that, Jake. She'll think you're starting to fall for me after all." Pam smiled and scanned the landscape. "Is she here? I should probably officially ask her if she's okay, too, just so I don't get in trouble for being here."

"No, Amanda left on Sunday, before Al's funeral. She needed to talk to her boss and make sure there wouldn't be any repercussions for the History Center."

"Tough boss, dragging her back on a weekend like that."

"I think she wanted to leave, to be honest. Pretty stressful here and Amanda is really happy with her job at the History Center."

"Long-distance relationships are tough, under any circumstances. Amazing turnout at the funeral, huh?"

"Yeah, that was something to see," Jake said. "All those people, dropping photos into the grave. Quite a tribute."

"Al was a special guy. I'll bet everyone in Donovan showed up."

"I saw Everett Kojarski there," Jake said. "He gave me a big bear hug and said how pleased he was that we had solved the Wardell case."

"Hmm. I didn't get a hug from him, but he did say he was awful proud and told the sheriff I'd better get a promotion when all this is over."

"So, unofficially, how is it going?"

"Pretty good. Maggie's attorney knows we have her dead to rights and I think he's just hoping for a decent plea deal. She keeps on rambling, even when he tells her to be quiet, and it's driving him nuts."

"Is that part of her plan? To act crazy and then get off on insanity?"

Pam shrugged. "Maybe, but I don't think it would work. She planned everything out so carefully, and she's almost bragging about it. It's hard to argue mental incompetence when you have evidence for premeditation. Anyway, that's for the courts and the lawyers to work out."

"Any idea when that might be?"

"It might not even go to trial, if we're lucky. In addition to the photo you saw, we found another dozen or so stashed among her paperwork. And two old cameras were tucked away in the back of one of the drawers. Look like the same models your assistant described, and I think Al's daughter recognized them."

"I'm surprised she kept them."

"Probably just didn't have a chance to get rid of them. Not like you're going to toss an antique camera in the trash and not have someone notice," Pam said. "Anyway, everything she's been telling us matches with what she told you in the hotel. After hearing about the new dig, Maggie started watching you and wondering if you were looking into Wardell's death. Your visit to Sheriff Kojarski probably sealed the idea in her mind. After that, everything you did just added fuel to the fire. You met with her old professor, Schumholtz, which really got her mad. Maggie was the one who ran you off the road after your visit, and she admitted trying to scare you and Amanda when you were walking back from dinner a few nights before that."

"I can't believe it," Jake said. "I never thought the two events could be connected. She could have killed me. And I suppose she was the one trespassing at the site, too?"

"At least some of the time. I think you had more than a few unauthorized visitors. In Maggie's head, you were responsible. So if she got something on you, to discredit your field school or maybe sabotage the dig, you'd go away and leave her in peace. Maggie did admit she broke into your campsite, though, when everyone else was gone."

"Well, that explains why nothing was taken. She was looking around, to see if we had anything incriminating about her. That's insane."

"The sheriff figures she wasn't thinking real clear at that

point, all wrapped up in paranoia and guilt. Been festering for years, most likely. All it took was you digging at Waconah again to set her off. She saw Mark Winters, Clark Kelley, the old NEWAS volunteers," Pam said, counting on her fingers. "All people from the old field school, showing up again. In her twisted version, it was all part of a conspiracy directed at her. And then you went to see Al, and that was the final straw."

"Al's death. This is all my fault, isn't it?"

Pam placed her hand on Jake's shoulder. "No. Definitely not. Devlin was bound to snap at some point and someone was going to get hurt whether you were involved or not."

Jake nodded, not entirely convinced. Pam watched him closely for a few moments before she continued. "Maggie knew Al from her dig, although it sounds like he wasn't treated real well over there. So he hung out with Wardell and her gang. Maggie got it in her head that he might have seen something that night, so she went over to search his place. He came back and Al was killed. It's not your fault."

"At least she's going to jail for what she did to Jacklyn Wardell. Finally."

Pam bit her lip. "Probably best you hear it from me. Jake, they may not pursue charges against Devlin for Wardell's death."

"Why not? She confessed, didn't she? And the red clay on her clothes ties Maggie to the murder."

"It puts her at the scene, yes. She admits stumbling and falling in the dark as she left the site. But what happened before that is up in the air. It could have been murder or it could have been an accident. Her attorney is pushing her to recant, arguing that she was under stress because of your badgering her."

"Badgering her? Who had the gun in that room?"

"I know, I know. Calm down. Thing is, other than her statement, there isn't any strong evidence to pursue one charge over another. Winters, Clark, Amy, and even Al, none of them were there when it happened, so no witnesses. No physical evidence, no DNA, no—"

"So after all that's happened, she gets off? No punishment for Wardell's death?"

"Devlin won't get off, not really. She broke into Al's place and caused his death. No denying that, her prints are all over the main room and she had his property in her hotel room. Multiple counts of trespassing, breaking and entering, attempted assault with a motor vehicle, and she took you and your girlfriend hostage, with me as an eyewitness. Don't worry, Jake. She's going to pay in full for everything she's done."

"I guess you're right," Jake said. "When you look at it that way."

"Of course I'm right. I'm the newest hero in the County Sheriff's Department," Pam said with a grin. She adjusted her cap and moved toward her vehicle. "You take care of yourself, Jake."

"You, too. Partner."

An outburst of whooping and hollering erupted from the midden, drawing Jake's attention. The students were clamoring around someone, yelling and gesturing for everyone to hurry over. Curious, Jake walked over, wondering what they could have possibly found that would garner so much excitement after a rich, full season of digging. Deep down, he hoped it wasn't a piece of human bone, especially not now, so close to the end.

As he neared, the crowd parted to reveal Michelle, wide-eyed, with the biggest smile Jake had ever seen. Her fellow students were praising her discovery and maneuvering for a better view. Cupped in her hand was the unmistakable missing half of the shellfish-effigy pendant recovered years earlier by Jacklyn Wardell.

Jake smiled, shaking his head in disbelief. "I guess this is one of those rare times when all the pieces fit together in the end."

ABOUT THE AUTHOR

Steven Kuehn is a professional archaeologist working in the Midwest and has over 25 years of field and laboratory experience dealing with the identification, excavation, analysis, and interpretation of prehistoric and historic archaeological sites. He specializes in the analysis of faunal (animal) remains and has examined bone and shell from sites across North America. After preparing hundreds of technical reports and scholarly articles, the call of mystery fiction grew irresistible and Steve began chronicling the adventures of Professor Jacob Caine, archaeologist and reluctant sleuth. One Jake Caine short story, *Talked to Death,* was published online in Mysterical-E. *Sunken Dreams* is his first fiction novel, with future novels in the works.